BOTH
of Us

AMBER KELLY

Cover Design: Sommer Stein, *Perfect Pear Creative Covers*
Cover Image: Scott Hoover, *Scott Hoover Photography*
Editor: Jovana Shirley, Unforeseen Editing, *www.unforeseenediting.com*
Formatter: *Champagne Book Design*
Proofreader: Judy Zweifel, *Judy's Proofreading*

For Kandace.
You are threaded throughout these pages. I miss you, my friend.
I will miss you forever.

CHAPTER
One

Brie

"SIS? WHAT DO YOU SEE? TALK TO ME."

I stand here, paralyzed, as I stare into Cross's eyes. *What is he doing here? He's not supposed to be here.*

"Brie?"

Nicco's voice is getting louder, and I can hear the alarm in his question. I blink from my stare-down and look to my brother. His face is full of concern. I look back up to the spot where I saw him, and he is gone, vanished into thin air.

Was he really there?

"A ghost."

"A what?"

"Nothing. I just thought I saw a ghost."

Nicco reaches up, grabs me around the waist, and plucks me from the stage.

"A ghost? Who? Was it Calvacanti?"

I blanch at the name. I didn't even think of Dante showing up here at Dawn's graduation party. Now, I am filling with panic. The room is crowded, and the voices are too loud. I need an escape. I need air.

"Calm down, *cara*."

"I need air."

"Okay." He looks up to Kelsey, who is still on the stage, dancing with Dawn. "Hey, Brie and I are going to walk out to the deck with all the desserts."

"Grab me a couple of cupcakes and a glass of champagne, and I will find you guys after this song," she shouts down over the music.

"Yes, ma'am."

He takes my hand and leads me through the horde of dancers and toward the exit. We pass by the place I thought I saw him, and it's empty, except for a waiter standing with a tray of glasses. Maybe my mind is playing tricks on me.

Once we are outside, he leads us to one of the tables and pulls out a chair for me. Then, he goes to the buffet. He returns with two plates filled with delicious cakes and goes back for flutes of bubbly.

It's a beautiful night. The sky is full of twinkling stars, but there is a breeze kicking up from the Pacific and what looks like clouds moving with it. I hope the rain holds off until after Dawn's party is over.

Chinese lanterns are strung across the patio, and the music from the ballroom is faintly drifting out. I take a deep breath in and try to calm my shaky nerves. I'm not sure what has me so on edge.

"Now, you want to tell me what spooked you in there?"

"Not really."

He gives me a look that says he will not drop it.

"I just thought I saw Cross standing on the side of the dance floor."

"Cross?" He looks confused.

"Yes, it's crazy; I know. I think I might be seeing things. I haven't slept much since I saw Dante, to be honest."

"Don't worry, sis. Now that I know he's in town, there's no way I am letting him get anywhere near you. Every man at every entrance here tonight has his description and his name and aliases. If he tries to get in, I'll be alerted right away. He knows I'm on his trail now. I don't think he's stupid enough to show up here."

I give him a look. A look that says we both know Dante is indeed that stupid.

Kelsey, Dawn, and Daniel come bounding up to the table a few minutes later. Sweaty and giggling.

"What happened in there?" Dawn asks.

"Nothing. I just got a little claustrophobic."

"Are you sure? I can find my dad and have Jake and Jessica Rabbit thrown out on their asses. He's not ruining this night for you."

"It's okay. I am pretty sure they were leaving anyway."

"I can't believe he brought her here."

"I'm fairly certain she brought him." I shrug. "It doesn't matter at this point. Even if I believe him, I need some time to straighten out my head, and I'm sure Carlie will use that time to shimmy her way right in."

"Excuse me for a minute, ladies." Nicco stands and walks to the other side of the deck as he answers a call to his cell.

Kelsey sighs as he walks away.

"That man sure knows how to wear a suit," she breathes.

Dawn and I both laugh at her.

"Stop it with all the dreamy sighs and googly eyes," I insist.

"I can't help it. Honestly, do you see him in that suit?"

"Oh, I see him," Dawn replies. "Damn, I wouldn't mind seeing him out of it either."

"Dawn," Kelsey and I exclaim in unison.

We look to Daniel, who shrugs and continues to eat his cupcake.

"What? There's absolutely nothing wrong with appreciating a fine male form."

"You are hopeless," I muse.

I love these girls. They know how to take my mind right out of that bleak place and bring me back into their world of love and humor.

I finish my raspberry cupcake and pick up my flute. I bring it to my lips as my eyes find Nicco. His conversation seems tense. I hope it's not a call telling him that Dante is trying to get in. He turns, and his eyes fall on me. He looks a little frantic or pissed off. This can't be good.

He ends his call, and he walks back in our direction.

"You wanna get out of here, sis? Maybe go hang out on the beach and watch the waves crashing in for a while? Clear your head?"

It's still early. Dawn's mom hasn't even called for the speeches or had the cake brought in yet, and Dawn hasn't opened any of her gifts. Leaving now would be rude.

"Not yet. I'm not opposed to ending the night on the beach, but we'll miss all the good stuff."

"Yeah, you guys can't just leave me here with my parents and all their dull friends," Dawn whines.

"I'm here," Daniel mumbles.

"I know, babe. I just mean that I want my friends here, too. You four are the only people I even like at this shindig."

"Then, why didn't we just have our own celebration at home tonight?" I ask.

"Duh, I get a band and food and drinks and presents from all these people. I've gone to all their lame-ass birthday and graduation parties over the years. They owe me. Besides, I'm hoping that maybe Daddy bought me a new car."

"I think the trip to Monaco is your gift," Daniel breaks it to her.

She pouts.

"You're probably right, but a girl can hope."

Nicco clears his throat. "How much longer before they do this cake-and-toast thing?" he asks.

"Why are you in such a hurry all of a sudden?" I ask, suspicion and a little bit of fear creeping in.

"No reason. I just thought it would be fun; that's all."

I'm not buying it. Something has him on edge.

"It will be. Just give us, say, one more hour, and everything should be wrapping up," Dawn guesses.

Nicco nervously looks around, and I'm now sure that Dante is here somewhere. He's trying not to alarm any of us, but he's definitely scanning every inch of the perimeter.

Perhaps leaving now is for the best.

"Hey, guys. Maybe Nicco is right. I have been a little freaked out in the crowd. We could head out, and you guys can join us in a bit," I suggest.

"Really?" Dawn asks, a little deflated. "I was hoping you guys would give the speeches. If my mom ropes my cousin Ann-Marie into it, she's going to do her best to embarrass me with stories of me wetting the bed when we were kids or something equally evil."

"I'll give a speech," Kelsey volunteers, ever perceptive, "and so will Daniel. You'll be fine."

She turns to me. "You guys go ahead, and I'll text Nicco when we're all done. We'll find you guys afterward."

"Thanks, Kelsey."

They get up to head back into the ballroom.

"I'm going to go find my friends Rick and Melanie and let them know we're headed out and to tell Mr. and Mrs. Martin thank you and good-bye," I tell Nicco as I start to head back inside.

"Okay, you do that, and I'll have the valet bring my car around."

He starts toward the exit, and I walk back inside the ballroom. I find Rick standing against the far wall.

"Hi, Rick. Did you lose your dance partner?"

"Nah, she just had to run to the ladies' room. I'm doing my husbandly duty," he says as he raises the jeweled clutch he's holding.

"Good man. Can you let her know that I am leaving? I am tired, and so is Nicco, so we're going to head on out."

"Sure," he says as he leans down and kisses my cheek. "I'm pretty sure she'll be ready to go soon, too. She's already tipsy."

"You guys deserve a night alone, full of inebriated fun." I waggle my eyebrows at him, and he starts to laugh.

"We'll see about that. I have a feeling my window will be closing shortly."

"Then, you'd better gather your girl and get the heck out of here."

"Will do."

I take off in search of Dawn's parents next. I don't see them in the ballroom, so I venture out to the Ocean Deck. The DJ is taking a break, and the deck is practically empty. No parents, so I turn to go back inside and stop dead. There he is.

"Hi, *Tesoro*."

My knees start to buckle, and I grab the edge of one of the pub tables to stay upright. He's here. I haven't laid eyes on him in over a year and a half. I've only heard his voice the one time when I accidentally answered Nicco's phone. I never thought I would hear it again. It echoes through me.

"Why are you here?" I choke out. "You can't be here."

"I needed to see you," he whispers into the night air.

"No, you don't exist here," I say in a shaky voice.

He starts taking measured steps in my direction.

"Don't—" My voice cracks as I throw one hand up in front of me. "Don't touch me."

He stops short of making it to where I stand.

"Gabby." It's a strangled plea.

"Gabby isn't here anymore. She's dead. You killed her some time ago."

We stand there in the silence with only the sound of our mingled breaths and our beating hearts.

Finally, he speaks, "Are you okay?"

"It's none of your business how I am."

He lets out a loud sigh. "Gabby—"

"Brie."

He raises his eyebrows.

"My name is Brie."

"Okay, Brie," he says like he is trying my name on for size.

I want to run. I want to run right past him and not look back, but I am frozen to the spot. Afraid he'll touch me and afraid he won't.

He takes a couple of more steps, and he is right in front of me, blocking me from the sight of anyone in the bar area. He reaches to touch my hair or my face, and I flinch. A look of hurt passes his eyes, and he pulls his hand back and slides it into his pocket.

"You can't be here, Cross. You can't taint this place, too. Please. I don't want to go home. I don't want to have to move somewhere else. I am so tired of starting over. Please don't take here away from me, too."

I hate how small the admission makes me feel, but I am tired of running.

"I'm not here to take you home, *Tesoro*."

I look up at him, confused. If he isn't here to take me home to Papa, then why is he here?

He takes a deep breath and closes his eyes.

"I'm getting married. I wanted to tell you myself, in person. You deserve that much from me."

My mind instantly flashes back to his loft and the ring I found in his T-shirt drawer. My ring. *Did he give someone else my ring?* Anger. Blinding, hot anger fills me.

"Married? You came all this way to tell me you're getting married? Really? Go to hell!"

I find my legs and start to march past him. He steps in front of me to halt my progress.

"You have to hear this from me."

"There's more? I'm sorry, Cross, but if you came to see if you could tear me apart again for old times' sake, you are wasting your time. You don't have the power anymore. There's nothing left in me to break. Do you understand that? There is nothing left in me to break. It's all already shattered. So, take your best shot." I stand there, waiting. "Go ahead, take it," I dare him.

"I'm to marry Adriana in twelve weeks."

CHAPTER
Two

Cross

AS THE WORDS LEAVE MY LIPS, I WISH I COULD SNATCH THEM OUT of the air and take them back. The look of pure pain and betrayal that rocks her hits me like a physical blow, and I watch in slow motion as she starts walking backward, clutching her chest as if she could grab hold of her heart and keep it held together. I step forward, intending to catch her before she falls, and she lets out a small, tortured cry. I stop, and I wait. I want her to scream. I want her to yell at me, and I want her to hit me. I want her to punch me over and over again. I deserve her anger. I deserve the pain. I want to take it from her and absorb it, but she doesn't do any of those things. She bows over and holds her hands to her chest, and I watch her break all over again.

This time is worse than the first when she begged me not to walk away before she got so upset that she vomited on my shoes. After I went to retrieve her at the hotel that day, I knew, when we returned to her father's house, I was going to have to break her heart. To break all the promises that I had made to her. The other family heads had decided that it was a bad idea for us to continue our relationship while I concentrated on taking over for Papa. They thought Gabriella was too much of a wild card, a distraction. In truth, they had just decided that they had another bride in mind for me. One who offered an alliance that would bring confidence to the other bosses and hopefully scare my father's enemies and keep them at bay. Vincenzo, Gabby's father, and Salvatore, Adriana's father, had made a deal, unbeknownst to me. In that deal, Vincenzo secured Gabby's safety because he knew that, if the other families wanted us apart and we refused, they would do anything they had to to get what they wanted, including hurting her. So, he forced my hand. They all had.

"*Tesoro*," I softly call to her.

She is lost in pain right now, and I want to help her, but I don't know how.

"What the fuck, man?"

I hear a roar from behind me, and Nicco storms across the deck to her. He gets on one knee in front of her, and he gently brushes her hair back as he talks softly. I can't make out what he's saying.

She jerks with her quiet cries, and I am helpless. I can't comfort her. I can't touch her. I can't soothe her in any way.

He looks back at me, and he has rage written across his face. He didn't want me to do this here, but I knew that, if they left, I might not get the chance to speak to her alone again. I had to catch her here. Because, as much as it hurts for her to hear, I couldn't have let her find out from someone else.

"I told you, not here. Fuck," he spits in my direction.

She lifts her head at his statement, and with a quivering lip, she asks him, "Not here? You knew?"

He turns back to her, and then he lowers his eyes and nods his head.

"How long? How long have you known?"

He looks back up to her and answers honestly, "I knew before I left New York."

She lets out another strangled cry, and I wonder how much more she can take. We keep throwing blow after blow, and she is still standing, but for how long?

"I am so sorry, *cara*. I was going to tell you, but you made me promise never to mention his name, and you were happy here. You were building a good life, falling in love, and I didn't want to bring all this hurt to your doorstep."

She cuts her eyes back to me, those beautiful coffee-colored eyes that I love so much. Then, she stiffens her back and wipes at her cheeks.

There's my girl.

"Well, you did what you came here to do. Thanks for letting me know. I mean, I would have hated to finally make that call to Adi that I have been contemplating for so long"—her voice cracks on Adriana's nickname—"and have her voice mail pick up and announce that I had reached Adriana Scutari's phone. I mean, how silly would I have felt? And what kind of person would I be if my best friend in the whole world got married and I didn't even send her a fucking card? Right?"

That's it, baby. Let me have it.

"I hope you have other business here in California because I would hate for you to have flown all this way just to see those few tears I had left."

"Tesoro."

"Stop calling me that! My name is Brie."

"Brie." I let the foreign name linger on my tongue. I've known for the last year that this is the new name she chose for herself. It doesn't suit her.

"What? What more could you possibly want to say to me?"

"I have something for you." I reach inside my jacket pocket and produce the box I had tucked inside.

She blanches when she sees it and starts to shake her head in protest. "I don't want anything from you."

"It's not from me." I frown in puzzlement. "It's from Una."

The box contains a necklace that was once Una's and then my mother's, and she insisted I bring it to Gabby.

She won't approach me to take the box, so I set it on the edge of the table and back away.

She walks over to it and carefully slides it open, and a tear rolls down her right cheek as she peeks inside. It's a stunning necklace.

"You should keep this and give it to Adi. It's a family heirloom, and it should stay in your family," she says softly as she fingers the delicate chain.

"Una won't hear of it. She said that my mother would want you to wear it."

"I can't." She is still caressing the necklace.

It is an antique locket that was handmade for my great-grandmother by a jeweler in Italy. Inside, there used to be a tiny photo of my mother and all of her boys.

She looks up. "I can't accept it."

"She wants you to have it. She removed the picture inside and said you could place your own precious memory in there. It's supposed to bring good fortune and protection on the one it holds. An old Italian blessing."

She squeezes her eyes tightly closed, and I see her filling with strength as she nods her head to herself. Then, she opens her eyes back up and looks at me again.

"Tell her I said thank you," she concedes.

Odd. I expected more of a fight.

"I will."

"Now, if you'll excuse me, I think I am ready to go home." She closes the box and tucks it into her palm.

"I'll take you." Nicco starts forward.

"No. I'll get myself home."

She's upset with him. I wanted to avoid that. Why did he have to tell her he had known about the engagement? He should have played dumb.

She turns and flees inside.

I face Nicco as a partygoer stumbles onto the deck from the other side.

"Brie," he calls, and then he stops and looks between Nicco and me. "Everything all right out here?"

"Yes, Jake, everything is fine. Go back inside," Nicco warns.

"Who are you?"

His attention is focused on me. As focused as it can be, as the guy is obviously drunk. So, this is Jacob Mason. Jealousy flares inside me. Intense jealousy and hatred. This asshole is the one who got to hold her. The one who could have spent the rest of his life making her happy. The one free to do that, and the motherfucker blew it.

"Christoff Scutari," I bite out.

He looks me up and down, and then recognition dawns on him. *How?*

"The criminal," he sneers.

What the fuck? Did she tell him about me? About us?

"Excuse me?"

I step closer to him, and the asshole doesn't even have enough sense of self-preservation to back up.

"That guy told me about you. You're the one her parents are trying to protect her from because they think you're dangerous. You're the reason she left New York. He said you'd come looking for her."

"Who told you this?" I demand.

He cuts his eyes to Nicco. "That guy, Lucas."

I look over to Nicco, and his jaw is twitching.

He looks back at me, and through gritted teeth, he says, "Dante."

Without thinking, I advance on him, and it takes him off guard. He stumbles backward, but before he can orient himself, I'm on top of him. I grab his lapels, and I back him toward the side to the bar.

"Cross, man, stop." Nicco has ahold of my shirt from behind.

"You brought that fucker back into her life?" I spit at him.

He has the decency to look remorseful.

"I didn't know," he tries to explain.

"He could have hurt her or her friends, and you were telling him where and when he could find her," I roar into his face.

"I thought he was working for her father."

I toss him to the ground. Frustrated. He's not even worth it.

He grabs on to the bar and pulls himself back to his feet.

"Did it ever occur to you to check his information?"

"Check it with who, huh? I don't even know her name. She let me into her bed, but she won't even tell me her real fucking name."

Fury. White-hot rage blinds me, and I hit him hard. Grab him by his neck and squeeze, and then I raise my fist to pound it into him again.

A small hand reaches and grabs my bicep. "No, Cross, don't."

I stand there with my hand still on his throat holding him in place. He's gasping for air, and she tugs at my arm again.

"Don't hurt him. He doesn't understand. He doesn't mean to show disrespect. He doesn't know who you are. Let him go."

I slide my eyes to her, and she pleads, "Please, Cross, let him go."

I drop him to his feet, and he falls on his ass. He sits there, sputtering and gasping for air. She goes to him and helps him up.

"Fuck, what the hell, Brie? Is this what you want?" he asks. "This guy?"

"Stop, Jake. Just stop."

"Listen to her," I bite out, "Jake."

He looks between her and me, and he pulls out of her grip. "You know what? Whatever. I don't need this." He looks her in the eyes, and he snaps, "I don't need this. He can have you."

Then, he turns and staggers back inside and into the arms of a woman waiting for him on the dance floor.

Gabby watches him go, sadness in her stare. She doesn't cry. She doesn't say anything. She just stands there.

Then, she turns to Nicco and whispers, "I forgot that you have my apartment keys in your pocket."

He digs into his pants, produces a keychain, and walks it over to her. "Please text me and let me know when you make it into the apartment and set the alarm, okay?"

She nods to him, and then she walks back inside, without sparing me another glance.

"You have a man on her, right?" I ask as I watch her go.

"Of course I do."

CHAPTER
Three

Bree

I FIND DAWN AND KELSEY JUST BEFORE THE CAKE IS BROUGHT OUT.

"Can I steal you guys for a second?" I ask them.

They follow me away from the crowd just as Dawn's mom announces for the waiters to bring out the flutes of champagne, so the toasts can begin.

"Change of plans. I think I'm going to skip the beach. I feel a migraine coming on, so I'm going to head back to our apartment and turn in for the night. I just wanted to hug you before I left. I can't believe I'm not going to see you for almost a month. I hope you and Daniel have the most amazing time in Monaco. Please call or text me or something to let me know when you've made it there safe and sound," I tell Dawn.

I wrap my arms around her neck and squeeze her as tight as I can. You never know when the last time you hug someone is the last time you will ever embrace them. I have learned to make even the most insignificant good-byes count.

"Thank you, Brie. I promise to touch base as soon as we land." She squeezes me back.

"Hey, are you sure you don't want me to come home with you? Migraines are no fun. I can tell Nicco that I will stay another night." Kelsey has a look of concern on her face.

"No, please, don't change your plans. I'm just going to go take some medication and lie down. A cool, dark, quiet apartment is what I need. I am sure Nicco will be a lot more fun than me tonight."

"Yeah, he will," Dawn chimes in.

Kelsey rolls her eyes and brings her focus back to me. "You promise to call us if you need anything?"

"I promise, and I'll see you tomorrow."

We come in for one more group embrace before Dawn's mom calls them both to the stage, and I slip out the front entrance. The wind has kicked up, and it looks like storm clouds have blown in. The horizon is dark and unsettling. I feel a tinge of foreboding as I walk to the Uber that is waiting for me by the door. I hop into the back seat and close my eyes. I wasn't lying about the headache. My head is throbbing.

The sky opens up just as we turn out of the parking lot, and rain starts pelting the windshield. It's coming down in sheets by the time we pull up to the apartment building. I shout my thanks to the driver over a loud crack of thunder as lightning illuminates the courtyard. Then, I take off sprinting for the steps to let myself in as quickly as I can.

I kick my heels off at the door and head to my bedroom to change out of my soaked dress and into a tank and shorts.

I keep playing the night's events over and over in my head—from Jake showing up with Carlie to Cross blindsiding me with his big news.

Why? Why would he marry Adriana? He could barely tolerate Adi when we were growing up, and she wasn't exactly his biggest fan either. *There is absolutely no way he is in love with her now. Is there?*

Would he do it just to hurt me? That doesn't make any sense. I left, and I haven't made any attempt to contact him or mess with his new life. *Has that new life turned him that cruel?*

I hold my cell phone in my shaky hand, and I type in her number. The phone rings three times in my ear before I hear her concerned voice pick up.

"Gabriella?"

"Hello, Una."

She sighs, and I know she is fully aware of why I am calling.

"He is there?" she asks softly.

"Yes," I answer.

"Are you okay?" she asks, concern clear in her voice.

"No, but I will be. Thank you for the necklace. You shouldn't have sent it. It's an heirloom, and it belongs in your family."

"You are my family, Gabriella."

"But I'm not." I sniffle. "You should give it to Adriana. She will probably give you lots and lots of great-grandchildren, baby girls, to pass the necklace down to."

"It belongs with you. You wear it, and you remember that I am always here for you both. I am sorry that you had to see him and that he brought such hard news."

"I wish you had just called me. I hate that he saw me breaking."

"I tried to stop him. He wouldn't listen."

"Why? Why her?"

"That I don't know. Does it even matter?"

"It matters to me."

"It shouldn't."

She is right. None of it should matter to me anymore. I have friends who love me. I have Rick and Melanie and Cassian. I have a future ahead of me here that does not involve either of them.

"It still hurts so much," I admit.

"I know, dear girl, but you are stronger than you realize, Gabriella. I am so very proud of you. This pain, too, will pass."

I know she's right.

"Okay. I'll try not to call again."

"You can call me anytime. I am always going to be here whenever you need me. Understand?"

"Yes."

I end the call, and then I type out a short text message and hit Send before I lose my nerve.

Congratulations to my BFF. I wish you nothing but happiness while living the life you stole from me.

Almost instantly, three little dots appear, and I go to my Contacts and block her number before she has time to finish her reply and hit Send. Nothing she could say would make any difference to me anyway. Our friendship is irrevocably broken.

Betrayal. It sinks into my bones, and I accept it. It is the only choice I have.

My head is still pounding, so I go to the kitchen and get two ibuprofen and a glass of water. I swallow them down and open the fridge. Nothing appeals to me. I return to the living room, grab a blanket, and curl up on the couch with the remote control. I restlessly flip through channels, trying to find something, anything, to lose my head in for a few hours. Nothing captures my attention.

My thoughts keep going back to Cross. He looked so different. Still as handsome as ever but definitely more poised and put together, slightly dangerous. There's a confidence to him that didn't exist before. He's not the same carefree man I knew. He has a very commanding presence now. It reminds me of Papa and the way he could set an entire room on edge just by stepping through the threshold. I always loved that about Papa, if I were honest. It made me feel safe. Like no one and nothing would ever dare harm me while Papa was around.

I laugh to myself.

Safe. What I would give to feel that way again. A little girl's childish fantasy. Cross used to make me feel that way, too. Now, he is here, somewhere in my city. It is like my body is humming with energy and in complete chaos because it can feel him near, and it feels anything but safe.

I turn off the television, and I close my eyes in frustration. Now what? I am too angry to sleep and too angry to cry. I want to hit something. I want to hit someone.

I can finally stand it no longer, so I stand, grab my keys off the table, and head back out into the storm.

CHAPTER
four

Cross

"WE NEED TO TALK. I'M STAYING WITH YOU TONIGHT."

Nicco walks past me without looking me in the eye and speaks through gritted teeth, "Fine. I have to let someone know I'm leaving. Meet me out front."

I walk through the crowd and head back toward the entrance. I watch as Nicco approaches one of Gabriella's friends and whispers into her ear. She wraps an arm around his waist and nods up at him as she smiles. He places a kiss on her lips and then walks over to Daniel.

That's an interesting development. One he hasn't told me anything about. I make a mental note to inquire about my friend's actual fucking life after we get all the ugly business out of the way. I hate that every relationship in my life takes a back seat to, or has been drastically altered by, my new position. It's like the man I was before my family was gunned down doesn't even exist anymore. I miss my friend.

Ten minutes later, we are in his car, headed south. The tension is thick as we ride silently. Rain is pounding the Jeep, and it sounds like a drumroll against the soft leather top. I can barely see the lines on the road. I hope Gabby made it home safely in this downpour. Nicco should have been more heavy-handed with her and taken her home himself.

His knuckles are white as he clinches and unclinches the steering wheel. He wants to let me have it. He is warring with himself.

"Go ahead. Speak your piece."

"I can't believe you came here. I asked you not to. You knew she didn't want you here."

"I wanted to see to this Dante situation. You can't handle it alone, and we need him secured as fast as possible. I have to get it done now before there are too many other distractions."

"Distractions. You mean, like your fucking wedding?"

"Yes. That's one of them."

He shakes his head. "You are un-fucking-believable, man. You should have called Tony. He would have taken care of Dante."

"I didn't want to get too many players involved. It's my responsibility."

"No, it's not. That's the fucking point. She is not your responsibility anymore."

He turns into a parking deck beneath a condominium building facing the beach and shuts off the engine. Then, he turns to face me.

"You're going to have to let her go, Cross. You're marrying Adriana. There is no coming back from that. You know that. You're going to have to let Gabby's family take care of her from now on. We'll watch over her. We'll take care of any threats she has. You are off duty."

"I'm the reason she's here. I'm the reason she left home. I will always"—I cut my eyes to him—"always, make sure she is safe."

He lets out an exasperated sigh. "Fine. Let's get inside and figure out our next move. The longer he's in the wind, the harder he'll be to find."

I grab my bag from the back seat, and we head to an elevator leading to his and Daniel's sixth-floor condo.

Once inside, I drop my things into his guest room, which has its own small, attached bathroom. I could have stayed in a hotel, but I've spent so many nights alone in hotels as of late, and I hate them. Plus, I wanted to spend some time with my friend.

I walk back to the kitchen, and Nicco is standing at the island that separates it from the living room, holding two open beers. He hands one to me as I sit in a barstool.

"Did you take care of the favor I asked for?" he asks.

"Yes, I was able to pull a few strings, and Marianna is now the new labor and delivery nurse at Mount Sinai."

"Thanks, man. It's always been her dream."

"You're welcome."

He gets a far-off look as he brings the bottle to his lips.

"You know, you don't have to stay here forever. I can send someone else to California if you want to come home."

"No. I'm starting to like it here. Besides, I missed the brat, and she's not going to let anyone else get as close to her as I am."

I nod. It's true. She doesn't trust easily anymore; however, I have a sneaky suspicion he is staying for more reasons than just to watch over Gabriella.

"I like your place," I comment as I look around. "It's nice, and it has a great view."

The living room has floor-to-ceiling windows that overlook the Pacific.

"Yeah, we lucked out when it became available. The girls like it because they can spend all day on the beach, drinking, and then crash here."

"The girls?" I raise an eyebrow in question.

"Gab ... I mean, Brie and her roommates. I expect to see a lot of them now that classes are out for the summer."

"Speaking of which, I saw you back at the party with, which one is it? The one with the long blonde hair?"

"Kelsey."

"Yes, Kelsey. You two seemed cozy. What's the story there?"

He shrugs. "It's casual. She was in the process of shaking off an asshole who'd cheated on her when I got here. I just helped make it a little bit easier." He grins.

"I bet you did. Does she realize it's casual?"

"Yes. We've discussed it."

"She's beautiful."

"She is and funny, too. Man, you should see the three of them together. It's nonstop laughter. Gabby has found a family out here. They love her."

"She's easy to love."

"Yes, she is."

We stand there in loaded silence for a few minutes, and then I decide to get to business.

"I had my people dig into Calvacanti's recent activities. It seems that, since we saw him last, he has become very unstable. Developed a painkiller habit after we busted him up. His family tried to help him for a while, but they lost their patience with him about a year ago, and his father released his trust fund and then cut him loose. They haven't seen or heard much from him since. Word has it, he got involved with the wrong crowd and has been snorting Daddy's money away pretty rapidly. As far as I can tell, he left New York about the same time Gabriella did, so I can only assume that he followed her straight here."

"That was almost ten months ago. That asshole has been lurking in the shadows and watching her for ten months? Damn it. We should have kept better tabs on him. It never occurred to me that he was still a threat after two years. Fucker has been lying low and biding his time, and when he knew we weren't paying attention, he made his move to get to her. Right under our noses."

"He might have been under our radar but no more."

"We should have killed him then."

"I agree." I laugh humorlessly. "Back then, it was a foreign concept, but, now, when we find him, it's done."

His phone dings on the counter, and he looks down.

"Kelsey will be here soon. Dawn and Daniel are dropping her off on their way to Dawn's parents'."

"Casual, huh?"

He looks up and grins. It's obvious he's very infatuated with this girl. I am happy for him for about two seconds.

"Wait, if your girl is staying here and Daniel's girl is staying with him, who is staying with Gabby?"

His grin falls away.

"Please tell me she is not in that apartment alone for the night?"

"She is. She was supposed to come back here before you showed up."

"Call her now, and send a car for her. I'll go to a hotel."

Both of our eyes go to the door as we hear the lock click, and the knob starts to turn.

In walks—or more like, stumbles—two giggly females. Nicco grabs them before they hit the floor as Daniel carries in an overnight bag.

"I'm gonna miss you guys so much. I mean, not too much, being as I'll be on the beach, drinking all the cocktails and gambling away all my graduation money in Monte Carlo, but at least a little bit."

"It's okay. I'll be staying here while you guys are gone, and I won't miss you that much either. Nicco and I plan to christen every surface in this condo while we have it to ourselves."

They both melt into a puddle of drunken giggles, and then Dawn notices me standing here. She eyes me up and down for a moment and then asks, "Whoa, who are you?"

I set my beer on the counter and extend my hand. "I'm Christoff, an old friend of Nicco's from back home."

She looks over her shoulder at Nicco as she takes my hand. "Damn, what is in the water in New York? Does that state even have ugly people? Average? No?"

She turns back to me. "Are you moving here, too? I'm running out of available friends at this point. Oh! Wait, Brie is free now. I bet you sure could get her over Jake real quick."

"Babe, I don't think Brie would appreciate you trying to play matchmaker." Daniel gives me a wary look. He knows who I am. He remembers all those summers at Gabby's parents' as well as I do, and by the way he's looking at me now, I'm sure he knows the rest of our story as well.

"Oh, come on. Look how well my skills have worked out for Kels."

"Hey, you did not set me up," Kelsey protests.

"I encouraged you to let Nicco here ravage you, so I'm taking a hundred percent credit for your recent experience with multiple orgasms."

"Whatever." She rolls her eyes and whispers in my direction, "Pretty sure Nicco gets the credit for those." Then, she covers her mouth with both hands and blushes from head to toe. She is adorable. No wonder he likes her.

"All right, that's enough embarrassing drunken Tourette's for one night. Let's go." Daniel tries to lead his girlfriend to the door.

"I hate leaving Brie here, all alone and heartbroken. I would have a much better trip if I knew Mr. Tall, Dark, and Handsome here was helping to lick her wounds while we were away."

There is genuine sadness and concern in her voice now. She is worried about Gabby.

I like this girl.

"Don't worry, Dawn." Kelsey stumbles over to her friend and wraps her in a tight hug that almost takes them both back down to the floor. "I'll take care of Brie while you're gone. Nicco and I won't let her sit alone, being sad. I promise. You guys go have the best time ever."

"Okay. I love you."

"I love you more."

"No, I love you the most."

Daniel walks over to separate the two of them as their laughter turns to tears.

"All right, this could go on all night. You both love each other equally. Now, give each other a high five, or whatever you guys were doing in the car, for all the sex you're both going to have, and let's go."

"Yes, sex-bump," Dawn squeals.

They fist-bump, and Dawn and Daniel head out the door.

Kelsey stares at the closed door with a pout on her face.

"Come on, baby. Let's get you to bed. You'll see her in a few weeks." Nicco takes her by the hand and leads her toward his bedroom door.

"I'm gonna miss her."

"I know you are. Tell Christoff good night."

"Good night, Christoff."

"Good night, beautiful." I wink at her as she follows him.

She turns to Nicco. "He called me beautiful."

"That's because you are beautiful," he confirms.

She buries her head into his chest and lets him lead her into his bedroom. I decide I need something a little stronger than the beer and pour myself a tall glass of scotch from the decanter I see on the counter. After a few minutes, he returns to the living room.

"Sorry about that," he apologizes.

I'm staring into the amber liquid swirling in my glass. "You're right. She has found a family here. They obviously love her."

"They do. She loves them, too."

"That makes me very happy. She deserves friends who are worried over her and won't be able to enjoy their vacation if they think she's at home, sad. She's never had that. Adriana was as close as she came."

"Yeah, and we know how that turned out. With a knife right in Gabby's back."

I look up at the statement.

"You know that this isn't exactly what either of us planned."

"Knife still pierced her all the same." He tightly purses his lips.

I swallow the rest of the liquid and let it burn down my throat. Then, I manage to choke out, "I don't like her being there by herself."

"She's fully guarded. I have a man on her. The apartment has a security system, and she knows to set it as soon as she walks in the door. We can't start treating her like a prisoner. Remember how well that worked out the last time?"

I could never forget. She'd run.

"I don't like it."

CHAPTER
five

Bue

I PULL UP TO ONE OF THE PARKING SPACES ACROSS THE STREET FROM Nicco's building, and I watch as Daniel wrangles a drunk Dawn into his truck. He's so gentle with her as he tries desperately to get all her slippery limbs into the truck while getting soaked. I love how he treats all the women in his life with such care. I hope Dawn realizes how fortunate she is to have that. I sit in the car, trying to talk myself into just going back home as I watch them drive away, when I see the lights in Nicco's room come on and then go back out about fifteen minutes later. I know Kelsey is up there, and I don't want to cause a scene in front of her.

My phone dings in my purse with a message, and I grab it and look at the display. The text is from Nicco.

Are you home? Alarm set?

I get out of the car and sprint across the street. By the time I make it to the building, I'm drenched. In my haste, I forgot to grab an umbrella. I take the elevator up, and nerves assault me as I knock on the door. I know he's here.

Nicco answers with a look of surprise on his face. He stares at me for a few heartbeats, and I can see the apprehension in his eyes. Then, he merely steps aside. Cross comes out of the guest bedroom, wearing just pajama pants. He opens the door to the room wider and silently gestures for me to go in. As I slide past him, he cuts his eyes to Nicco, and he gives him a slight nod. Then, he follows me inside.

I stand with my back to him, facing the opposite side of the room. I say nothing as I hear the door shut, and the lock clicks into place.

What am I doing here? Why am I doing this to myself?

I start to shiver uncontrollably as the adrenaline leaves my body in a rush. My clothes are soaked through, and my teeth are chattering as I feel the cold air from the vent near my feet wash over me.

I hear him walk into the bathroom and back, and then his hands come around me and start to peel my T-shirt from my body.

"Arms up," he softly commands. "We need to get you out of these wet clothes."

I raise my arms without protest and let him remove my shirt.

He wraps a big, warm towel around my shoulders, and then he gently turns me. He pulls the string on my sleep shorts, and they fall in a soggy heap on the floor. He pulls the towel all the way around to cover me and then takes a second towel and starts drying my hair.

It feels familiar. Too familiar. So right, and yet it's all wrong. This isn't who we are anymore.

I bring my hand up and clutch his wrist, halting him. He looks down at me, his piercing green eyes heavy with the same sadness that is sitting on my chest like a cement block.

He looks weary, like a man who has the weight of the world on his shoulders.

He drops the towel he was holding, and I step into him and out of the towel he wrapped me in. He places his hands on either side of my face.

"Hi, baby," he whispers.

I whimper and grab the waist of his pants with my fists.

I lean my forehead onto his bare chest and stand there, fighting with myself. Then, I stand on the tip of my toes and I crush my mouth to his.

He lets me kiss him. He doesn't move or try to take control. He opens for me to take, and I do. I take because I need him to ease this ache. I need him to dull this pain. Everything hurts, all of me, and I need him to make it feel better even if it's only for tonight.

My arms go tightly around his neck, and I pull him to me. He clasps my waist and lifts me off my feet. He walks us back to the bed and sets me on the edge. He disengages and kneels in front of me. He brushes my hair behind my ears, and then he looks up into my face and waits. I reach behind, unclasp my bra, and slide the straps from my shoulders. I watch his face as his eyes follow my hands. A single tear escapes and rolls down his cheek.

Grief pulses through me, and every single intake of breath feels like a cluster of tiny knives piecing my lungs. I bend down and catch his tear with a kiss to his chin. He pulls me in and holds my face to his throat with his hand at the back of my head. I bring my hand up and place it on his chest between us, and I can feel his heart beating. I wonder if it hurts him, too.

"What do you need, *Tesoro*?" he whispers into my hair.

"A good-bye," I murmur into his neck.

He looks down at me, and I see the pain and regret. The last time we said good-bye, he was so cold. He didn't even look at me as he tore my world apart. I don't want that to be the last memory I have of him— the one I carry with me forever.

He stands and removes his bottoms as I watch, committing every inch of him to memory. He tosses them aside and joins me on the bed. He hesitates as he brushes my hair from my shoulder.

"Are you sure?" he asks.

I reach for him in answer, and he bends his head to mine and kisses me. It is not a hurried or frenzied kiss. It's slow and full of emotion. Neither of us is in any rush. His hand glides down my side and whispers over my hip, and I wonder if he knows. *Can he tell that my body has changed? Does he know it no longer belongs to him alone?*

He kisses his way down my chest and stops when he makes it to my hip. On the left side sits a small tattoo of a bleeding heart being pierced by a cross. A reminder of why I left and can never go back home.

He comes up on his knees as his fingers flutter over the ink. "Oh, baby." It's a strangled curse.

I come up to an elbow and extend my hand to him.

He follows me back down, and I wrap my legs around his hips as I kiss him more urgently. He finds my entrance, and I'm wet and ready for him. Always wet and ready for him. He slowly enters me as I expand around him. I forgot how good it feels to be filled by him. I groan at the pleasure and raise my hips to bring him fully inside. The stretch is a wonderful pain, and I want so badly for him to pound into me, to make it hurt until I can't feel the ache in my heart anymore, but he doesn't. He is gentle.

He peppers my neck with kisses as he steadily increases his thrusts, and this time, I commit everything I can to memory and file it away in that secret place in my heart. The smell of his skin, the rhythm of his breaths against my neck, the way the scruff on his face scratches my cheek, the feel of his weight on top of me, the way the muscles in his back flex and contract as he moves inside of me. I watch the sweat beading on his upper lip and the way his eyes dilate as he gets close to coming. I take it all in because I know it's the last time that I'll have the opportunity to see him like this.

I pour all of myself into this moment. I love him with every inch of my body. This time, I will brace for the slice of pain that awaits me in the morning. I won't fight it. I won't try to hold on because my happiness doesn't matter anymore. His happiness is all that matters now. So, I'll be ready for tomorrow, but tonight, I'm not holding anything back.

He continues to rock inside of me. He brings his hand between us and starts to massage my clit with his thumb. He knows my body so well. He knows exactly what I need to relieve the sweet tension growing inside me. It's exquisite torture. I dig my nails into his back as my orgasm hits, and I cry out as he pulls pleasure from me. He continues to pump in and out of me as my cries turn to trembles. A few heartbeats later, and he arches his back and growls as his release follows mine. He empties himself into me before collapsing on top of me, entirely spent.

I reach up and start to run my fingers through the damp hair at his nape. "Thank you," I whisper.

He raises his head and gives me a questioning look.

"Thank you for replacing the last memory I had of you. I needed this. I needed closure."

"A good-bye," he states mournfully.

"A good-bye."

He rolls to my side, and he pulls me into him. He kisses the top of my head and whispers, "Sleep, baby."

I snuggle in close and close my eyes. I don't want to fall asleep. I don't want the morning to come because I know that, once the sun rises, he's lost to me forever. Till then, he is right here. I have him. I want to savor every second, but I'm so exhausted, and no matter what I do, I can't stop the sun.

CHAPTER
Six

Cross

I AWAKE FROM THE BEST NIGHT'S SLEEP I'VE HAD IN MONTHS TO HER snuggled beside me with her long, dark hair fanned out on the pillow and her arm draped across my chest. Her soft breath on my shoulder.

She is still the most beautiful thing I have ever laid eyes on, and for a moment, I think I'm dreaming.

I carefully slide out from under her.

I want to leave her sleeping peacefully. It's the cowardly thing to do, but I know, if I wait until she's fully awake, the moment will be unbearable.

Selfishly, I kiss her forehead and tuck the blankets around her.

I whisper, "Good-bye, *Tesoro*. You will always have my heart. Always," against her cheek.

Then, I dress silently and walk out of the room as quietly as I can. Nicco is standing at the kitchen island, holding a cup of coffee. I can't look him in the eye as I walk over to the front door. I need to get out of here. Out before I change my mind and run back in there and crawl back into the haven with her.

"You just going to sneak out and let her wake up to find you gone, huh?" he questions.

"You know I have to," I say to the door.

"Funny, I thought you were in charge now. Doesn't the boss man get to make all the rules? You know how badly this is going to hurt her," he barks.

I turn and stride toward him, anger fueling my heavy steps. "Of course I do. Everything I do hurts her. Do you think I'm unaware? Every single decision I've ever made has been for her! I hurt her to protect her. I don't want to leave. I damn sure don't want to marry Adriana, but I will, for her. To keep her safe, I would do just about anything."

"Then, you really shouldn't have come here. You should have left her alone," he challenges.

It's the truth. I didn't have to come.

"I told you, I didn't want her to find out about the wedding from anybody but me. I thought she deserved that much from me."

"Liar. You know good and well that you coming here was about you wanting to see her. Hearing about you marrying her best friend was going to kill her, no matter how she found out. You being the one to deliver that blow didn't make it any easier."

I don't deny his accusations because, even though I convinced myself I was doing the right thing in telling her myself, on some level, I know he's right. Coming here was for me. Una tried to stop me. I wouldn't listen.

"I'm sorry, Nicco. I'm sorry I keep doing this to her. I'm sorry you keep having to pick up the pieces. I wish things could be different. I do."

He nods. "Yeah, I know. Me, too, man. Me, too."

"I need a favor." I know I'm pushing my luck with him, but there's one more thing I need to take care of before I can get on a plane. "How do I find Jake Mason?"

I have my driver drop me off at the corner. I don't want Mr. Mason to be alerted to my arrival, so I walk the block up to the address Nicco gave me.

Jake is not the one to come to the door when I knock, so I'm able to get into the house by saying I'm a friend of his. The guy who does answer is on his way out, so he tells me to go on in, that Jake is in the shower and should be down shortly. *What an idiot.* He gives me unfettered access to his home and his unsuspecting friend without so much as getting my name. It must be nice to be so unaware of the evil in this world.

Lucky for him, I only want to have a man-to-man talk with his roommate.

Jake descends the stairs about twenty minutes later and bellows, "Shawn, man, please tell me you started the coffee. I think I might be dying."

Death by hangover, I presume.

"Sorry, Shawn left, and unfortunately, he didn't start the coffee. I could use a cup myself," I answer.

He stops short at the sound of my voice. When he spots me, his face turns red with anger.

"What the hell are you doing in my kitchen?"

His eyes start darting around the room, as if looking for an escape or perhaps a weapon.

"Calm down, Jake. I only want to have a little chat. How was the shower? Did it work?" I inquire.

"What do you mean, did it work?" he asks as he walks the rest of the way into the kitchen.

"Were you able to wash her off? I'm assuming you brought the redhead from last night home with you, no?"

A momentary look of guilt sweeps over him, and then he glares at me, which is confirmation enough.

"I thought so. Probably sounded like a great idea last night. Gabby pissed you off. I pissed you off. So, you might as well take the hot, willing woman home and fuck her brains out to make yourself feel better. Right? Felt good last night, didn't it? You sure showed us. But then you woke up this morning, and the person lying beside you in bed was not the one you wanted. I bet you couldn't jump out of that bed fast enough, could you? Thought a nice, long, hot shower could help wash her off of you. Her smell. Her touch. Did it work?" I ask again.

He leans against the counter and crosses his arms on his chest. Remorse burns in his eyes as he glares at me, and I know that I hit a nerve and that I have his attention.

"What exactly do you want, huh? To rub salt in the wound? To laugh in my face over the fact that I fucked up? Who are you anyway? I mean, I know you're the ex. The one she supposedly left home over, because you hurt her so badly, but why the hell did she act like that? Like she was scared of you or scared you were going to stab me or something? What am I missing?"

"Who I am is a tale for another day. All you really need to know is that I'm not someone you want to cross. I don't make empty threats. Ever. You really fucked up last night. I ought to choke you, but I can see that you are in a world of pain already. See, I know what it's like to lose her. I know what it's like to wake up, hungover, next to a third-rate replacement." I shake my head at his pathetic state. "She deserves better than you; better than the both of us. Do you have any idea how lucky you were? You had her. She was yours. And you risked it for what?"

"Like you care. I saw the way you looked at her. Hell, I saw the way she looked at you. I'm not stupid."

"I disagree. You are very, very stupid. And it has nothing to do with me. You were already out with your date before I arrived. So, what did he offer you?"

He looks confused. "He?"

"Yes, Dante. I know you were in cahoots with him. Now, tell me, how do you know him and why the hell did you agree to get close to Gabby for him?" I slam my hand down on the counter to keep from grabbing him.

I need information. My instincts tell me this guy does care about Gabby. The way he reacted to my presence last night said all I needed to know, but he somehow ended up in Dante's snare, and I need to know how.

"Ugh, that guy? I told her it was nothing." He throws his arms in the air, exasperated. "I told her brother everything I know. I tried to explain it all to her, but she wouldn't listen to me. Then, she wouldn't see me or return any of my calls. Who the fuck is he to her? She is so full of secrets, and I don't understand any of this."

I can tell he's frustrated with being kept in the dark. I don't blame him. He can't love her and protect her like he should if he doesn't have all the facts. But do I trust him enough to tell them to him?

"He's an evil man from her past. He has hurt her before. I won't go into the details, but he's been obsessed with her for a long time now, and he scares her. We thought ... I thought that he was no longer a threat. I guess he isn't as smart as I gave him credit for. Coming here, seeking her out, was a big mistake on his part. A mistake I will deal with, but right now, I need to know your part in it."

I can see the moment he resigns to tell me everything. He has nothing left to lose at this point.

"He approached me months ago. Before I met Brie. She was a new hire at the club, and he said that he was a friend of her father's. That the father was a wealthy businessman in New York and was willing to pay big money for a little insider information on his daughter's life. She'd had her heart broken by a guy back home." He looks up at me. "Some loser named Christoff, who turned out to be a criminal and was using her because of her family's money. He said she was angry and was going through a rebellious stage as a result because she blamed her parents for the split. Apparently, they had him pegged from the beginning and disapproved of their relationship.

"She took off to California after that, and her father was concerned. She wasn't talking to him or her mother, and they wanted to give her time and space. It all sounded believable to me, and he did have the cash. I'd heard the new girl was a knockout, so I thought, *Why not?* I arranged to take some tennis lessons from her and see if I could win her trust. I didn't expect to fall for her like I did. It didn't take long though. I only met with the guy a few more times before I told him to go fuck himself."

"I bet he didn't take that very well. What all information did you pass on to him before that?"

"Minor shit. He already knew where she lived, went to school, and worked. I told him the names of the friends she had made and some of the places they liked to hang out. Gave him her work schedule for a couple of weeks. Seriously, nothing that he couldn't have found out for himself. I quickly became suspicious of his motives, and I wouldn't tell him anything that wasn't public knowledge. It frustrated him. I didn't give a shit, and finally, I told him I was done. He didn't like it, but I threatened to go to the police if I caught him anywhere near her or the club. He backed off, and I didn't see him or hear from him again.

"Not until he walked into the locker room and cornered me the other day. Brie showed up as I was trying to get him out of the club without causing a big scene. I didn't even see her; I didn't know she was there that day. I just wanted him out of there, so I pretended to be willing to hear him out, and I walked with him to his car. He was still feeding me the concerned-parents bullshit and trying to throw more money at me. I agreed to meet him later for drinks, which I never intended to actually do. I made my mind up to confess everything to her and tell her about him.

"I knew something was very wrong with him at that point and that the story he had been telling me was bogus. But the next thing I know, I get a text from her, saying we're over, and she refused to talk to me again. I couldn't get her to listen to me. She just shut down completely. I tried. I tried to get Daniel to talk to her. Nothing worked. I don't know what else to do." He pauses for a moment and pleadingly looks up at me. "What do I do, man? What do I do?"

He's cracking, but he's showing me what I need to see. He does love her. It's like a knife slicing me in two, but it's obvious. He didn't do this on purpose. Dante had tried to pay someone to be his inside eyes and ears in her life and never considered that person would grow to care for her. Once Jake Mason fell in love, he shut Dante down.

"She's scared. Dante has hurt her before, and someone she loved very much betrayed her once."

"You?" he accuses.

"Me," I admit. "I lost her. I broke her trust. It's not something she gives easily, at least not anymore."

"I don't think she's going to let me back in," he says in despair. More to himself than to me.

I can't help but feel bad for the guy. I know exactly where he is.

"No, she won't. She cares for you, but she doesn't trust you anymore. Neither do I. You fucked up. You have to accept it and move on because if I hear of you making this any harder for her, I will end you. Do I make myself clear?"

He chuckles under his breath as if he isn't taking my threat seriously. "Yeah, crystal."

The redhead comes sauntering down the stairs like she owns the place. We both turn as she enters the kitchen.

"Jake, baby, I woke up all alone. Come back to bed."

"I'll let you handle this unpleasant business," I say as I excuse myself.

I head toward the door, leaving him to take the trash out.

I call my car to pick me up, and I have to force myself not to head straight back to Nicco's place and back to her. I can't.

I won't put her any more at risk. I have enemies—faceless ones. Greater threats than Dante could ever be. Not enemies of my own making, but inherited enemies. The moment they know that something or someone means more to me than my own life, they will use and abuse it to break me.

So, I made a choice to let her go. I broke her, so they couldn't.

CHAPTER
Seven

Brie

I WAKE UP ALONE. BEFORE I EVEN OPEN MY EYES, I REACH FOR HIM, and his side of the bed is empty and cold. I sit up, taking the sheet with me, and blink away the sleep. I can still smell him on the sheets and my skin. Grief hits me but just for a moment. I knew he would be gone, so I pull myself together, get up, and make my way to the bathroom.

As I look at myself in the mirror I think, *How did I get here again?* I promised myself I would never be broken again, and yet I feel battered and bruised.

"You can handle this, Brie. You're not the same weak girl you were before," I say out loud to my reflection.

I start the shower, and step in, letting the scalding hot spray wash over me. Everything that happened last night replays in my mind. *What a strange twenty-four hours it has been.*

I honestly thought nothing could shock me anymore. I was so wrong. When Cross said Adi's name, I felt the wind get knocked from me. And then there was our last good-bye. I'm not sure where I go from here.

After I'm dressed in my shorts and one of Nicco's old sweatshirts I found in the bathroom, I head out to face the world. Nicco is standing in the kitchen, in front of the stove. The smell of bacon wafts through the air, and a fresh pot of coffee is sitting on the counter.

I clear my throat, and he turns to face me. I'm embarrassed. Embarrassed that I was so weak last night.

"Hey, sis," he starts and then stops. He looks toward the door. "Um, he, uh—"

"He's gone," I finish for him. "It's okay, Nicco. I expected to wake up to him gone."

He gives me a sympathetic look, and he sighs. "He just ... shit, I don't think he could face you this morning," he tries to explain.

"I shouldn't have come here last night. I know that. I couldn't stay away. I needed to see him one last time. I knew that, when he left, it would be the last time I ever saw him, and I wanted more time. I know that makes me sound a little pathetic, but please don't judge me," I plead.

"I'm not judging you, sis."

I feel a sense of relief at his words. I need my big brother to understand.

"I think your bacon is done." I point to the stove. "When did you start cooking anyway?" I question him.

"When I moved out of Mamma's house. Don't look so surprised. It was either learn to scramble an egg or starve to death."

"Starve, huh?" I giggle.

He scoops some eggs and bacon on a plate and sets it down in front of me. "So, what now?" he asks.

I let out a heavy sigh because I have no idea. "I don't know. I want everything to go back to the way it was before Dante showed up because, honestly, I don't want to run again."

"You never stopped running, Gabby. Being here. Lying to everyone. Pretending to be someone else. It's running every damn day. Don't you see that?"

"I have my reasons, Nicco."

"Really? What are they? Because, if you think for one second that Dawn and Kelsey are going to love you any less if they know your real name, you're crazy. I haven't known them half as long as you have, and I know they would throw themselves in front of a bus for you."

"Yeah, well, there used to be a time when I thought Adi would do the same."

"Don't do that. Don't compare them to Adriana. They don't deserve that. Adi has always been about Adi. Yes, you were close, but she was never selfless or dependable."

"I never thought she would betray me like this."

"Then, you never knew her as well as you thought you did because it doesn't surprise me one bit."

"How long have you known?"

He blows out a long breath. "About the engagement? A few months. But they were living together before I left."

Before he left. So, they were living together before Christmas.

"When did it start?" I ask.

"Gabby, don't ask questions you don't want to know the answers to."

"I need to know, Nicco."

"Right after you left," he admits.

I nod and let it sink in. Two years. They have been together for almost two years, which is way longer than he and I were together. He'll build her the dream house, and she'll be the one to fill it full of babies. I let the knowledge settle deep into my bones. I think some part of me always hoped that we would find our way back to each other one day, but it can never happen now. Not after this. He's made his choice, and it's not me.

"Thank you for telling me."

"I would have told you sooner, but you insisted that I never bring up his name, and I just didn't want to hurt you anymore."

"It's okay. I am not mad at you."

"Truly?"

I can hear the relief in his voice.

"Truly."

We hear his bedroom door creak open, and our conversation comes to a halt.

Kelsey scoots into the kitchen, yawning out her greeting, "Good morning, guys."

"Good morning, sunshine." I grin at her disheveled appearance.

"I don't know about that sunshine business. I kind of feel like I was hit by a truck last night," she whines.

"I bet Dawn feels a lot worse," I assume.

"No way. She can drink like a frat boy and still function. I don't know how she does it." She takes a seat at the island with her head in her hands. "I didn't expect to see you this morning. How's your head?" she asks.

"My head?"

"Yes, I guess your migraine subsided if you were able to drive over here this early. I was worried about you last night. You looked miserable."

Nicco and I exchange a knowing look.

"I felt miserable, but I guess a massive dose of ibuprofen and a good night's sleep did the trick. I feel much better now."

"I'm glad. You didn't happen to bring any of that magic ibuprofen with you, did you?"

"I think I have some in my bag."

"Awesome."

I collect the medication and hand it to her with a cup of coffee.

After swallowing it down, she looks over her shoulder to the guest room door. "Babe, is your friend still here?"

"No, he had an early flight this morning, so he snuck out a few hours ago," Nicco fibs.

"Bummer. I really wanted you to see him, Brie. He was beautiful."

"Beautiful?" Nicco asks.

"Yes, beautiful. Tall, dark, and brooding. He had the most incredible green eyes. Like the color of sea glass. I thought Dawn was going to faint when she saw him."

"Hate that I missed that." I can imagine Dawn's reaction to Cross.

"Oh well. There are lots of fish in the sea. Speaking of, I say the three of us spend the day on the beach. We need to kick-start this epic summer with a bang. No worrying about asshole exes—you or me—and no feeling sorry for ourselves because we are not in Monaco with the Ds," she insists.

"That sounds like a fantastic idea. Tell you what. You ladies grab your suits and a change of clothes and come back here and set yourselves up on the beach. I have a little business to attend to. When I come back, I'll take my two favorite girls out to dinner, and we can all stay here tonight," Nicco says as he sets a plate in front of Kelsey. He goes to his room, comes back with a spare key, and hands it to her.

I wonder what business he has to attend to, but I am probably better off not knowing. Plus, I am sure Cross is still in California, and he wants to spend a little more time with his best friend before he leaves for home.

"What do you say, Brie? A little hair of the dog on the beach?" she asks.

"Sounds good to me."

CHAPTER
Eight

Cross

MY PHONE VIBRATES IN MY POCKET, SO I PULL IT OUT. IT'S A CALL from home. Probably Una wondering how everything went.

"Hello?"

"Where the hell are you?"

"You know, Adriana, it's customary to return a greeting when given one."

"Whatever. Hello, honey. How are you? I miss you madly. Please hurry home. Just answer the fucking question. Where are you?"

"I am in Los Angeles on business. I'll be back sometime tonight."

"Business, huh?"

"Yes, business. What do you need?"

"Does this business have anything to do with Gabby?"

How does she know this? Una would never tell her, and as far as I know, she has no idea where Gabby has ended up.

"I'll take your silence as a yes," she huffs into the phone.

"Why would you assume that?" I ask curiously.

"Oh, I don't know. Maybe because I got a text last night from an unknown California number, congratulating me on our engagement and wishing me happiness in the life I stole from her."

Well, fuck.

"I'm sorry. I didn't think she would contact you," I admit.

I feel like shit. I should have told Adriana that I was coming.

"You didn't think she would contact me when she found out I was marrying the love of her life? You didn't think she would let me know how badly I was betraying her and how we both broke her fucking heart? Really? Sometimes, I wonder if you ever knew her at all. How could you tell her and not warn me?"

"What good would that have done?"

"At least I would have been prepared. Damn it, Cross. You're not the only one riddled with guilt over what we're doing to her. I'm in this, too, you know."

"You're right. I should have told you I was coming to tell her."

"What exactly did you tell her?"

"That we're getting married. Nothing more. What did you tell her?"

"Nothing. I sent her a reply, just asking if it was really her and if we could talk, but I didn't get a response, so I called the number, and apparently, she'd blocked me. I was going to use one of the guys' phones to call, but I assumed she wouldn't answer any unknown number from New York anyway. I don't even know if she got my reply."

"It's for the best."

"Probably, but that doesn't make me feel any better about her finding out. God, she must hate us."

"That's probably for the best as well. It'll be easier for her to move forward if she hates us both."

There is a pregnant pause as we both let the guilt settle between us.

"Look, I have to go. Nicco is messaging me. I'll see you tonight. We can talk more then."

"Fine."

I hang up and open the message from Nicco. He wants to meet at a restaurant in half an hour. I have my driver head back into the city.

We order lunch and then launch straight into business. My plane leaves in three hours, and we need a plan in place.

"How did it go with Jake this morning? Is he still breathing?" he asks, only half-joking.

"Yes, of course, he is."

He raises an eyebrow as if to say it wasn't a given. "That's good, I guess."

"I just went to quiz him about Dante in case there was something he'd forgotten to tell you or some clue he had to his whereabouts."

"And?"

"And he pretty much told me what he'd told you, verbatim."

"Do you believe him?"

That's a question I've been asking myself all day. As much as I want to hate the guy, he seems genuine. I feel sorry for him at this point.

"Yes. I don't think he meant any harm to come to Gabby or the girls. He's not dangerous, just stupid."

"I don't even think he's stupid. He didn't know what he was dealing with when it came to Dante. He was conned. I'm telling you, man, I've seen him with Gabby. He loves her. He would never intentionally let anything happen to her."

I growl. Yes, growl.

"He loves her, yet I found him this morning with another woman in his bed," I angrily point out.

Nicco sighs. "Yeah, well, she was in your bed last night," he points out.

"Don't," I warn.

I pin him with a furious glare. He places his hands in the air.

"Just stating the facts, man. The entire night was a shit show on all fronts. I don't think any of us should be passing judgment based on what was done last night."

He's right, and it pisses me off, so I change the subject.

"Let's talk about Dante, shall we?" I ask through gritted teeth.

"I think you need to talk to Tony when you get back to New York."

I start to interrupt him and object, but he continues, "Hear me out. I know you want to take care of this, and you think she doesn't want her family involved. That might very well be true, but he has resources out here, and we keep hitting dead ends. I want to find this asshole before he makes a real play for her. Because you and I both know that's exactly what he plans to do. I can't track him down and keep up with her and the girls at the same time. I have two guys here, and one has to have his eyes on her anytime I'm not there. He's watching her and Kelsey now, so we can have lunch. I need help, Cross. Tony will provide that aid. We're her family, and she needs us whether she wants to admit it or not. I get that she wants to live here and not in New York. I get that she wants to be as far away as possible, and maybe that's healthy, but I do not understand her changing her name and pretending to be someone else. It just doesn't add up for me."

It makes perfect sense to me. Our business has far-reaching legs. Even out here, the Mastreoni name carries weight.

"I can send more men," I offer.

"Good. The more, the better. But talk to Tony. If you don't, I will."

I relent because I know he's right. Whatever it takes to get our hands on Dante as soon as possible. That's all that matters now.

"Okay. I'll call a meeting with Tony as soon as I'm back in New York. As long as he keeps your father out of it because, if Vincenzo gets wind of any of this, he'll have our asses for not telling him what happened back then, and he'll have her dragged back home against her will. I can't do that to her. I can't let him do it to her. The farther away she is, the safer and happier she is."

"Agreed. I'm sure Tony knows that, too. He won't involve Papa."

"How was she this morning?" I ask, not sure I want to know the answer.

"Fine. Better than that. I think she's going to be okay. You know, it amazes me how resilient she's become. She keeps getting back up and moving forward. She's not a little girl anymore. I'm so fucking proud of her."

"Me, too."

"How are you?"

"Me?"

"Yes, you. Don't forget I know you. Being here can't be easy. I can see the toll this is all taking on you. I give a shit about you too."

"I'll be just fine as soon as Dante Calvacanti is six feet under."

"What about the other stuff? Any progress on finding Atelo?"

I shake my head.

"No, it's like he vanished into thin air. Obviously, he doesn't want to be found. Can't say I blame him."

"Yeah, well, fuck him. Any leads on the shooters?"

"Nope," I bite out, my frustration evident. It's been almost two years, and every lead has turned out to be a dead end.

He nods. "It'll get easier, Cross."

"What will?"

"All of it."

It won't, and it doesn't even matter to me anymore. My life has been reduced to meeting my obligations and going through the motions. I've just resigned myself to never having the happiness I once thought I was going to. Gabriella is gone forever. I'll never get to build her a home. Never watch her walk down the aisle to me. Never see her swollen with our child. I hope she finds all those things. I won't be the one to give them to her, and living with that, will never get any fucking easier.

CHAPTER
Nine

Bree

KELSEY AND I HAVE SPENT THE ENTIRE AFTERNOON LYING IN THE sun and splashing in the ocean. It is therapeutic. A carefree day with my friend is what I needed after the emotional roller coaster of the past few weeks.

"Mmm, this is so nice," she sighs as we face each other while lying on our stomachs.

"It really is. I haven't been this relaxed in a long time," I agree.

"How are you doing with everything? I know seeing Jake last night had to be hard."

"Yes, a little, but honestly, I went into that relationship, holding back, so I wouldn't fall completely apart when it did," I voice the thing I knew all along.

Her head rises at my admission.

"That's my biggest fear," she starts, "that I'll do the same thing. It's like I am so afraid of liking Nicco too much or not enough or even just the right amount. I know that sounds crazy."

"It doesn't sound the least bit crazy. Brad was your first love. Maybe not your first boyfriend, but your first love."

She nods in confirmation.

"Things are always so simple with our first love. We go all in and completely give ourselves to them—heart, body, and soul. We hold nothing back because we don't know we need to. Our hearts have never been shattered, and our lives have never been torn apart. We've never had to gather the scattered fragments and try to piece them back together before. So, we don't know to have a wall, a part of us that we don't give them. Our first loves, we love without fear. With utter abandon, we give them everything, and once that trust is betrayed, we never love like that again. We always hold something back for ourselves."

She lifts her head and rests it on her folded arms as she considers what I said. "You're right. It sucks."

"It does, but we will heal, and we will love again. Madly and deeply, I hope. Just never quite the same."

We lie in silence, pondering our romantic misfortune a while longer, when she changes the subject.

"So, what are our plans for the summer?" she asks.

"I have several catering jobs lined up—from children's birthday extravaganzas to summer dinner parties—courtesy of your mother's friends. She wasn't lying when she said she could drum up business for me."

"Trust me, she has no shortage of bougie friends who are more than willing to spend ridiculous amounts of money for little Jimmy's fifth birthday party." She rolls her eyes.

"Thank goodness. I can use all the practice and extra cash I can get."

"Do you want any help? I mean, not the cooking part, but the setup, serving, and cleanup parts? I'm an excellent hostess."

"Sure, but you don't want to be working all summer, especially at your mom's friends' parties. Besides, I can't afford to pay much."

I'd hate for her to spend her summer working for the measly salary I could pay. I intend to find some high school kids who would do a horrible yet affordable job for me.

"Why not? I don't mind working hard. The only reason I don't work during classes is because Mom and Matt insist. They pay for everything, so I can concentrate on my studies."

I consider her offer more carefully.

"If you're serious, I would love to have you. It would be fun to do it together. I can pay you a third after paying for supplies, and then we'll split the tips. Would that work?" I ask, suddenly hopeful.

She comes up onto her elbows. Her long blonde hair blowing into her face, she grins, and genuine excitement lights her face. "Let's do it. I'll even be your sous chef and assist while you cook. I'd enjoy learning how to make some of your recipes. When is our first job?"

"A Memorial Day dinner at the American Legion Yacht Club in Newport Beach. It's a two-hundred-dollars-a-plate dinner to raise money for their Wounded Warrior fund. It's the Friday night before Memorial Day. It pays well, and they have a good budget for food, so we can go all out. Their staff will be handling all the serving and cleanup, so we don't have to hire for those, which means more profit for us. Plus, it has a large kitchen, so we don't have to try to prepare and transport that much from our kitchen."

"Perfect! We can work on Friday night and have the rest of the holiday weekend to enjoy ourselves. I think this is going to be the best summer ever," she squeals.

I hope she's right. I hope Cross and Nicco can track down Dante or that he's fled far away. I don't want to spend the summer looking over my shoulder or being followed by bodyguards.

We settle back down and start talking menus and uniforms. It's nice to have a partner in crime.

About an hour later, Nicco walks up and squats down between us in his board shorts, tee, and sunglasses. He looks way more at ease than he did this morning. I hear a little sigh come from Kelsey. He is a handsome sight with his massive arms and tanned skin.

"How are my favorite girls doing?"

"Amazing. We were just about to go for a swim to cool off. Care to join us?" Kelsey asks as she brings her hand up to shield her eyes and gaze up at him.

He peels off his T-shirt and stands. Then, he extends his hand to her. She gets to her feet and turns to me.

"You coming?" she asks.

"You guys go ahead. I'll be there in a minute."

She grins, and they take off for the water. I watch from my towel on the sand as he picks her up and throws her into a wave, and she comes up, laughing. She jumps on his shoulders, trying to dunk him. Her efforts are futile though because his massive frame is not budging. I smile at the happiness my friend and my brother are beaming with. I think maybe her heart is beginning to heal after all. That's what's most important to me now, that everyone I love, including myself, heals.

"Hey, Brie, come on. Hurry! I need help," Kelsey yells to me from the water as Nicco picks her up once again to toss her.

"On my way!" I get to my feet and take off flying through the sand. I launch myself at my big brother.

Together, Kelsey and I manage to get him to his knees as he wraps us in his tree-trunk arms like he is a god. I think maybe he is a real-life Hercules.

Nicco has to take a shower and run into the city for an unexpected meeting, so we have to cancel our dinner plans.

He's been getting an expansion office for one of our family's marketing companies off the ground here in LA. Therefore, the last few weeks have been full of last-minute meetings and handling construction and contractor issues.

Kelsey and I decide to head back to our place and make a late lunch, and then I'm going to teach her how to make French macarons from scratch. We stop at the market on the way back and grab all the supplies we need.

"This is going to be so much fun. I've always wanted to learn how to bake. I mean, I can bake a boxed cake with the best of them, but to bake from scratch … not so much," she admits as we load our cart.

"My mother and grandmother taught me how when I was little, but when I lived in Paris, Sacha took me under his wing and fine-tuned my skills," I tell her.

"Sacha?"

"Yes, he was the pastry chef at the café my aunt managed. He was an artist. I learned a great deal from him, like the tricks to making the perfect macaron. You have to always separate your egg white in advance and make sure they are room temperature before you start. And you sift the cocoa powder and powdered sugar when making chocolate macarons. You think they're already fine enough, but you're wrong. Then, you pipe the cookies onto a baking mat, not wax paper. Most importantly, open the oven halfway through baking and let the steam escape. Once they are done, let them cool completely before piping your buttercream in the middle and refrigerate before you serve them. They taste better that way."

"Wow, so much goes into baking one little cookie. I don't know how you keep it all straight."

"It's like riding a bike. Once you get your hands in the dough or your whisk in the batter, it all just comes naturally."

"I don't know about that, but I can't wait to learn."

We spend the rest of the afternoon and evening baking. Kelsey is a pretty quick study and very interested in all the aspects. I patiently teach her each step, and she masters them all.

"You're a natural."

"You think so? I've thought about taking a few cooking classes at LaVarenne, but I don't know. I don't think I've quite decided what I want to be when I grow up yet. Dawn has always known she wants to work at a magazine. She loves fashion and gossip and all things magazine-ish. I'm just coasting with a Liberal Arts major until I can figure out what I want to do."

Dawn is taking her communications degree and starting as the new social media manager for an online fashion magazine based out of LA. It's the perfect job for her personality, and she's excited to get started.

"You should definitely look into culinary classes. One thing I've learned for sure is that you either love to cook and enjoy the entire process or you hate it and do it because you have to. My nonna always said that you could taste the love in food like it was an ingredient."

"I do love to cook. I love being in the kitchen, and I love to feed my people."

"Then, I think you have your answer."

She smiles to herself as if the thought pleases her. "Maybe, one day, you and I could own a restaurant together," she says.

I find that I like that possibility. "Why stop at one? We could have our own chain one day."

"And Dawn can do a feature for our grand opening in her magazine." She grins at me.

"We're going to rule the world one day," I inform her.

"Yes, we are."

CHAPTER
Ten

Cross

I'VE BEEN PUTTING OUT FIRES SINCE I RETURNED HOME. WHEN I TOOK over for my father, everything was a mess. Getting the books in order and restoring confidence within our organization was a massive undertaking, but in the past two years, the Scutari family has grown stronger, and our businesses are once again thriving.

I am sitting in my office in the estate I took over from my father last year. He is still wheelchair-bound, and I found him a handicap-accessible condo in a fancy building across town and employed a full staff that takes exceptional care of him. My grandparents have stayed on here, and Adriana moved in about six months ago when the engagement was announced. Since then, the manor has been a whirl of activity, as she has redecorated every single room, one by one. It has cost me a fortune, and the mess has been irritating, but it keeps my new fiancée distracted, so it's worth the trouble.

"When did you get home?"

Adriana is standing in the doorway. I set the report I have been scanning aside and lean back. She comes in and sits on the edge of my desk.

"Late last night."

"How did the rest of your trip go?"

I rub my temples, trying to ease the headache that has been plaguing me all morning. I know she wants details about Gabriella, and I'm not in the mood to share.

"I don't want to discuss it, Adriana."

"Fine. Don't tell me," she huffs angrily.

"Can we talk about it later?" I ask because I know she won't drop it.

"I suppose so. I have a dress fitting today, and then I have to meet with the bakery and the caterers to finalize the cake flavors and menu. Do you want to come with me?"

"No. I'm swamped here." I motion to the papers scattered across my desk and under her ass.

"Can't you spare a couple of hours? This is your wedding, too."

She's pouting now. I hate it when she does that. It might have worked on her father to get what she wants, but it won't work on me.

"You know I don't care what cake you get or what food you serve. Get whatever you like."

Her face falls.

"What?"

"It's just no fun, planning it all by myself; that's all."

"Why don't you call your bridesmaids and have them go with you? Isn't that part of their duties?"

I have no idea what bridesmaids are supposed to do or what their actual purpose is, but she has chosen a dozen girls, so the very least they can do is save me from having to do anything but show up on the day of the ceremony.

"Ugh, no. I can't stand any of those bitches," she sneers.

"Then, why did you choose them to be in your wedding party? You should have chosen your friends."

"My mother insisted I include all my female cousins and her best friend's daughters. They don't like me, and I don't like them."

"Then, call some of your actual friends and ask them to accompany you."

She sniffles and turns her head away. I hate to see a female cry. Any female.

"This sucks," she whispers.

"Honestly, I thought you were excited to plan this."

I'm confused by her behavior. She has an unlimited budget, and this wedding and party are all about her, which is precisely how she likes things.

"I was. I am. I've been planning my perfect wedding since I was ten years old. I was going to be married in the grand ballroom at The Plaza in front of about five hundred people. I wanted to wear an original Vera Wang. I planned to walk down the aisle to 'Ave Maria,' and white doves were going be released at the reception, which would be held in the courtyard of Tavern on The Green. I wanted Papa to hire Maroon 5 to play. The whole thing was going to be the social event of the year and make *Page Six*."

"Well, you have your dream venues booked and the dress you wanted, so what's the problem?"

"Gabby was supposed to be my maid of honor, and I was supposed to be hers. Of course, she wanted some lame beach wedding with just a few guests and to walk to her groom to 'A Thousand Years' by Christina Perri." She rolls her eyes as she smiles. "She is such a Twi-nerd."

She's lost me. I have no idea what that is.

"She picked out this simple Grecian dress and wanted to wear flowers in her hair instead of a veil with just a clam bake and dancing on the beach at sunset for her reception." She pauses and laughs. "It's so Gabby. Simple elegance. Damn, we're so different. It's just not the same, planning it without her, you know?"

The last thing I want to do is picture Gabby in a wedding dress. Her hair blowing in the seaside breeze and joy beaming on her beautiful face as she walks to some other man's side. *Fuck, why did Adriana have to put that image in my head?*

My mind goes to the ring in my safe. The one I bought for her. The one I can't seem to get rid of.

"Yeah, well, you're going to have to make do with one of your bridesmaids. Sorry. Just pick the one you dislike the least and call her."

She sighs at that and hops off my desk. "Fine. If you really won't go with me, at the very least, you can pick and hire the band for the reception."

"What, no Maroon 5?"

She snorts. "I've outgrown that fantasy. Besides, I only chose them for Gabby. She's the one who always had a hard-on for Adam Levine."

My headache is getting worse.

"Okay. I will take care of the music," I concede.

She walks around the desk and leans down, and I kiss her on the cheek. I'm making an effort to try to be more affectionate with her. It's been almost two years, and it's still awkward as hell for me.

"Dinner?" she asks.

"I have a dinner meeting in the city. I'll be home sometime afterward."

She frowns but doesn't say anything. She leaves the office, passing Tony as he saunters in.

"Adriana," he clips in acknowledgment of her with a bite in his tone.

He's made his distaste for Adi very clear as of late. All of Gabby's brothers have.

"Tony." She exaggerates her own bite as she disappears into the hallway.

Tony comes and sits across from me. His face is a mask of disinterest. I'm not exactly his favorite person either. He blames me for Gabby taking off, and he has no intention of getting over it anytime soon.

"I'm here. What is so urgent?" he asks.

"I need your help."

"With?"

He's not going to take any of this news well. I brace myself before I start.

"Dante Calvacanti."

His jaw jumps at the mention of Dante's name. "What help do you need with that fucker?"

"His father cut him loose. Apparently, he's had his nose in some bad business, and he's become an embarrassment and a liability," I start to explain.

"And I care, why?"

"He was last seen in California at the club where Gabriella works."

That gets his attention. He sits straight up, and rage fills his expression. "What? That motherfucker can't be that stupid."

"He is. He even hired a guy with connections to her new life to give him information on her."

"I should have killed him when I had the chance. I would have if you hadn't stopped me."

"I stopped you because she'd begged me not to let you," I remind him.

He shakes his head. "They were right to force you two apart. She's your weakness. A blind spot. We all have one, and she is yours. You could never tell her no."

"I told her no plenty." I meet his glare.

"Not once you had her. I should have shot you in the kneecap back then."

"Wouldn't have kept me away from her."

"Nope, but it would have been fun."

"Can you imagine Gabby's reaction if you had shot me?"

He grins. "She would have handed my ass to me. She's going to put me into an early grave, that one." His face turns serious. "Did you take care of this?"

"Nicco tried to pin him down, but he's in the wind. I made a trip out there, and I have several men following leads now. The problem is, his family cut him loose and released his trust fund to get rid of him. He's obviously still obsessed with Gabby, and he has nothing to lose. My intel says he got into drugs and burned through a lot of cash, so my guess is, he has to be getting low and desperate. We need to find him fast."

"Where is she now? Did you bring her back with you?"

"No. I have twenty-four-hour surveillance on her, and Nicco is there."

"Not good enough. You should have brought her home," he snaps.

"We can't force her to come home."

"The fuck we can't. I'm going to get her." He stands up and starts for the door.

"Tony, wait. Please, sit back down. We need to work together here."

He stops and turns. "No, we don't. This is Mastreoni business. I'll handle it from here. You concentrate on your wedding. Gabby is none of your concern anymore."

"I contacted you out of courtesy, Tony. Her well-being will always be my concern. We don't need to fight. We need to work together to find him. I've sent all the men I can spare to California, and I need you to send anyone you can. I want to do this without disruption to her life. She is happy there. She has friends who love her. She's in school and working and thriving. Dragging her back to New York is just going to hurt her. Haven't we all hurt her enough?"

He glares at me for a few seconds and then takes his phone from his pocket and dials. "Nicco. Cross just briefed me on the Dante situation. I'm sending Stefano and his crew to you. Stef is the best tracker on the planet, and he will find him. Brief them as soon as they arrive. Yes. I am in his office now. Don't let her out of your sight."

He closes the phone and puts it back in his pocket

"Please, Tony, we have more to discuss. Come sit back down."

He reluctantly does as I asked.

"I heard the Irish are in town," he states as he settles in.

"Yes, I'm meeting with O'Neill tonight at La Palinas."

La Palinas is a quaint little Italian restaurant I own in Brooklyn. It has good food and friendly and discreet staff; therefore, it also serves as the perfect meeting place. The back room is soundproof and secure and fully wired.

"You need backup?" he asks.

"Yes, but I don't want to bring anyone else to the table. Matteo is accompanying me, and I would like some armed men in the restaurant. I'm sure he'll have his own. If things are going well, we'll move the discussions to the back room. I would appreciate you being there."

Matteo is my right-hand man, as he was my father's before me. He and Papa are the best of friends, and he helped me secure the O'Neill deal.

"Are you bringing Salvatore in on this?"

"No. You and I control the docks in Staten Island. The Irish want access and protection for their trade. Salvatore doesn't need to be there."

He laughs. "Salvatore thinks he needs to have his nose in everything."

"I know, and it's time he learns to stay in his lane."

Salvatore Ferraro is Adriana's father and has an overinflated sense of importance. When I first took over, I needed him as an ally. Both his and Gabby's father, Vincenzo's, support was instrumental in boosting the confidence of the other family heads in my ability to quickly transition as head of our family's affairs. It's the reason I agreed to the relationship with Adriana. To solidify the alliance. Lately, he's been pushing to partner more and more, and I've been reluctant at best. I just don't care for my future father-in-law.

Now, I've moved beyond needing his backing, and he's just become a nuisance.

"Good. I don't like the guy. Never have. What about the Paulino situation?"

This is the part I hate. Running the businesses and negotiating deals I'm good at, but the dirty work still turns my stomach.

"He has to be taught a lesson."

He nods his agreement. "Want me to have it taken care of?"

Tony doesn't have the same qualms I do.

"No, I need to be the one to do it."

"He'll be at the carnival tomorrow night. Out in the open. It'd be a perfect time."

"Not with his family there."

"Cross ..." he starts to interject.

"I said, no. Not in front of his children and not when they or his wife could get caught in the cross fire."

"Okay. Then, when?"

"I'll have my men fetch him and bring him to the Bowery warehouse. We'll interrogate him and find out who he's selling us out to before we take care of him."

"Your call. You need to send a very clear message that you do not tolerate rats."

"I will," I bite as I cut my eyes to him.

As much as I hate this part, I know he's right.

CHAPTER
Eleven

Bree

THE AMOUNT OF SECURITY THAT HAS MADE A SUDDEN appearance in my life is ridiculous. I swear, men sleep in a car across the street from our apartment building every night. Two days ago, a new state-of-the-art alarm system was installed, replacing the perfectly good one we already had. To Kelsey's credit, she has taken it all in stride and hasn't let it freak her out. She and Dawn both know about Dante, and they know that his sudden presence in Santa Monica scared me. I'm sure Nicco has filled in the parts I didn't tell her. At least, some of them. At this point, I'm just thankful the two haven't asked me to find other living arrangements. They didn't exactly sign up for all of this.

Melanie and I are perusing the wares at the Santa Monica Farmers Market. I have a few new recipes I want to try this afternoon, and nothing beats the fresh, organic produce at the market. I brought a couple of large newsboy sling bags from home, and I'm checking the ripeness of some heirloom tomatoes when I feel the hair prickle at the back of my neck. I look up and scan my surroundings. I don't see Melanie and the baby, nor do I see Nicco's man, Gino, who has been staying a few feet back but within eyesight all morning. There are throngs of people crowding the street between the tents. I feel a little silly for my unease, so I pay the lady, place the tomatoes in my bag, and go in search for Mel. I turn a corner, and as I start to look at a selection of fresh herbs that caught my eye, I feel a hand slide up the back of my thigh.

"Hey, don't touch me!"

I turn and shove the offender as hard as I can. His body doesn't budge. Instead, he clasps my wrist and pulls me in close.

Dante.

Panic hits me like a physical blow. I start to struggle, and before I can scream, he pulls me behind a nearby food truck. He traps me between his body and the cold metal of the truck, leaning into me with one hand over my mouth. I'm thrashing and banging my foot against the side of the truck, trying to get someone's, anyone's attention, but the sound of the generator running beside us mixed with the roar of the crowd makes it impossible for anyone to hear me.

"Calm down, Gabriella. I'm not going to hurt you."

I inhale deeply through my nose and settle my body down as much as I can as my thoughts go to Melanie and the baby. I have to be smart here. I can't let him get anywhere near them even if it means complying with him.

"That's my girl."

He leans in closer, puts his nose into my neck, and inhales deep as he plays with the tendrils of hair escaping my ponytail at my nape. I'm close to hyperventilating. My body is shaking.

"Mmm, I've missed the way you smell, baby, and I love the way you tremble when I touch you."

He still has one hand covering my mouth. He takes a slight step back and looks me over from head to toe. Then, he glides his free hand over my hip and across my stomach.

"Still so fucking beautiful."

I take a moment to really look at him. He is still handsome, but his black eyes are wild, and he seems very unkempt, like a man who hasn't slept or maybe even showered for days.

"I'm going to remove my hand, but you're not going to scream. Understand? I have a gun at my hip, and I will use it, Gabriella. You

don't want me shooting you or shooting into this crowd full of innocent people, now do you?"

I shake my head as tears of panic start to sting my eyes.

He drops his hand, and I begin to gasp in air as a small sob bubbles
up from my chest.

"Shh … don't cry, baby." He reaches and gently wipes a tear as it
falls. "God, I've missed you," he says as he caresses my cheek.

I don't say anything. I turn my head and avert my eyes. I watch as
people walk right past us and never look behind the truck to see us.

"Look at me." He grabs my chin and turns me back to face him.
"Why do you make me chase you, Gabby? Why?"

"I don't want you to chase me, Dante," I rasp out.

"Then, stop running from me." He leans in and nuzzles his cheek
against mine. "We belong together. I knew it the moment I met you, all
innocent and doe-eyed. Fucking beautiful. It was instant. I know you
were confused by our connection, and I know you thought you were
in love with Christoff then, but look at what he did to you. He threw
you away like you were nothing and made you leave. It was never him.
You never belonged with him."

He leans back and looks me in the eye. "It's time to come home to
me, sweetheart."

He is delusional. This is not the Dante I knew. No, this version of
him is much more terrifying.

"Here's what we're going to do. You're going to be a good girl and
walk to my car with me. You will not struggle, and you will not cause a
scene. We will go back to my place and spend the evening making up.
Then, in the morning, we'll book our flights back home."

"This is home," I try to tell him.

"No, it's not. We are going back to New York, where we belong."

I change tactics. "Okay, but I don't have any of my things, and I
want to say good-bye to my friends," I plead.

"I'm sorry, baby. You'll have to leave everything here. Your brother
has your apartment being watched like a fucking hawk, and we can't

risk him stopping us. I'll buy you anything you need, and your friends can come to visit us once we are settled."

"Don't you think they'll come looking for me when they realize I'm gone?" I try to reason with him.

"Yes, but by then, we'll be long gone, and once we are back in New York, we'll have protection. I have a friend who's going to help us. After we take care of all your enemies, your father and brothers will see that I am good for you and how in love and happy we are. They'll realize that keeping us apart was wrong. We will marry, and my father will welcome me back. Then, everything is going to be so good. You'll see."

"My enemies? I don't have any enemies."

"Yes, you do. We both do, and Scutari is going to pay. I'm going to make him pay."

"Cross didn't do anything to me, Dante. We dated, and we broke up; that's all. Couples break up all the time."

"Don't defend him. He destroyed us both. We are both here because of him." He caresses my cheek and then runs his hand down the column of my neck as a look of sadness washes over him. "He misread what was happening between the two of us that night. Took you from me and then brought your brothers back the next day. Do you know they put me in the hospital?" he asks.

"I'm sorry they did that, but he didn't misread anything, Dante. You were assaulting me."

His sadness is replaced with anger. "No, you were enjoying yourself. I know you were. We were having a good time. I was going to show you how much I loved you—until he showed up."

"That's not what that was, Dante. I didn't want that. You drugged me."

"To help you relax. I knew you were nervous; that's all. But you were there willingly, were you not?"

"Yes, but—"

"Yes, you were. He had no right to barge in on us like that. He had no right to take you from me. Then, he proceeded to ruin my life. I had to drop out of school. My father was livid. I was supposed to become a partner in his firm and take over one day. He fucking disowned me, and it's all Scutari's fault. He ruined my life, and now, I'm going to ruin his. I'm going to take everything from him. Everything."

I don't want him, or this friend he has, doing anything to hurt Cross, his grandparents, or his papa.

So, for now, I'll play along until I can figure out what to do.

"Okay, Dante."

The tension leaves him at my agreement, and he kisses me. I have to force myself to relax and let him without gagging. He pulls back and grins a satisfied grin.

I resolve myself to leave with him. Anything to get him out of here and away from Melanie and Cassian.

He takes my hand and turns to lead us back into the open market when the door swings open beside us, and a huge man in a hairnet and apron comes barreling out of the truck.

"What are you two doing back here? You aren't allowed in this area," the man grumbles.

"We are leaving, sir."

Dante pulls me toward him, and he begins walking just as Gino is passing the truck with Melanie and the baby in tow. He spots us and pulls his gun.

Dante puts me in front of him and draws his own, just as the cook yells, "What the fuck is going on here?" and starts to advance on us.

Dante turns his attention to the guy, and that is when I take my opportunity to stomp on the arch of his foot and jerk free. His left leg gives a little, and he loses his grip on me. I run past Gino and into the crowd. Dante curses and then darts in the other direction when the two big guys collide. He turns back just in time to see me launch myself in front of Mel and Cassian. His eyes meet mine as I pull Cassian in my arms. He pauses for a split second, and then he's gone.

CHAPTER
Twelve

Cross

I STROLL INTO THE BACK OF THE BOWERY WAREHOUSE WHERE MY men have Paulino secured to a metal chair. He sees me approach, and his gaze fills with confusion, but he puts on a brave face.

Two of the last five shipments of arms we received were hit in transport. That was two shipments that we were unable to deliver on time to our Irish friends. O'Neill was understanding, but his patience is running thin, and so is mine. Only a few trusted people knew the time and destination of those shipments. One of whom was Paulino. One hit could have been a coincidence, but two? It's a setup. Never in a million years would I have thought Pauly would be so foolish. I've known him since we were kids, and I was there when he married his high school sweetheart, Leesa.

I hate this part. The part where I have to extract information from someone I consider a friend. The part where money became more important to him than loyalty. Loyalty is prized above all else in my world, and disloyalty simply can't be tolerated, or people die.

"Hello, Pauly. How are Leesa and the girls?"

"Gooood. They are good, boss," he stutters.

"That's good to hear. Any trouble at home you want to talk to me about?"

"No, sir. Nothing comes to mind."

I nod and start to circle his chair. He cranes his neck, trying to follow my progress.

"Are you happy, working here for me, Pauly?"

"Yes, Cross. I've always been happy here. You're family."

"Family. What does that mean to you?"

"It means that I love you."

"Tell me, Pauly, do you usually sell out people you love for money?" I ask calmly.

I watch as the sweat starts to bead on his brow, and his pupils dilate in fear.

"I would never ..."

"Before you finish that sentence, I want you to remember how much I despise liars."

"I'm not lying." He swallows hard and looks around at the other men surrounding the large room. "I swear, Cross." He takes a few deep breaths and meets my eyes.

"Who?"

He doesn't reply, and I walk in front of him. I put a bullet into his right foot, and he screams out in pain.

"Who?" I calmly ask again.

"Please, Cross. I have no idea what you're talking about. I would never betray you."

I pull off another shot. This one hits the cement near his other foot. The bullet ricochets and hits the metal of the chair under his ass. He hunches over, and I think he might have passed out. I motion for one of the boys to check on him, and he raises his face to me.

"Who? Do not make me repeat myself, Pauly."

"Why-why are you doing this? I swear."

I look into his pleading eyes, and I want to believe him.

"Two of the shipments were hit and not by petty thieves, but by men who had known exactly what was in those trucks. They had to have known the pickup and drop-off points and the schedule. The only people who knew that schedule were me, Matteo, Tony, and you."

He looks nervously between Tony and me, doing the math. "I

didn't tell anyone."

"Are you saying Matteo or Tony did?" I ask casually.

"No! I would never accuse." He lowers his eyes again.

"Someone had to leak the info, Pauly."

He looks up once again, and I can see him frantically trying to figure out who it could be. I lower my gun, and he exhales a breath of relief.

"Cross?" Tony's voice comes from behind me in question.

I turn to him. "He's telling the truth."

"How can you be sure?" he asks.

"I just am. He didn't do this."

"Then, who did?"

"I don't know, but I'm sure as hell going to find out."

I turn back to Pauly, who is turning pale as blood pools on the floor at his feet.

"I'm sorry, but I had to be sure."

He nods as if he understands.

"I promise to make this up to you. There will be deposits made into the girls' college funds tomorrow morning."

He nods again.

"Pauly"—I get his attention—"I'm sorry I doubted you."

"It's okay, boss. I'm just grateful you believe me."

"Take the next week off and recover. When you're ready, we'll relocate you to the warehouse midtown. It's closer to your home and the girls' school. We'll make sure you're compensated for your missed hours and pain and suffering."

"Thank you, boss."

I turn to one of my men.

"Clean him up and get him to Doc quickly," I command.

Pauly sags in relief.

With that, I walk out of the warehouse, leaving the cleanup to the rest. We're back to square one now. All I do is run into brick walls at every damn turn.

I walk into Vincenzo's study. He's waiting for me.

"Christoff, welcome. Please sit."

I move to one of the chairs across from his desk and take a seat.

"Brandy?" he offers.

"Yes, thank you."

He pours us both two fingers and comes to sit on the chair at my left. "You wanted to discuss your father and Emilio."

"Yes. Giovanni remembered something from that night. He said that, earlier in the day, before they left for dinner, Emilio and he had a meeting. Emilio mentioned going to see a man named Aguilar that morning."

Giovanni is our family's financial advisor, for lack of a better term. He was a good friend of my brother, and Emilio trusted him with some of the more delicate matters pertaining to our business. When I took over, Gio helped me as I navigated the books and worked at moving the majority of our interest toward our more sound investments. I still entrust a good deal of responsibility to him.

I see surprise cross Vincenzo's face before he reels it in.

"You're certain of this?" he asks.

"Yes. Does that name ring a bell?" I watch him closely.

"Diego Aguilar heads a large drug cartel out of Cuba. He runs most of the heroin trade in New York."

"Why would Emilio have been meeting with him? We don't mess with drug trafficking. Never have."

Vincenzo shrugs. "Perhaps Emilio was trying to get into the drug trade, or he could have just been meeting with him to offer him protection or to supply weapons. Have you asked Marcello?"

"No, not yet. I wanted to see if it was anything of concern before I burdened him with it. He remembers very little from that night, and it agitates him."

The truth is, I try to protect Papa from as much as I can.

"Do you think this guy could have had something to do with the hit?"

He considers the question for a moment. Then, he shakes his head. "No. Doesn't seem his style. Unless Emilio double-crossed him in some way. Diego likes to keep a low profile. He has a very lucrative business here, and as long as his men don't cause any problems, the police leave them alone."

"Do you know how I can contact him?" I ask

"Careful, Christoff. This is not a man you want to trifle with, and it's dangerous to throw around accusations with no proof."

"I just want to talk to him; that's all—to ask what his relationship to Emilio was. I'm not going to accuse him of anything."

He gets up and walks back behind his desk. He takes a seat, and I watch as he tries to decide whether or not to help me. I can see the hesitation.

"Okay, I will make contact on your behalf and arrange a meeting."

"Thank you, Vincenzo."

"You're welcome, son."

Son. The word slices through me like a knife.

"I paid a visit to California last week," I blurt out.

He looks up in surprise. "Did you now? Do you think that was wise?"

"Probably not," I admit.

"And how is my *bambina*?"

"Better. Still wounded. A little more so at the news of my upcoming wedding."

He sighs. "I can only imagine."

He seems to have aged so much the last few years. Losing Gabby has taken its toll on him. He played the bad guy, so he could get her out of the line of fire, and her anger at him has beaten him down. He loves her so much. I know exactly how he feels.

"One day, I hope she will forgive me and come home. Her mother misses her terribly. She drinks now. She has never been a drinker." A pained expression overtakes him.

"I'm sorry. I didn't mean to upset you. I just thought you'd want to know that she's doing well there. She has good friends, and she seems truly happy."

"Good. Is very, very good," he mumbles more to himself than to me.

He's lost in his thoughts for a few moments before he pulls himself back together.

"If that is all …" he says as he stands.

I stand in acknowledgment that we are finished.

I follow him from the study, and he walks me through the kitchen to the back door. Being in this house is hard. All I see is Gabby. Cooking with Nonna in the kitchen. Sitting at the dining room table, doing homework. Cheering as the boys and I played basketball in the driveway. Her ghost is everywhere here.

Lilliana is at the stove when we walk past her.

"Christoff," she acknowledges as she walks over and pulls me into an embrace. "Have you talked to my son lately?"

"Yes, ma'am. I just returned from visiting him."

A look of concern crosses her face. "A visit. To California?"

"Yes. He has a gorgeous condo overlooking the beach. You would like it very much."

"I am sure I would," she says hesitantly.

"He is well. Everyone in California is doing well."

Her eyes fill with unshed tears, and she smiles a relieved smile.

"Yes, well, thank you for letting me know. Please tell Nicco to call his worried mother more often when you talk to him again."

"I promise I will."

I kiss both her cheeks and leave.

CHAPTER

Thirteen

Brie

MELANIE AND I RUSH TO THE PARKING LOT WITH GINO ON OUR heels. He was unable to catch up to Dante, and he didn't want to leave us unguarded to go in search of him.

"Brie, what is going on? What happened back there? Who was that?"

Melanie is a little freaked out, and the last thing I want is to scare her worse, but I have to be honest.

"Dante."

"Dante? I thought he had taken off?" she says with panic in her voice.

"So did I. I guess he decided to try his luck with Cross and Nicco after all."

She stops before we make it to the car. "Are you okay? Did he hurt you?"

"I'm fine. He didn't hurt me. He just … he's lost his mind. He has some fantasy that he's going to take me back to New York, and we're going to get married. Then, Papa will welcome him into the family, and the two of us will live happily ever after."

"He's unstable," she surmises.

"Yes. He always has been when it comes to me, but this was different. This was a desperate delusion or something. I think he might have seen you and Cassian."

"In that chaos? I doubt it. Even if he did, how would he know we were together? There are hundreds of people here."

"He looked back before he disappeared around the corner, and I swear, he looked right at me as I made it to you guys."

"Calm down. Even if he did see us, he has no idea who we are."

She's probably right, and even if he does know who they are, they're just people I work for. They're not relevant to him. He wants me. Only me. Still, I can't help but be a little nervous for them. God, I hope Nicco is able to find him soon.

I drop Melanie and Cassian off at home and head back to my apartment with Gino's SUV close behind. I'm not surprised to see Nicco's Jeep in the parking lot when I arrive. He's waiting for me when I let myself in.

"Sis." He wraps me in a relieved hug. "Are you all right?"

"I'm fine. A little freaked out but okay."

I sit and give him a rundown of what happened at the farmers market.

"He appeared out of thin air. I have no idea how he knew where we were," I tell him.

"I don't either. We have this place under constant surveillance, and he hasn't shown his face anywhere near here, but it can't be a coincidence that he was there. Damn it, he's so fucking slippery. Why didn't you scream or beat on the damn truck or something to get someone's attention? Gino said you looked like you were willingly leaving with him."

Now is my chance to tell him. To come clean with all my secrets. Nicco is the one person I can trust, but I can't seem to get the words out.

"I think I was in shock, and he had a gun and threatened to shoot in to the crowd. I didn't want Melanie and her son or any of the other families there to get caught up in my mess and get hurt, so I just kept my cool and let him think I was going to go peacefully with him," I explain, hoping that he will let it go.

He seems to accept it, even though I know he wants to yell at me.

"I'm sorry, sis, but until we find him, I think you're going to have to avoid public places, and I'm going to have to send more guards with you. One isn't enough. Gino was trying to watch you and your friend and her baby. All it took was for him to take his eye off you for one second, and Dante was able to grab you. I know you hate being followed, but—"

"I get it now," I cut him off. "I'm okay with the extra security, and I won't leave the house, except for the catering jobs I already have lined up. You can send whoever you want to tail me. I won't fight it."

He looks relieved. I didn't notice before how worried he truly was. I don't make any of this easy on him. I'm sure being my protector is a particularly tricky challenge.

Guilt washes over me. I could be a tad more compliant for his peace of mind.

"All right, I think I'll be spending the nights here with you and Kelsey for a while, and I'll tell her as little as possible but enough for her to be on alert and aware of her surroundings, too."

"Can you spare guards for her and maybe Rick and Melanie, too?" I ask.

"I'll make sure Kelsey is covered. I don't think your bosses have anything to worry about though."

"But he saw them with me today. I don't want him to mess with them."

"If you are concerned, maybe you should quit and have them find another babysitter."

"Nanny. I told you, I'm a nanny."

"Yeah, whatever you say."

He smirks at me, and I can tell he's trying to lighten the mood and dispel some of my fears. As much as it kills me, I think he's right. I'll have to tell Melanie that I can't watch the baby or see any of them for a while, maybe a long while. My heart breaks as I consider never seeing them again. I'm going to have to find the strength I don't feel I have to let them go.

"You're right. It's not fair to put them in danger, too. I'll quit, and I'm sure they can find someone else to watch Cassian." A sob escapes me as I try to reel in the sorrow I feel.

"Hey, don't cry. I'll help with your bills until you can find something else."

He pulls me into his arms as I fight the grief crashing into me.

"It's not that. I've just been watching him since he was born—well, since he was a few months old—and they're like family to me now. It's going to hurt never to see them again."

He tightens his hug and lays his chin on top of my head.

"I'm sorry, *cara*. I am so damn sorry that you keep having to lose everyone you love. It's not fair. Maybe, if they haven't found someone else after we're able to take care of Dante—and we will take care of him—you can start working for them again."

I squeeze him back.

"Your life keeps getting dragged into my drama, too. I'm so sorry, Nicco. I don't know how I keep finding myself in these situations. I'm always running from something or someone. It's ridiculous. I bet you're seriously regretting that move from New York right about now."

"Pain in my ass. Since the day you were born. I swear." He shakes his head in fake exasperation.

I sock him in the stomach. He coughs out a laugh.

"Kidding. I regret nothing. You're my baby sister, and it will always be my job to look after you and beat up all the boys who make you cry."

The door opens, and Kelsey walks in.

"Hey, guys. What's up?" She tosses her purse and a bag from Chef Ming's Kitchen in the chair as she heads toward us.

"I didn't expect you tonight," she tells Nicco with a pleasant surprise in her voice.

"I hope you don't mind," he says as he releases me and walks over to kiss her on the top of her head. "I was missing my girls."

She looks up at him and smiles huge. "Of course I don't mind. I stopped for takeout for lunch, and we should have plenty." She looks to me. "I know you wanted to try those new recipes tonight. Maybe Nicco here can be our guinea pig later."

"About that, I wasn't able to find all the ingredients I needed at the farmers market today. Mind going to the grocery store for us, big brother?"

"Not at all. What do you need?"

After we eat, I make a grocery list, and Nicco heads out to go by his condo and grab everything he needs to move in before going to the store for us. Kelsey goes to take a quick shower while he's gone, and I dial Melanie's number.

"Hey, Brie. Everything okay when you got home?" She's been worried.

"Yes, Nicco was here. Gino had already called him and filled him in. He's going to stay with us for a while."

"Thank goodness. I was worried about you girls being there alone."

"He suggested that I quit my job with you," I blurt out in a rush before I can overthink it.

"Quit your job? What?"

I sniffle as I deliver the news, "As your nanny. He said if I was worried about Dante messing with you guys and the baby, then I should quit and let you find someone to replace me—at least for now."

"Oh, I see."

"I think maybe it's for the best. Just until he is far, far away from here. It'll be safer if we aren't seen together."

"It's going to be okay, Brie. I have Rick's mom if I need anyone to watch him, and it's not like Cassian will forget who you are."

"He might if it takes too long. He'll wonder where I went and why I just abandoned you guys."

"I promise, I will show him your picture every single day and remind him how much his BB loves him."

I fall apart then, and Melanie spends the next fifteen minutes comforting me. I pull myself together, and I tell her that I'll let her know as soon as I can see them again. I add that, in the meantime, if there is any emergency at all, she can call, and I will be there, danger be damned.

When Nicco returns a few hours later, I'm sitting at the kitchen island with a glass of wine.

"Ready to cook for me, women?"

"Definitely."

Kelsey and I start preparing a new spicy beef Wellington recipe I created. Losing myself in cooking is what I needed. It grounds me.

As I place the creation in the oven, I think to myself, *This too shall pass*.

Nonna used to tell me that anytime I was upset as a little girl, and she was always right.

CHAPTER
fourteen

Cross

I OPEN ONE EYE AND BLINK AT THE CLOCK AS MY PHONE STARTS ringing. I am in my old loft, and the television is blaring an infomercial. I must have dozed off while watching the movie. It's three in the morning. *Who the fuck is calling me at three a.m.?* I roll to my side and grab my cell off the coffee table. Nicco's number is on the display. I accept the call as I leave the couch and walk into the bathroom.

"Nicco?"

"Sorry to wake you up, man. I know it's late there, but I waited until the girls were asleep to call."

"Is something wrong?"

"Yes. Calvacanti got his hands on Gabby today."

"What? How? Is she okay? Does he have her?"

A million scenarios pass through my mind in the three seconds it takes for him to answer.

"No. She got away. She was at the local street market with a friend, and while Gino was distracted for a split second, he grabbed her and tried to get away with her. She was able to escape, and Gino tried to chase him down, but he couldn't follow him and get Gabby and her friend to safety."

"Fuck. He is getting ballsy. How the hell is he finding her? The guys haven't spotted any tails, have they?"

"None. He's smoke, man."

"Damn it."

"It gets worse."

"Worse? Did he hurt her?"

"No, not that she told me, but she was going to leave with him. Willingly."

"What?"

"Yeah, man. She wasn't putting up any fight in order to distract him because she was worried about the innocent people at the market and the friend who was with her. He had a gun and threatened to shoot into the crowd. Fucker knows exactly how to manipulate her. Thank God Gino spotted them before he could get her to his car."

"We're going to have to force her to leave. It's too dangerous for her there," I tell him what we both already know.

The last thing I wanted was to make her leave her new home, but clearly, she can't stay there any longer. It's not safe for her or her friends.

"I've moved in. Until this is resolved, I'm not going anywhere, and she has promised that she will only go to work and home from now on."

"Do you think she will actually comply, or did she agree to pacify you?"

I know her too well. She hates to be ordered around, and she hates to be treated like a prisoner in her own home.

"I'm pretty sure she means it. She was completely shaken up. She said Dante was acting more erratic than she remembered him to be. He was talking nonsense about taking her back to New York and them getting married and everything going back to normal. He scared her, more for her friend than for herself though."

That sounds like Gabriella. She has never had a strong sense of self-preservation. It drives me insane. We are not only fighting the danger, but also fighting her to keep her safe. Infuriating woman.

"I don't like it. We need to get her out of there. Temporarily."

"I have two men on her now at all times. I am here at night. Plus, Gino has his guys outside, doing surveillance at night. I also have a man on Kelsey, and I'll brief Daniel and get a man on Dawn when they get home week after next."

"That's a lot of bodies that are doing a lot of babysitting and no searching for Dante." There is a bite in my statement. Bite born of concern, not anger.

"I know. But, at this point, I think it's necessary. He got to her in broad daylight while she had other people and Gino in tow. He doesn't give a fuck about discretion anymore. He doesn't think it's warranted because he thinks Gabby belongs to him, and as soon as she comes back and tells everyone, then life will be fucking peachy."

I growl. Gabriella does not belong to him.

"When you find him, I want to be the one."

"You are going to have to stand in line. I called Tony first and wouldn't be surprised if he was on a plane now with Stavros and Lo close behind." He pauses. "If he had gotten her into his car ..."

I close my eyes tightly, trying not to see her in that hallway two years ago with him pressing her into the wall and his hand up her skirt while she begged him to stop.

"I know."

"I think he is unhinged enough to really hurt her this time, Cross."

So do I.

"Then, we stop him."

I splash cold water on my face and stare at myself in the mirror. The last thing I want to do is lie back down. I am wide awake now, so I jump into the shower.

When I walk into the main house, it's a quarter till six, and Adriana is curled up on the couch in the living room, staring into a glass of wine.

"What are you doing up at this hour?"

She looks up at me. "This house makes noises. Did you know that?"

I take a quick look around.

"It's an old house. I'm sure there is probably a draft, and the rattling is just some normal settling."

"I hate it. It's too … Amityville-ish."

"I didn't take you for a scary movie fan."

"I'm not. Gabby used to force me to watch all those cheesy horror flicks. She loves them."

"Yeah, she made me watch one or ten myself." I move and sit down beside her.

"Not sure there is anything I can do to make the house less noisy. Maybe you should get a white noise machine or something for the bedroom, so it won't disturb you when you sleep."

She lays her head on my shoulder and brings her wineglass to her lips. "It's just not my house. It's your father's house, and even with all the redecorating, I can't get the old, cold feeling out of it. I never wanted a house anyway. I always wanted a three-story penthouse in Manhattan that had a three-hundred-sixty-degree view of the city. One floor for me, one floor for my husband, and one floor for the children. Hell, I'd prefer my and Gabby's fifth-floor walk-up in Hell's Kitchen to this place."

I look around the grand living room. She's right. It has no heart. It's big and stately, and it's my father's over-the-top taste. However, it's owned by the family; it has room for us, my grandparents, children; it has my office; and the grounds are secure. My loft is still above the garages, and I still wander out there from time to time to be alone.

"Maybe we can remodel. Tear it down to the bare bones one room at a time and make it into something you love."

"Really? You'd let me do that?"

"It's your home now. I don't want you to be miserable, Adriana. I know this isn't exactly what you wanted, but we can fix it up and make the best of it. Then, hopefully, one day, we will at least feel at home here."

"Okay. We'll remodel."

She starts looking around the room, and I can already see the wheels turning as she begins planning.

"I can't believe our wedding is only a few weeks away."

"It came fast."

She sits up and turns to me. "Do you think you could ever love me?"

I sigh and look her in the eye. "I'm not sure I'm even capable of love anymore. I care about you, and I don't think we have to always be at each other's throats. We don't have to be enemies, but I think we both know it will never be love. I gave my heart away over twenty years ago, and she never gave it back."

She sighs deeply. "It's a business deal. Not exactly what every little girl dreams of, but we'll make the best of it. Right?"

"I can promise you that I will always treat you with respect, and I will always use discretion."

"Same. Although you might want to knock before entering if you hear noises coming from behind the door, buddy. I'm not checking into hotels when I have my bedroom and master bath exactly as I want them. I'll have a side door added or something, so my sexual minions can come and go, undetected, at my whim."

I chuckle as she jokes. She is nothing if not resilient. I'm beginning to see why Gabby loved her.

"Can I take you to breakfast?"

"Yes, I am starving, and I need some food in my stomach to soak up all this wine."

I stand and extend my hand to help her up. "Come on; let's feed you then."

CHAPTER
fifteen

Brie

KELSEY AND I ARE ON THE COUCH WITH A BLANKET UP TO OUR noses, watching an episode of *American Horror Story*. Nicco is in the kitchen, popping popcorn, when the doorknob starts to turn. Then, someone begins furiously shaking the door, and it sounds like they're pounding into it with their shoulder. We both let out a terrified scream.

Nicco comes charging in with his gun drawn, and that causes us to scream again. Then, we hear a high-pitched wail from outside and a myriad of loud cursing. Nicco looks out the front window and curses under his breath. Then, he places his gun back in its holster before unlocking the dead bolt and swinging the door open wide. We come up behind him and peek out to see Gino with Daniel in a choke hold and Dawn beating on his back with her purse while kicking him in the back of the knee. All while insulting every member of his family tree all the way back to the old country.

"You mind, boss?" Gino looks to Nicco for help.

"Let him go, Gino. They live here," Nicco demands.

The big bear of a man lets go of his hold on Daniel, and he falls to his knees in the breezeway and starts gasping for air. Lights come on next door, and our neighbor peeks out to see what the commotion is all about.

"Sorry, Mrs. Dixie. We weren't expecting Dawn home tonight, and they gave us a scare," I whisper-yell the apology.

The older lady glares at me through the crack in her door and then slams it shut.

"What the fuck is going on here? Why didn't my key work, and who the hell is this?" Dawn gestures to Gino as he reaches down to help Daniel up, apologizing.

"It's a long story. Come inside, and we will explain everything." Nicco is scanning the surroundings. He does not like us being out here, exposed.

"I have to run back down and grab Dawn's bags out of the truck. I was walking her up first," Daniel says as he rubs his neck.

"Gino and I will help, and we will fill you in. You girls go back inside and lock the door behind you. We will be back up in a few minutes."

The three of them hurry off.

Dawn watches as they descend the steps and turns to us. "What the fuck?" she asks.

We shuffle over to her and wrap her up in a three-way hug.

"What are you guys doing here? We didn't expect you back for another seven days," I question.

"Inside!" we hear Nicco's command yelled from the parking lot.

"Let's go in, and we will explain everything." I push them toward the open door.

Dawn lets me guide her in, eyeing the newly installed dead-bolt lock and the new alarm panel as we go. "I guess I missed a few things the last couple of weeks, huh?"

"A little bit, yes. I'll go get a bottle of wine," Kelsey offers because she knows we will all need it.

Dawn looks at me as I sit nervously on the couch. "Okay, I am listening."

The door opens, and Nicco and Daniel come in, carrying Dawn's and Daniel's suitcases.

"Why are you bringing your stuff in? I am not doing your laundry. You are a big boy with a washer and dryer of your own at home. I'm not your mother." She stomps her foot and places her hands on her hips.

"Looks like I am moving in, babe," Daniel calmly states.

She raises an eyebrow and looks around at us all. "You guys had better start talking. Now."

We all head into the kitchen and sit around the island. I explain to Dawn and Daniel, like I had to with Kelsey last week, precisely who Dante is and what happened with us in the past. Then, I tell them about him attempting to kidnap me while Melanie, Cassian, and I were at the farmers market a couple of days ago.

"That son of a bitch!" Dawn is fighting mad. "How dare he lay a finger on you without your permission." She turns to Nicco. "I blame you."

"Me?" Nicco looks taken aback.

"Yes, you. Why the hell didn't you take care of him two years ago?" she asks accusingly.

"I, um, we thought we had—" he tries to defend himself.

She doesn't let him finish. "I, um … apparently, you didn't. Really?"

Nicco stands there and takes her anger.

Then, she turns her focus to me. "Are you all right? Did he hurt you?"

"I am fine. Other than slamming me against a metal food truck and forcing his tongue in my mouth, he didn't hurt me."

"Fuck …"

That comes from Nicco. I didn't exactly tell him every detail.

"I wish I had been the one with you instead of Melanie. I would have kicked his ass," Dawn declares, murder in her tone.

With that, I start to giggle, imagining her jumping on Dante's back and beating him in the head with her purse. The laughter is contagious, and pretty soon, we are all howling.

Once we recover, Dawn looks at Nicco again. "So, what's the plan, handsome? You and Daniel are staying here to be our bodyguards, and you have wired this place up like Fort Knox. What else?"

Nicco looks at me and then back at my wild-card friend. Kelsey and I were a breeze to wrangle compared to her, and he knows it.

"Our family sent men to look for Dante. They also sent men to guard you ladies anytime I can't. Daniel and I are going to be staying here with you until he is found. I would appreciate you three not fighting us on the guards and not making any additional plans that will have you out in the open and exposed. I don't think Dante would try to grab anyone but Brie, but she is worried for you guys, and it's better to be safe than sorry," Nicco explains.

She sits there, nodding in slow motion. Her lips pursed, she moves her eyes from me to Nicco to Daniel. I can see the wheels turning. This can't be good.

She starts speaking, very controlled, "Your family sent some men—big, scary men, like the steroid twins outside—to look for this Dante character and to 'guard'"—she uses finger quotes on the word guard—"us girls until he is found. No police report on the attempted kidnapping? No harassment charges filed? No restraining order? The family is just going to take care of things?" she asks condescendingly.

Then, I see the lightbulb come on.

Nicco waits as she finishes putting two and two together, and then he answers, "That's correct. The family will take care of Dante. The family will protect you guys."

She tilts her head in acceptance, and then she turns her attention to Daniel. "You and I are going to have a long chat about this family that I am marrying into and why exactly I am just now learning about it."

Daniel lifts an eyebrow and grins.

That's when it hits us.

"What did you just say?" I ask.

"Yeah, what was that?" Kelsey moves in beside me.

Both of our gazes zero in on our friend's left hand, and that's when we see it. A stunning gem perched on that all-important finger.

"Oh my God!" I look at my cousin, who is wearing a look of pure joy.

"You proposed in Monaco?"

"I sure did, and she said yes." He beams, proud as a peacock as he kisses the side of her head.

The kitchen erupts in peals of female squealing as Kelsey and I rush to Dawn. All three of us are jumping up and down and blubbering like babies.

Once we get all of that out of the way, we settle back down and wait for the story.

"We had been there for about a week, and I swear, I was about to secretly pack Daniel's bags and have him carted off to the airport by some locals while he slept because he had been acting so strange and jumpy all week. He was killing my relaxed vibe. So, one night, we got in a huge argument because I wanted to go to one of the casinos in Monte Carlo, and he wanted to stay at the resort and have dinner on the beach. I said we could have dinner at the casino. He kept insisting, and I might have called him a few unflattering names and implied he was an old man and no fun anymore and that he was ruining my graduation trip. He got angry and went to his suitcase where he pulled out the ring box and flung it at me. Then, he started taking all his clothes out of the drawers and stuffing them into his suitcase like a drama queen." She pauses and rolls her eyes. "I opened the box and saw this gorgeous ring nestled in the velvet, and I fell in love instantly. He'd had a romantic dinner set up for us on the private beach with live music, and he'd planned to have the ring hidden in the champagne flute when dessert was served or some lame-ass shit. I ruined it. Blah, blah, blah. I told him he was welcome to leave, but the rock stayed. Then, I put it on my finger."

We sit there with our mouths agape, looking between the two.

"Oh, don't look so upset. He didn't leave, and we had the most amazing makeup sex before he finally took me to the casino," she brags.

I look over at a smirking Daniel, and he winks at me and shrugs.

"That's the best engagement story I have ever heard," I tell them both.

"Damn straight." She grins.

I am so happy for my friend and my cousin. They are the best couple I know. No one could handle Dawn better than he does. They restore my faith in real, lasting love.

CHAPTER
Sixteen

Cross

I SPEND THE MORNING WITH PAPA. WE POUR OVER BOOKS AND ledgers. He is old school, and everything has a paper trail. He doesn't trust computers, neither their ability nor their security. I assure him that all my files are encrypted and secure, but he is still uneasy with the technology, so I appease him.

I'm working very hard to move as much of our money and focus on our legitimate ventures. Our restaurants, nightclubs, steel foundries, and New Jersey casinos are thriving. The shipping business is getting more and more accepted bids, which helps to hide the illegal gambling, loans and arms smuggling—for now. Scutari & Sons Construction has won several large contracts for hotel construction and remodeling in Manhattan, and because the costs of materials and labor can be easily manipulated on paper, especially with our own foundries supplying castings, those contracts have helped me to clean a lot of cash quickly. Our coffers are full to overflowing, and money is power. Papa has supported me in scaling back on the illegal activities. Losing his wife and two of his sons to the criminal underworld has vastly changed his stance on our family's business focus.

I hate the toll the shooting has taken on him. He was such a strong and formidable man and a great father and leader. Between the recovery from his injuries and the grief from losing Emilio and Atelo, he is a shell of his former self at only sixty years old. As I watch him struggle to get from his wheelchair into his recliner, I vow to myself anew that I will find the person responsible for the hits on my family, and I will make them pay.

He gets settled. I let him do it on his own even though my instincts are to rush to his aid. The last thing I want is to emasculate him any further.

Once he is in his chair, he adjusts it and starts to speak, "Has there been any word on Atelo?"

My middle brother vanished after surviving the bullets meant for him the night Emilio and Papa were hit. We assume he went into hiding.

"No, nothing yet."

"I never thought him to be a coward," he says as he lowers his eyes from mine.

"I don't think going to ground after surviving a spray of gunfire makes him a coward," I try to defend him.

"People get shot at. It happens, but you do not run. You do not abandon your family. He should be here, helping you."

"I don't blame him, Papa. I'm not angry. I just hope that, wherever he is, he is safe and happy."

At that, he looks up at me. "And are you happy, son?"

I calculate my reaction and give him a practiced smile. "Of course I am."

He knowingly nods his head. "Your wedding is coming up soon, no?"

"Yes, it's just a little over three weeks away."

"I wish your mother and brothers were going to be here to see it."

I swallow the lump in my throat. I, too, wish all my family were here. I miss them.

"Or maybe it's for the best that your mother isn't here. She would never stand for you marrying a woman you do not love." He cuts his eyes to me.

"I do care for Adriana, Papa. She is going to make a beautiful bride and an excellent wife," I insist.

"She will make an amiable wife. Yes. She'll be a dutiful wife. Yes. I even believe she will be a trustworthy wife. Definitely a favorable pairing. Especially for her family. I am sure Salvatore is quite pleased with the alliance the marriage of you and his daughter will make. Which I am assuming is why you are going through with the wedding?" he asks the question on his mind.

I have been playing the charade so long now that it comes natural, but I decide not to insult him with lies.

"It is indeed," I admit.

"And what of your Gabriella?"

He was hospitalized for a long time and was incapacitated when all the initial plays were made to secure the family and transition me into power in his stead. He doesn't know the whole story of how it all went down.

"I had to end that. She didn't take it very well. I hurt her badly, but the other families were concerned about our relationship, and I didn't want that concern to become any bigger." I take a deep breath and continue, "I didn't want the other families or your enemies to target her, and neither did Vincenzo. I broke her heart, and so did he. She took off as a result. She lives in California now."

"And are things still so volatile that you can't go and get her now?"

"Things are better, much better, but she is gone now. Settled. Safe. She will never have to look the other way when I do something she doesn't like, and I will never have to worry about her being gunned down in a restaurant or on the street." I give voice to my biggest fear. The real reason I agreed to all of this. I have dreams that involve Gabby and me out to dinner with my father and brother. I have watched a bullet go through her chest a thousand times while I helplessly stand there.

"You don't think that you could protect her." It is not a question. He is stating the fact that he sees on my face.

"I would rather her not require protecting at all," I admit.

"Have you thought to give that choice to her?"

"She left, Papa. She made her choice then. She decided that she wanted nothing to do with this life. Not even to stay with her own family. She left everyone. Not just me. I think that says all it needs to."

"Doesn't sound at all like the little girl I remember. That little girl loved her brothers. That little girl loved you. I think that, given the option, she would return."

"I don't think she would. She is happy."

"Are you certain, son? Because I can tell you one thing that you do not know. That pain you feel now, it will never go away. When you lose the love of your life, it's like a piece of your soul is ripped from your body, and you will walk around half a man for the rest of your days."

He gets a faraway look, and I know that he is speaking of his own torment.

"You will try to mend it with women and booze and work, but it will torture you. I don't want that for you, Christoff."

I see the loss of my mother reflecting back at me in his eyes. I know that he was never quite the same after her accident. We lost a part of him, too, that day. He just shut down emotionally. He tried very hard to rally for us boys, and he did the best he could to be there for us, but there was never a day when we didn't see the pain written on him.

"You still miss her."

"I will miss her until I breathe my last," he confirms.

I see my fate in him.

I sit with him for a little longer.

Matteo arrives to have dinner and play a game of cards with Papa, and that is when I take my leave.

I arrive home to find Una and Adriana in the living room with the wedding planner. The last thing I want to do right now is face the decisions

I must for this ceremony. I wish we could just go to the courthouse and get the deed over with. Adriana and her parents insist on a high affair. It is the least I can give her, seeing as I have no intention of being an actual husband.

"Hello, ladies," I greet them with a fake smile.

"There is my wayward fiancé." Adriana stands and walks over to kiss my cheek.

"What are we discussing today?" I ask.

"Flower arrangements and seating charts."

"Sounds like fun," I lie.

Adriana rolls her eyes at me. "I'm sure you think so."

"Do you need my input on any of this?" I ask, begging her with my eyes to say no.

"No, we have it covered. Although you might have to take a look at the seating chart once we are done and make sure I haven't placed any sworn enemies next to each other. I don't want anyone being stabbed with the Tavern's good silver during our first dance," she deadpans.

I look over to the sofa, and our guest has turned an alarming shade of white.

"I'll look it over when you are done. Now, stop scaring your event planner," I whisper.

"You're no fun." She spins on her heels and returns to her spot on the sofa.

Una rises and addresses them, "Ladies, if you don't mind, I need to go over a few things with my grandson."

They distractedly wave her off, and we head toward my office. It's strange. I used to hate the office when it was my father's. Now, it is my sanctuary.

Una comes in, carrying her glass of wine. "Follow me, Christoff," she requests.

"Where are we going?"

"To my rooms."

I do as she commanded without question. I have always obeyed her.

"How is Marcello?" she asks after Papa as we walk.

"The same. Good—or as good as can be expected."

"I think we should make the west wing handicap accessible and move him back into the manor. I don't like him being exiled in that condominium across town."

"He is not exiled, Una. He wanted to move into a space of his own. He doesn't like being treated like an invalid."

"I don't like it. Family stays together. He has to be lonely out there."

"He has friends and full-time nurses, and I am fairly certain that he is screwing his night nurse," I amusingly add.

"Can he still do that?" she asks.

"Yes, his legs no longer work, but everything else works just fine."

"Hmm. Good for him."

We make it to my grandparents' wing. They have their own rooms, sitting room, library, and office. She leads me into her bedroom and to the closet. She enters the code to her personal safe and then opens the door. She slides out a velvet-lined drawer. Her jewels are laid out in a row. Diamonds, rubies, emeralds, and pearls in a variety of settings— necklaces, earrings, bracelets, and brooches.

She steps aside and lets me get a better look at her treasures.

"I want you to pick a piece to give to your bride on your wedding day," she announces.

I walk over and assess the choices. All beautiful and all I have seen worn by Una at one time or another. Each one holding sentimental value.

"You don't have to," I say.

"I do. She is going to be my granddaughter-in-law, and she will be the mother of my great-grandchildren. I want her to have a piece she can wear on her big day and pass down to your daughter to wear on her wedding day."

I try to imagine Adriana as a mother. It's not a pleasant thought. I'm sure any children we have will be raised mainly by nannies or Una— God willing she is still around for their formative years.

"Can I ask you a question, Una?"

"Of course."

"Why did you send Mother's locket to Gabriella?"

The question has been nagging at me since she placed it in my hand and insisted I take it to California with me.

She sighs and folds her arms on her chest. "Because it belongs with her. Your mother loved that locket. She kept her most beloved treasures in it. The greatest loves of her life … her boys. So you would always be close to her heart. And the ones it holds within it are under God's protection. I told you this."

"You did, but don't you think Mamma would have wanted my wife to have it? For it to be passed on to one of her grandchildren?"

A look of sadness washes over her, and she quickly beats it back. "I think she would have wanted it to be worn by the greatest love of your life. Even if it is a love lost. Besides, it was mine before it was hers, and I want Gabriella to have it. She always loved it. When she was little, she would sit in my lap and open the locket and have me tell her the story of your mother and father over and over again."

I remember.

I bring my focus back to the baubles in front of me.

"Please, just choose something you would want me to give Adriana. I don't have a preference. Whatever you don't mind parting with." I put the choice back on her.

She leans in and picks up a pair of teardrop diamond earrings. "These. They suit Adriana. They will look stunning with her wedding gown. They can be her something old."

She carefully places them in my hand, and I close it around them.

"Thank you. I am sure she will adore them."

I bend down and kiss her on both her cheeks. I love her very much, and I strive to make her proud. In many ways, she is my mother. She raised me.

CHAPTER
Seventeen

Brie

FTER WE ALL CALM DOWN FROM THE EXCITEMENT OF THE engagement announcement, the boys go to SaMo Pizzeria to pick up our dinner, and I sit the girls down and finally come clean about almost everything. Now that their lives are being turned upside down because of me, they deserve to know my story.

"So, your real name is Gabriella? That's beautiful, and it suits you." Kelsey rolls my name off her tongue just like my family.

"Yeah, but I don't think I'll be able to call you Gabriella now," Dawn adds.

"I don't want you guys to change anything."

"I guess Brie is kind of short for Gabriella as well. Oh, is that why you chose it?" Kelsey asks.

"Yes. I wanted to choose a new name that was easy for me to remember, so I didn't out myself, and I guess to keep me a little connected to my family. That's why I chose Masters as well. Me leaving was never really about them. I love them. I just had to go," I admit.

"I get it. I think. Although I don't understand all the secrecy. I mean, it's not like your family was going to hurt you or anything. I get wanting to move to avoid running into Cross, and this demon spawn ex–best friend of yours, but changing your name and all that seems a bit extreme," Dawn voices her suspicion.

"I just needed a fresh start, and I didn't want the weight of who my family was to influence my life and relationships here," I continue.

It is a tiny lie. A half-truth. One I hope makes sense to them.

"Wait a minute …" Dawn jumps to her feet.

"You said this Cross character showed up at my party. Was he that hottie, Christoff, who was at Daniel and Nicco's condo that night when we dropped off Kelsey?"

"The one and only," I admit.

"Shit." She sits back down in stunned silence.

"That man was sexy as hell. Ah, honey, you had to walk away from all that? Come here." She opens her arms up wide, and I lay my head on her chest. She sympathetically pats my back.

"You poor thing. Had I known, I would have kicked him in the balls for you instead of trying to set you up. No wonder Nicco was trying so hard to shut me up."

"I'm so sorry I brought all this down on you two. You thought Tonya was the roommate from hell. At least she didn't put you in harm's way. I wouldn't blame you if you hated me and tossed me out on my ass."

"Are you kidding? Don't ever compare yourself to that disloyal tramp again. I knew, when you stepped through that door the first day with your one suitcase and your face full of secrets, you were going to bring excitement into our mundane lives. Granted, I never expected Mafia hits and kidnapping plots. I just thought maybe you were a stripper or some sleazy senator's side chick or something. This is way better. It's like we are living in the real-life version of one of those thrillers you love watching so much," Dawn muses.

I love them. I don't think any other roommates could have heard my sordid tale and been so supportive. How lucky am I that I landed here with them?

When the boys get back with dinner, Nicco pulls me aside in the kitchen.

"How did it go with them?" he queries.

"Great. I expected them to be angry or scared and maybe even ask me to leave, but they didn't. They took the entire story in stride."

"Sis, you have got to stop expecting everyone in your life to abandon you. Those girls love you. They aren't going anywhere."

My mind drifts to Adriana. I thought the same of her once.

Like he can read my thoughts, Nicco adds, "They aren't Adriana, and to be honest, I don't think Adi is the villain you think she is."

"Don't. Don't try to defend her to me."

He holds his hands up in a placating gesture. "I'm not. I'm just pointing out that, as of late, we have all been forced into situations we didn't exactly plan or ask for. Maybe she is no different."

"Like you coming here to babysit me?" I finally ask him the question that has been plaguing me since he arrived in California.

"I'm here because it is where I want to be." He wraps an arm around my neck and pulls me in for a quick kiss atop my head. "Now, stop questioning my motives. Just accept that I'm here, and I'm not going anywhere."

"All right."

We join everyone back in the living room, and I pass out paper plates for our slices. SaMo makes the best pizza in Santa Monica. Still, it pales in comparison to Champion Pizza or Lombardi's in Manhattan, but it's damn good for California.

"So," Dawn begins as she blows across her slice, "how locked down are we exactly?"

We all turn to Nicco for the answer.

"I prefer you not to go out in public any more than truly necessary. Why?"

"Well, here's the deal. I have always dreamed about wearing a one-of-a-kind Catalina Omar wedding gown on my wedding day. The problem is, she is impossible to get an appointment with. She has a two-year waiting list. But my mom talked to Kelsey's mom, and she was able to pull some strings through one of her set designer contacts who happens to know Catalina personally. She got us an appointment with her for this weekend, in New York," she explains excitedly. "Dad wants to fly me, Mom, Kelsey and her mom, and Brie into Manhattan for the long weekend. That's why we cut our Monaco trip short and came home early. It's the only appointment I'll be able to get. If I cancel this, there is absolutely no way I will get another one."

"Oh, Dawn, you can't cancel. You guys go, and I'll stay here," I offer.

"No way. You guys both have to be there. You are going to be my maids of honor after all, and I need you. While we are there, we can shop for your dresses, too. Plus, we are kind of counting on you to be our Big Apple tour guide. Kels and I have never been to New York before. While I am there, I want to see and do and eat everything."

She turns pleading eyes to Nicco.

"I think it's a great idea. I have been debating on whether or not to send Brie away until this disruption is handled. Hopefully, with you guys tucked safely across the country, Gino and I will have time to actually help track Calvacanti down and put an end to this ordeal. What do you say, sis? Up for a trip home?"

I fidget with my crust and mull it over in my head. Am I up for it? It's not like I have to let anyone in New Rochelle know I am coming to the city. New York is a big, crowded place, and the likelihood of me running into anyone I don't want to see is slim to none. Plus, getting away from this prison of an apartment for a while would be a welcome relief.

"Please, Brie. Mom will charter a private plane, so there is zero chance of your stalker finding out you are flying anywhere. Pretty please." She moves in front of me with her hands folded in prayer.

"Okay. I am in."

"Yes!" she squeals.

I turn to Nicco. "You can tell Tony I am coming into the city. I'd love to see him, Stav, and Lo if they have time, but tell him not to say anything to Mamma or Papa. And, if you are going to put guards on us, make sure they are discreet. I don't want Aunt Susan or Dawn's mother catching on that we are being followed."

Dawn jumps to her feet. "Yay! I have to call Daddy and tell him to get everything set up."

Daniel watches her as she heads to her room to retrieve her phone.

"She is going to be the biggest bridezilla," I tease.

He turns to me with a massive grin on his face. "I know. It's her day though. Whatever she wants is exactly what I want her to have. As long as she walks down that aisle to me, I don't care if she wears a dress crafted by fairies, using handspun unicorn hair."

Kelsey and I both sigh at his statement. That's the kind of love every girl dreams about.

After Dawn talks to her parents, we start packing. Our plane will leave first thing in the morning. I am both excited and terribly nervous to be heading home.

About thirty minutes later, we hear a knock at the door. I peek my head out of my room and listen as Nicco answers. He looks down the hall at me.

"Jake?" he states with a question in his voice.

I nod to him to let him know it is okay to let him in.

Jake cautiously walks through the door as he eyes the gun in Nicco's hand.

"I cause the need for that?" he asks.

Nicco holsters the weapon. "No, but you sure didn't help the situation," Nicco answers.

Jake shakes his head. "I am sorry, man. I never meant for any of this to happen."

"I know you didn't." He pats him on the back. "I am going to go see if Kelsey needs any help packing."

He excuses himself and heads down the hall. As he passes me, he says, "Give him a chance to say his piece, sis." Then, he disappears into Kelsey's bedroom and leaves us alone.

I make my way to the kitchen and start to uncork a bottle of wine. I set two glasses on the island in silent invitation. Jake follows me and sits in a stool across from me. Neither of us says anything for several moments.

Then, he finally begins, "I'm so sorry for showing up wasted at Dawn's party. Fuck, I'm sorry for so much shit."

His head is down, watching his hand twirl the wineglass.

"So am I," I murmur.

At that, he looks up at me.

"What are you sorry for?" he asks.

"For not telling you everything. I never intended to end up in a relationship. The way I felt about you took me by surprise, and I didn't know how or what to share. I knew, eventually, I would have to tell you about my life. I just wasn't ready. It was unfair of me to expect you to understand something that I never explained to you."

I see the tension leave his shoulders. He expected me to be defensive. Even I'm surprised that I am not.

"It was too soon for me, but I liked you so much that I jumped in anyway. That's on me," I acknowledge.

"And I should have told you about the Lucas guy right away, but I was afraid that you would think my feelings for you were a charade, and they weren't. They never were. I might have approached you at his urging, but that's where it ended. Every single interaction after our first was genuine. I swear to you."

His eyes are begging me to see his truth.

"I believe you," I reveal.

I have had some time to think it all over, and I've realized that he was sincere in every way. Had he not been, I know I would have felt it. His sincerity was one of the things that helped me let my guard down. I trust my instincts.

"Does that mean you forgive me?"

I don't miss the hope in his question.

"I do," I start cautiously, "but, like I said, it was all too soon for me, and now, with everything happening, I need to sort myself out."

I see and feel his disappointment.

"I assumed that you would," he admits. "I just had to make sure you knew how fucking sorry I was. I never meant to hurt you or put any of you guys in harm's way. I love you, Brie—or Gabby. It doesn't matter who you are or were. I just love you. All of you."

I nod my head at his admission. Honestly, I needed to hear it.

"I care about you, too, Jake. You gave me hope that I could move on, that I could feel again, when I'd thought that was impossible. I will always be grateful for that."

He stands. We look at each other for a long while.

Then, he breaks the silence. "I am going to go now."

I can tell he is trying to hold back tears until he escapes. I walk around the island to him. I wrap my arms around his middle and hug him tightly. We hold on to each other for a long time.

Finally, he kisses my forehead. "I hope that, one day, you are ready for what we could have been. When you are, you know how to find me."

With that parting statement, he releases me and walks straight to and out of the door.

I take a deep breath and let it out. With it, I let Jake go.

A few minutes later, Kelsey tiptoes into the living room.

"Is he gone?" she asks.

"Yes. He left a few minutes ago."

"I thought I heard the door shut. Are you okay?"

"I am. I think we both got our closure."

She smiles.

"Well, how about we finish packing and get some sleep? Because, tomorrow, we are headed out on a great adventure."

I lift my glass. "I'll drink to that."

I down the remaining wine, and she and I march to our rooms to finish packing.

CHAPTER
Eighteen

Cross

"**S**HE'S COMING TO NEW YORK." NICCO'S VOICE COMES OVER the line, telling me of Gabby's recent plans.

Relief sweeps over me. I have wanted her out of California for weeks now.

"She and the girls and their mothers will be on a nine a.m. flight tomorrow morning. It should land at JFK sometime around five p.m. your time."

"Airline and flight number?" I ask.

"Private jet, which works well. No tickets, no passenger list, no paper trail. Dante can't possibly know she's leaving or where she is going."

"Good. That's very good. Do we know where they are staying yet?"

"Kelsey's mom is arranging a hotel suite in the city. Not sure which hotel yet. I'll let you know when I do. She wants to see our brothers while she is in town, so Tony will have her itinerary, and he will arrange for protection. I don't want them to be on edge or to feel suffocated. I want the three of them to enjoy the hell out of themselves and not to worry about anything going on back here. I think they will be perfectly safe there. I just want a light detail on them; that's all."

"I agree. Gabby loves the city. I'm sure she is going to love getting to show her friends around."

"Don't seek her out, Cross." His tone is stern.

"Excuse me?"

"I mean it. I know you are going to want to, knowing she is there. Fight the urge."

"I have no intention of disrupting her trip," I say, offended by his tone.

"Good. And she doesn't want our parents to know she's there either. So, do not tell Papa."

"Understood."

"Hopefully, we get our hands on Dante while they are there and can put all this bullshit behind us. I want him found before school starts back. The last thing she is going to want me to do is send bodyguards to class with her."

I laugh at the mental picture. Gabby flanked by Gino and Frankie while her professor nervously lectures.

"Can you imagine Gino sitting in a desk in the back of a classroom?" I snort.

"The professor wouldn't dare give her anything less than an A," he answers.

We both laugh.

"I have to go; the girls are coming in. I'll keep you posted."

"Thank you, Nicco."

I can hear Gabby and her friends excitedly chatting away before he disconnects. I am jealous. As much as he complains, I know that he enjoys every second with them.

This house is void of laughter and chatter.

Tony is seated at the table across from me as the wine is being poured. We just finished up a meeting with a few of our mutual business acquaintances and are now awaiting my dinner guests.

"I take it, you know Gabriella will be in town tomorrow?" he states.

I incline my head. "Nicco called to let me know."

"I will be in the city the four days that she and her friends are here, keeping an eye on them, so you are going to have to oversee things at the Bowery warehouse. Paulino called this morning."

"And what did he say?"

"He changed the pending schedules, like we talked about."

Good. Now, we wait and see if anyone hits the dummy shipments. No one else is aware of the switch.

"O'Neill called as well. Said he was contacted by a gentleman in Queens who wanted to supply him with arms at a much better rate than he is getting from us."

"So, they are stashing our stock somewhere in Queens. They have to have help. Who do we know there?"

"Vitagliano's got a few warehouses up there. If anything is moving in his neighborhood, he will know about it."

Vitagliano is an old friend of my father. He, Papa, and Matteo grew up together, and the three of them would play golf often. Their mutual love of adult clubs and cigars bonded them.

"Call him and arrange a meeting. I'll meet with him while you are in the city with the girls."

"Want me to send Stavros with you? He and Carlos go way back."

Carlos is Vito's oldest son.

"Yes. That would be a wise move. A familiar face is always a good play."

"You got it."

"If the dummy shipments are hit, make sure our guys know to bring everyone back alive if possible."

Tony grins. "Of course."

Our waitress approaches and announces that our other guests have arrived, and we move on to other business.

Adriana walks in, wrapped in a form-fitting black cocktail dress.

Her black hair is slicked back from her face, and her lips are bright red. She looks stunning. She approaches our table with my new business associate, Benjamin Sutton, on her arm. He is smiling down at her, wholly enraptured in whatever she is saying. Tony and I stand to greet them. Adriana comes to me, and I kiss her on her cheek and pull out her chair.

"Thank you, darling." She beams. "I hope you don't mind, but I ran into our guest, waiting out front, and decided to escort him in myself."

She is being flirtatious, and Benjamin is basking in the attention.

He is the CEO of one of the largest distributors of steel in the country, and I am hoping to make a deal with him for raw materials for our foundries that will be very beneficial for both of us. It will bring me one step closer to taking our family in a more legitimate direction. A lot is riding on this dinner.

"Of course. I hope you weren't waiting long?" I focus my attention on our guest.

"No, not at all. My car had just dropped me off when your lovely fiancée found me."

Adriana lights up at his compliment.

"Benjamin, this is my friend Tony Mastreoni. We have a few joint business ventures, and we were just going over a few details."

At that, Tony stands and shakes his hand. "It is nice to meet you, Benjamin." He turns to Adriana. "Adi, always a pleasure. But I must take my leave. I will attend to the matters we discussed, Cross. I hope you all enjoy your dinner."

We all say our good-byes as he leaves, and then I turn to my dinner companions.

"Well, let's order some cocktails and food and get down to business, shall we?"

Once our drinks hit the table, we start negotiations. Matteo and I worked out a contract, which would benefit us all nicely, on all our current projects and left open the possibility for future ventures.

After an excellent meal, we leave the restaurant two hours later with a signed steel contract in my jacket pocket. I want to say my negotiating skills sealed the deal, but I have a sneaky suspicion it had more to do with my future bride's charm than it did with anything I said tonight.

I open the door to our waiting car as we bid good night to Ben, and I slide in after Adriana.

"You were perfect tonight. I can see why your father and Vincenzo thought you would be an asset. You handled yourself exactly as I needed you to."

I can tell the praise pleases her.

"You're welcome. It was easy. He was charming and not hard to look at, so batting my eyelashes at him all night was not a hardship."

"You truly are remarkable, Adriana. I keep treating you like you are the same spoiled-rotten, troublemaking teenager who used to infuriate me when you would drag Gabby into your antics, but you're not that child anymore. I have to start giving you more credit."

"Oh, I think a little bit of the troublemaker is still in here somewhere." She looks at me and winks.

"I'm sure she is, but you have matured."

"Yeah, it sucks ass, being a grown-up. I wish I could go back," she confesses.

"So do I."

"It's awful, missing her all the time, isn't it?" she asks.

I tilt my head in agreement.

"No offense, but being married to you is going to be my own private hell because, every time I look at you, all I see is her. She was the only real friend I ever had, and now, I have no one," she adds.

"If it makes you feel any better, I will be right there with you in hell. At least we will have each other."

She smiles a satisfied half smile. "It does make me feel a little bit better. Misery loves company after all."

"That it does. That it does."

CHAPTER
Nineteen

Bree

I HAVE NEVER BEEN ON A PRIVATE JET BEFORE. I HAVE FLOWN FIRST class many times, and I thought that was the only way to fly. I was so wrong. The plane is so over-the-top extravagant with its wide, swiveling leather captain's chairs, full wet bar, giant televisions, two sofas, queen-size bed in the bedroom, full bathroom with a shower, and a kitchen. It's like a traveling hotel suite with a first-class staff.

Before we even taxi out, our flight attendant brings us all mimosas and takes our breakfast orders. I order an egg-white omelet with portabella mushrooms, red onion, spinach, and Gruyère cheese with a side of home fries and rye toast. Try ordering that on an American Airlines flight.

We are all brimming with anticipation. The girls are chattering on and on about all the things they want to see and do in New York City. Kelsey wants to sightsee and visit all the landmarks, including the Empire State Building, One World Trade Center, the 9/11 Memorial Museum, Central Park, the Statue of Liberty, and the MET. Dawn wants to see Saks Fifth Avenue, Bloomingdale's, Bergdorf Goodman, Macy's, Tiffany & Co., and every single restaurant she has found while researching Manhattan eateries online. It will undoubtedly be a full four days. My goal is to get them to as many places on their lists as possible, but I also plan to take them to all my favorite out-of-the-way places in the city. The areas the locals love that you would never find littered with tourists stopping every five minutes to take selfies or to make some silly I Heart NYC souvenir purchase.

Several hours and several cocktails later, the pilot comes over the loudspeaker to tell us we are about to make our descent into JFK Airport.

A thrill shoots through me.

"Oh, wow, look at how beautiful it is." Kelsey points out the window to the impressive Manhattan skyline. It is indeed a sight to behold.

"There is nothing like it," I admit with pride.

I am suddenly hit with a major case of nerves. Home. I am about to be home for the first time in over a year. Oh, how I have missed it. I don't think I realize quite how much until I look out and see the buildings reaching up into the clouds like beacons between the rivers.

We all get seat-belted in for our landing, and I say a silent prayer that everything goes smoothly while we are here.

Susan rented a car service, and the driver is waiting when we land. We are ushered directly to the car, and our bags are swiftly loaded. Man, a private jet is definitely the way to travel. I have never made it through this airport so quickly.

It takes about forty minutes to make it to the hotel. The car pulls up in front of The Plaza, and the hotel's valets are instantly at our door.

"Is that the park?" Kelsey asks as she glances across the street.

I explained on the flight over that there are many beautiful parks in the city—Bryant and Battery to name a couple—but that Central Park was the largest and most beautiful. It is the heart of the city.

"Yes, ma'am. The one and only Central Park," I confirm.

"Exactly how big is it?" she asks.

"Eight hundred and forty acres."

Her eyes bulge out as she remarks, "That's a lot of acres."

I laugh. "Yes, it sure is."

"How are we ever going to see all of it this weekend?"

"Oh, I don't think you ever really see all of it. You could spend months here and visit the park every single day and always find something new. It has music venues, restaurants, fountains, athletic fields, a lake, ponds, walking and running trails, bike trails, and even a zoo."

"Really? A zoo?" She looks at me in fascination.

"A zoo," I repeat.

"Wow. I heard there was a carousel, too." Her eyes are filled with wonder.

I look back across at the park and try to see it through her eyes. It is magnificent. There is a reason it's the most filmed location in the world. New Yorkers don't appreciate it as much as we should.

Dawn's mom, Carolyn, calls down to us from the steps of the hotel, "Come on, girls; our suites are ready."

We follow her up the red-carpeted steps as she hands us our key cards. We follow across the stunning mosaic tiled floor toward the entrance. The girls are in awe of the beautiful lobby with its dazzling stained glass ceiling and crystal chandeliers. It is quite spectacular. I imagine even more so if it is your first time taking it in. It's like stepping back in time, into old New York glamour.

We make our way to our rooms. Carolyn and Susan are sharing a suite across the hall, and the three of us are sharing a gorgeous three-bedroom suite with an insane view of the park. This setup had to set Dawn's dad back several grand a night. I have always loved The Plaza. I have never stayed here before—there was never a need to when Adi and I lived in the city—though I have had several meals here and many a dirty martini in The Rose Club or a cocktail in The Champagne Bar.

"I want to live here," Dawn declares as she drops her purse on the sofa and looks around.

"No, you don't. You would be broke in a few weeks. Even your father would be penniless. The Plaza is opulent, and you pay heavily for that opulence."

"Well, we are here now." She twirls. "I guess we are just going to have to soak it all in while we can. Room service anyone?"

She hands us each a menu, and we order a king's ransom worth of decadent food before we decide to call it an early night, so we can be well rested for tomorrow's shenanigans.

I was able to get us a reservation for brunch at Norma's. It is my absolute favorite brunch spot in the city. It is in the Parker Meridian Hotel. The venue is tiny, and the wait is insane if you don't plan ahead. However, the food is fantastic and absolutely worth it.

"Is there really a two-thousand-dollar omelet on this menu?" Dawn asks in disbelief.

"That can't be right. Where do you see that?" Kelsey asks as she scans the menu in her hand.

"Right there." Dawn points to the ostentatious breakfast option. "It even says, *We dare you to expense this.*"

"You would be surprised how many people do expense it," I inform them.

"That omelet had better come with a Louis Vuitton handbag and an orgasm for that price," Dawn loudly exclaims.

The patrons at the table to our left all glare at her.

"What? I bet none of you are eating that omelet either, so get your noses out of our conversation."

"Dawn! Inside voice," Carolyn scolds like she is ten years old.

We all erupt into uncontrollable laughter.

An hour and a half later, we are sitting and waiting for the check.

"That was the best food I have ever put into my mouth," Kelsey muses.

The table is littered with plates. None of us were able to decide between the sweet, mouth-watering breakfast options or the savory lunch items, so we ordered a little bit of everything and shared.

"Oh, you just wait," I tell her. "You haven't seen anything yet. By the time we leave for home, you are going to have so many favorite restaurants in the city. I can't wait to take you guys to Little Italy. It's heaven on earth."

"This is going to be the best trip ever," she declares.

After brunch, we head out to do the shopping portion of our trip. Susan and Carolyn are as excited as Dawn to see all the exclusive storefronts on 5th, Park, Madison, and Lexington Avenues. They rival that of Rodeo Drive. We are only a few blocks in, and they each already have their arms weighed down with bags.

Two hours later, and Kelsey and I are helping tote their loot. We have just been window-shopping.

As the others make their way into Hermes, we wait outside on the sidewalk.

"Don't worry, Kels; tomorrow, I am taking us to SoHo and Tribeca. That's where all the funky, eclectic, independent shops are. Much more our style," I whisper to her.

"I don't mind. Let them have their fun. I'm just soaking up the sights and sounds of the city." She beams.

I look around us at all the people whizzing by, and for the first time since I left, I feel a real pang of homesickness.

"Hey, are you okay?" Her free hand reaches for my arm and her face fills with concern.

"Yeah. I just didn't realize how much I missed the city. California is great and I love it there. I do," I start as tears threaten to spill.

"But it's not home," she finishes for me.

"No, it's not. It sounds crazy I know. LA is so beautiful, lush and green, but I prefer my concrete jungle."

"It doesn't sound crazy at all. I can see it. You are different here. You glow."

After grabbing a quick lunch, we head back to the hotel to drop off their purchases before our appointments at the Guerlain Spa. We are having the works done—massages, facials, wraps, waxing, and then hair and makeup for our big night out. We are going to see *Something Rotten!* on Broadway. I couldn't let them come to New York without seeing a show. It's one of my absolute favorite things to do. Adi and I used to stand in line for hours at the TKTS counter in Times Square to try and score tickets for our favorite shows for a steal.

Afterward, we are having dinner at one of my favorite restaurants in the Theater District. I debated on taking them to Tavern on the Green. There is nothing quite like dining in the beautifully lit court-yard in Central Park at night. I wish we had a couple of more days here. I want to take them everywhere I love.

"This is the life," Dawn practically singsongs.

We all have our hair wrapped in towels and faces slathered with a thick green cream and our eyes covered with cucumber slices. We are wearing the softest robes ever created, and we each have a girl working on our nails.

"Isn't it?" Kelsey breathes. "I might be too relaxed to get dressed after this," she moans.

"I'm sure they have someone who can do that for you," Dawn adds.

We all giggle.

"We'd better slow down on the champagne, or none of us are going to be able to dress ourselves," I say as I tilt my glass up and swallow the last sip.

After we are all polished and buffed and dressed in stunning cock-tail dresses, we head down to the car that is waiting to take us to the theater.

"Oh no, I forgot my clutch." I remember just as we arrive at the lobby.

"No problem. You girls go back up and grab it, and we will go meet the driver," Susan offers as they exit the elevator.

"Thank you. We will only be a minute."

I press the button to take us back up to our suite.

Five minutes later, the three of us have made it back down. The lobby is a whirl of activity in the evenings. Crowds of people are meandering around, waiting for tables in one of the restaurants or for seats to open in the bars or clubs. We quickly make our way toward the front entrance and are about to step outside when we hear a voice ring out from behind us.

"Gabby?"

Then, again but closer, like she has given chase.

"Gabs, is that you?"

I stop at the sound of my real name being called. Dawn and Kelsey come to a stop as well, and we all turn around to face the voice. It's like we're moving in slow motion, and before I even see her face, I know precisely who it is.

"It is you," she says as she walks hurriedly toward us.

Fuck.

Adriana.

CHAPTER
Twenty

Cross

I SIT IN MY OFFICE AND TRY TO BUSY MYSELF WITH PAPERWORK. NICCO called last night to let me know the girls had made it safely to New York. It has taken everything I have not to get into my car and head to Manhattan. It's like my soul is humming because it knows she is here, and it wants to seek her out. I can feel her in my bones.

I pick up my glass and stare into it. I should probably not have any more. If I get drunk, then all bets are off, and I will probably end up at Gabriella's hotel door.

I leave the glass sitting, and I head up to my room. I change out of my suit and put on a pair of jeans and a tee. Then, I head out back to the garages. I take the stairs to the loft I used to call home. Everything is the same as it was the day I moved out. I make my way to the couch and turn on the television. Perhaps a baseball game can distract me for a few hours.

I try to concentrate on the game, but my focus keeps shifting around the room. Gabby is everywhere here. Memories of a determined ten-year-old kicking my ass at Guitar Hero. The awkward fourteen-year-old scarfing down pizza and soda and forcing me to watch those terrifying *Saw* movies while she hid under a blanket or crawled behind my back. The crazy-beautiful sixteen-year-old who drove me insane and almost got me shot. The sexy-as-hell nineteen-year-old who rocked my world and made me the happiest man on the planet. I see her smile, I hear her laughter, I feel her silky hair against my shoulder, and I swear, I can even smell her skin. I don't know why I keep this place. It's sweet torture every time I come here.

I pick up my phone and call Lorenzo. He is staying at his parents' home while he waits to close on his new apartment in Brooklyn. He oversees his family's interests there now and decided to move to Williamsburg.

"Yo, Cross. What's up?"

"I am bored and hungry. Just wondering if you want to go grab a bite and a couple of beers with me?"

"Nonna just pulled a lasagna from the oven. The cheese is still bubbling on top. Come over and eat. Then, we can go get a few drinks at Murray's."

"You sure there is enough?" I ask as I turn off the television and gather my keys and wallet.

"Are you shitting me? Nonna still cooks like all five of us kids are living at home. I don't think the woman knows how to cook for just the four of them." He chuckles.

"Okay, you had me at bubbling cheese. I'll be there in a few minutes."

Lo answers the door and leads me into the dining room. Vincenzo and Lilliana, Nonno and Nonna are already seated. Lo and I sit at the other end of the table, and before my ass even hits the pad of the chair, Nonna has gotten up, placing a heaping plate of lasagna in front of me and pouring me a glass of Chianti.

"Thank you, Nonna."

She leans down, and I kiss her age-lined cheek as she pats my arm.

She shoos me. "Eat, eat. You are looking way too thin, Christoff," she chastises me.

Same Nonna. She has been telling me I am too thin for as long as I can remember.

"Glad you could join us, Christoff. Where is your blushing bride-to-be this evening?" Vincenzo asks.

I see the wince slide through Lilliana at the mention of Adriana. She hates us both—the two people who hurt her baby girl so badly.

"She is in the city, finalizing a few wedding details," I answer.

He nods. "Good. Is good. Not too long now before you are a married man."

"No, it is rapidly approaching."

I keep my eyes focused on my plate as I take my wineglass and empty it. It is awkward at best to speak of my upcoming nuptials with Gabriella's family.

"So, did you catch the Yankees game today?" Lo changes the subject, and I give him an appreciative smile.

We speak of the game and other small talk while we eat.

Lilliana finishes her dinner and excuses herself before dessert. Never once acknowledging me.

"Come, boys. Let us have a brandy and cake on the patio, shall we?" Vincenzo invites.

Lo and I follow him outside, and he pours us each a drink. It's a gorgeous night. Clear and not too hot. I shouldn't be so on edge, yet I can't shake myself out of it.

"What do you two have planned for the evening?" Vincenzo lights a cigar and sits back in a chaise as he waits expectantly.

"We are just going to go have a few drinks and maybe play a few rounds of pool down at Murray's to blow off some steam, Papa," Lo answers.

"So, you aren't going into the city then?" He asks the question casually, but it's anything but.

Tony must have told him she is here. Either that or he has his own eyes on her, which does not surprise me in the least.

I look him in the eye. "We hadn't planned on it, sir."

"If you do decide to go into the city, I hope I can count on you both to use good judgment." He stares back at me, and I don't miss the command in his statement.

"Of course, Papa," Lo reassures him.

I nod my concession.

He inclines his head in approval. "Then, I will not keep you from your fun. My lovely wife awaits me to start our show. She doesn't realize it, but I watched the last two episodes while she was at the salon today, so I watch them again and pretend it's the first time. This is what a husband does." He dispenses his wisdom, and then he clasps us each on the back as he walks us back inside.

"So, Papa knows Gabby is in town, and so do you apparently," Lo says once we are seated at Murray's.

The bartender sets our bottles in front of us.

"Yeah, Nicco let me know they were coming. I am glad she is out of Santa Monica. Here is much safer for her right now."

"She didn't want Papa to know, but he has his ways, I suppose. Tony, Stav, and I are having dinner with her and her friends tomorrow night. I can't wait. I miss the brat, and I hear her roommates are hot." He grins a mischievous grin as he lifts his bottle to his lips.

"I would be careful. One of them is engaged to your cousin Daniel, and the other is sleeping with your brother." I let the cat out of the bag.

He coughs and chokes on his beer as he raises an eyebrow at that news. "Really? He omitted that fun fact when briefing us on them. Are you sure?"

"Saw it with my own eyes."

"What?" he exclaims.

"Not the literal act, but the interaction between them, and she stayed the night with him when I was in California."

"Good for him. He didn't need to spend any more time moping around over Marianna."

"True enough," I agree.

My phone starts to buzz in my pocket, and I pull it out and check the screen.

"Speak of the devil." I raise my phone, so he can see Nicco's name flashing. "I'll be right back," I tell him as I stand to seek out a quieter location to answer the call.

He waves me off and turns to whisper to the brunette on his left. I head to the back and into a private booth tucked in the corner.

"Nicco?"

"Hey, man. Just wanted to let you know, we found where Dante has been staying. Stefano tracked him to a place in La Mirada. He has been renting it week to week and paying cash, tossing the building super a little extra to keep it off the books."

"Please tell me you have him."

"He wasn't here when we got here, but he will be back, and we will be ready."

"Thank God. Let's get this done before the girls fly home. I'll let Tony know. Call me as soon as you have him in your hands."

"Cross, we found some things here," he says carefully.

"What kind of things?"

"Hundreds of photos, all of Gabby, a couple of burner phones, debit cards, and receipts for cash wires."

"Okay …" I say with a question in my voice. I am not sure why any of that has him on edge. None of it sounds surprising.

"It seems that Matteo di Rossi has been sending him large sums of money."

What the fuck?

"What? Matteo? Are you sure?"

"Positive. He has his contact info in a folder with the wire receipts."

"How in the hell do Dante and Matteo know each other, and why would he send him cash?" I wonder aloud.

"I've racked my brain, and I can only think of one thing that could possibly benefit them both," he begins cautiously.

"Getting rid of me," I finish.

"It would seem so. Matteo would get control, and Dante would get ..."

"Gabby," I confirm.

As the pieces start clicking together, the entire thing comes into clear focus. Matteo was with my father and Emilio the night of the shooting but had luckily gotten up to take a phone call before the shots were fired. He is the only other person who has access to the schedules of the Irish arms shipments other than Tony, Pauly, and me, and he has knowledge of Gabby's whereabouts. The questions are, how does he know anything about Dante, and how would helping him find her benefit Matteo?

My father's best fucking friend and right-hand man. *Has the key to all the answers been under my nose the entire time?*

Fuck me.

CHAPTER
Twenty-One

Brie

ADRIANA LOOKS LIKE SHE HAS SEEN A GHOST AS SHE APPROACHES us. I quickly back away. Dawn can read my expression, and she immediately steps between us.

Adi looks impeccable. She's dressed in a white pantsuit, perfectly tailored to her body, and nude stiletto Louboutins. Her black hair is pulled back in a sleek, low ponytail, and her makeup is airbrushed perfection.

Just goes to show, you can dress betrayal up in head-to-toe Chanel, and it will still be just as ugly.

"Who are you?" Dawn clips as she curiously eyes Adi.

"Who am I? Who the fuck are you?" Adi smarts, never one to be out-attituded.

"We are Brie's roommates," Kelsey chimes in from behind me.

Adi looks confused for a moment as her eyes move from Dawn to Kelsey and back to me. "Brie? Who the hell is Brie?" She looks to me for an answer.

"What do you want, Adi? What more could you possibly want from me?" I ask instead.

Her face falls at my question. "I'm just surprised to see you; that's all. Can I talk to you privately for a minute?"

"There is nothing for us to say to each other."

"Please, Gabby, five minutes," she pleads.

She confidently looks at me, but she lets her mask slip, and for a second, I get a glimpse of the broken girl I used to know. I consider giving her five minutes, but before I can answer, a woman in a heather-gray jacket with a clipboard under one arm and a glass of champagne in each hand approaches us.

"Miss Ferraro, are you ready to finalize all of your and Mr. Scutari's rehearsal dinner plans? I spoke with him this morning, and he said to give his beautiful fiancée anything she wanted, so this should be a lot of fun!"

Adi nervously looks at me as she addresses her, "I, um ... yes, thank you, Pamela. I'll be just a minute."

"Of course. I'll be waiting in The Champagne Bar when you are ready."

At that, she smiles at us and then hands Adi one of the flutes before walking off into the lobby.

"Gabby, I—" she starts.

"Don't," I cut her off. "I can't do this with you. I can't ever do this with you," I angrily retort.

I see the pain run through her. *Good.* I hope it hurts like hell to hear those words. *Honestly, what did she expect?* It's not like she wasn't there for everything. All of it. She knew how this was going to kill me.

"I never meant to ..." she starts with a quiver in her voice.

"Yes, you did."

"No, Gabby. I didn't. It's been over a year. I thought you had moved on."

Her bottom lip is trembling. I have never seen her so contrite. I almost believe her, but I can't let myself fall for it. She knew exactly what she was doing when she helped run me out of my home, out of my life, so she could slide right in. She might miss having me follow her around like a little puppy, but that's all it is.

We stand there in a stare-down for several seconds with Dawn standing guard between us when we hear Aunt Susan call us from outside.

"I have to go. Enjoy your wedding planning," I quip as I turn from her.

Then, I rush from the hotel to the car with Dawn and Kelsey on my heels.

The car pulls up to the Shubert Theatre on West 44th Street about a half hour before the show. The lobby is filled to capacity with excited spectators grabbing refreshments and Broadway souvenirs before curtain.

"Are we overdressed?" Kelsey looks down at her cocktail dress.

"Maybe a little, but we are going out to a fancy restaurant after the show, so we are fine. You don't really have to dress up for the theater. I mean, I wouldn't wear shorts and sandals, but ballgowns, furs, and diamonds are usually reserved for the opera, not Broadway. Broadway is more dressy casual instead."

She peeks over at her mom, who has on a long jade mermaid gown and is dripping with emeralds and diamonds. A small circle of adoring fans has surrounded her, and she is signing a few ladies' cocktail napkins and taking selfies.

"I'm not sure my mother knows the meaning of the words *dressy casual*," she observes.

"I think you are right, but who cares? She's famous and she's fabulous."

"Yeah, she kind of is, isn't she?" she agrees.

"Come on. Let's get in line and get us all a glass of vino while she entertains her adoring fans. Then, we can head in."

We grab our wine and a couple of packs of Peanut M&M's and make our way to our seats, all giddy with anticipation. We managed to get dress-circle seats. I wanted the best seats in the house because this is Dawn and Kelsey's first show, and nothing beats dress-circle seats.

As we all settle in, Dawn leans over and whispers, "Are you okay? After that scene at the hotel before?"

"Yes, I'm fine. I just wasn't anticipating running into anyone I knew. Of course, in a city of eight million people, I would walk right past her."

"So, I am assuming that was the ex–best friend who is marrying your man, huh?"

"Yep, Adriana Ferraro, in the flesh."

"What a bitch. For the record, you are way hotter than her."

"Way hotter," Kelsey agrees from my other side.

Adriana is stunning; I know that, but I appreciate them trying to make me feel better.

As the lights go down and the curtain rises, we turn our focus to the stage. The show is a hilarious musical comedy, following a couple of brothers in the 1500s, who are trying to write the world's first musical, but they are competing with a manipulative rival playwright known as William Shakespeare. It highlights everything one loves about Broadway. We laugh until we are breathless.

When the lights come on for intermission, Dawn looks at me, confused. "Is that it? They didn't even get their musical done. And who knew William Shakespeare was such a dick?"

"It's just intermission," I tell her.

"Intermission?"

"Yes, it's a fifteen-minute pause before the second half of the show begins."

"So, it's like halftime? You can run to pee and grab more beer before the game starts back?" she surmises.

"Yes, it's exactly like halftime."

"Awesome! Let's go! I'll grab more wine while you guys go to the restroom." She stands and leads the way for us.

After the show, we head to Legasea at the Moxi Hotel. It's a fantastic seafood restaurant near Times Square and one of my favorite dining spots in the city.

The show was amazing, but I didn't honestly get to enjoy it. Luckily, I have seen it a time or two already.

I kept replaying the run-in with Adi in my mind over and over. It is real. The wedding is really happening. As long as I was tucked away in California, I didn't have to face the reality of it, but Cross and my best friend are getting married in a matter of weeks. I have to face the fact.

We are seated at our table, and the hostess places menus in front of us. The space is something else. It's decorated in deep chocolate leathers and copper accents. The nautical theme is classic and subtle with low lighting to give a glowing ambiance.

We order an appetizer and a round of drinks before our meals. As soon as it hits the table, we all dig in and start discussing our plans for tomorrow.

Lost in my thoughts as they chatter away, I start when Aunt Susan addresses me with concern in her voice, "Brie, darling, is there something wrong with your food?"

At her question, I look down and see that I haven't touched my entree or the second cocktail that arrived shortly after we ordered.

I was pondering the possibility of Adriana still being at the hotel when we return. Surely, her meeting is over by now, but what if she's waiting to ambush me? I don't think I can face her.

I look from my plate and back up at Susan. "No, ma'am. It is wonderful. I think I just ordered too much; my eyes were bigger than my stomach," I deflect.

I pick up my fork and twirl the pasta. Then, I scoop up the succulent piece of lobster and pop it into my mouth. It is divine, and I am angry with myself for letting anything ruin this lovely evening.

"Well, don't force it. You have to save room for the chocolate tiramisu and the buttermilk panna cotta." She grins.

"I always have room for panna cotta," I declare with a wink.

I put all things Adriana and Cross out of my mind and decide to be present with these women who love me fiercely and treat me like I am family.

Once we are finished, we walk up to Times Square, so they can see it all lit up at night. It's like a mini Vegas strip. Dawn and Kelsey beam as they take it all in. The crowd is elbow-to-elbow, as it tends to be on warm evenings. We all snap a million photos together, and Dawn gets a few with the street performers. She even chases down the infamous naked cowboy and loses her shit over him. I have to video the two of them together as he picks her up and informs Daniel in the message that he is running off with his bride-to-be.

As we walk, I look over to the left and see the neon sign above Havana Central lighting up the side street, and a shiver runs down my spine. *Thanks for ruining my favorite Cuban restaurant for me, asshole.* One more reason to hate Dante Calvacanti. I miss those empanadas and coconut mojitos so much. I will go back there one day, just not today.

"Whatcha looking at?" Dawn comes up beside me and links her arm with mine.

"Nothing, just soaking it all in," I fib.

"Thank you for coming. I know it's kind of hard for you to be here, but this trip wouldn't have been the same without you. I love seeing this place through your eyes." She snuggles into my side.

"I wouldn't have missed it for the world."

CHAPTER
Twenty-Two

Cross

AFTER A FEW MORE DRINKS AT MURRAY'S, LO AND I HEAD HOME. I need a good night's sleep. I have to figure out this Matteo situation. *Could he honestly be behind the hits on my family? And what is the connection between him and Dante? How do they know each other, and what exactly is their end game?* It doesn't add up.

Matteo is one of my father's closest men. They love one another like brothers. He was like an uncle to me, Emilio, and Atelo, growing up. I knew he wasn't exactly thrilled when I took over operations from Papa. He thought I was too young and that I was not ready for such responsibility. Rather than step up and help me ease into the position, he backed off. It confused me a little, but he and Papa remained close, and as I proved myself to be capable, he eventually came around.

Now, he is my closest associate, as he was Papa's. I trust him with a lot of responsibilities. One of which is our New Jersey casinos. He makes an excellent living. I pay him well. *So, why is he organizing hijackings of our shipments for the Irish and now bankrolling Calvacanti?*

My instinct is to bust into his apartment and drag him to one of our warehouses to let my men coerce the answers out of him, but I have to control the urge. Old-school men like him don't sing easily, and with his relationship with my father, I want solid proof of his betrayal before I act. I hope I am wrong. I hope this isn't what it seems.

I'm just coming in the door when I notice a light on outside, off the sitting room. I find Adriana sitting, wrapped in a blanket on a swing on the patio, crying into a half-empty bottle of vodka. At hearing my approach, she starts talking before I'm even able to ask what's wrong.

"I ran into Gabby today. Did you know she was in New York?"

"Yes."

"Of course you did. You know everything."

She takes a drink straight from the vodka bottle. I move to sit on the lounger across from her and let her talk.

"Apparently, she has new friends now. They look like fucking Barbie dolls. How droll."

She rolls her eyes, but I can see the hurt underneath the flippant comment.

"I'm sorry. I should have told you she was in town, but I didn't think you would run into her."

"She's staying at The Plaza. I had a meeting at The Plaza this evening with the event planner, remember?"

"I thought you had a meeting to discuss the menu. Shouldn't that have been at Tavern?" I ask, confused.

"I was meeting with the caterer at The Plaza regarding the rehearsal dinner's menu. Not the reception's menu. Do you listen at all when I speak?"

In all honesty, I tune out about ninety percent of what she says when the wedding plans are the topic.

"She looked at me like I was Cruella de Vil, trying to steal her puppies."

She takes another gulp. I move to take the bottle from her hand, and she wrenches out of my reach.

"She hates me," she whimpers. "I tried to get her to sit with me for five minutes, and she wouldn't."

"What did you hope to accomplish by speaking with her?"

"I don't know. I was just so fucking shocked to see her, and I didn't want her to go."

"Nothing you say is going to change anything. You are never going to be friends again."

"I know."

"You did everything you could to protect her. Just like we all have done." I try to ease her guilt.

"Did I really? You don't honestly think that I'm the only Mafia princess who could've been found to marry you, do you? They would have been lining up at the door. You're gorgeous and wealthy and powerful. But Salvatore saw the opportunity and pounced on it before anyone else could. He's power-hungry. Always has been. He wants to hitch my wagon to yours because he sees the potential you have for success, and he wants a piece of the pie. I'm the means to an end for him, and I lost the one person who ever really gave a damn about me in order to please him. I have been doing it my entire life, but nothing is ever good enough."

She laughs bitterly.

"Maybe marrying you will be."

"You don't have to go through with the wedding."

"Ha! Yes, I do. I have to be the good little girl and do just as I'm told, or he will cut me off at the knees. What do I have to lose at this point anyway?"

"I wouldn't let him."

She snaps her eyes to me. "Would you go to war for me, Cross?"

"Yes."

She laughs bitterly. "We both know that isn't true. You wouldn't even go to war for Gabriella, and you loved her."

She hit her mark. That feels like a kick to the gut.

"I did go to war for Gabby. I let her go. I loved her enough to let her go."

"Keep telling yourself that, but that wasn't love. That was fear. Love fights. Fear lets go." She slurs the last sentence out, and I know she has had enough.

I am sure running into Gabby was traumatic.

I stand and walk to her. I remove the bottle from her grip and set it aside. Then, I lift her in my arms and carry her to bed.

"I miss her," she whispers into the dark hallway.

"I know. So do I."

She passes out before I even cross the threshold of the bedroom. I gently lay her down, cover her, and turn off the light before I head into the shower.

I wake with the sun after a fitful night of sleep. I change into my sweats and go for a run. I am hoping the fresh air and physical exertion will clear my mind and help me to focus. Tony is meeting me in a few hours to discuss what Nicco found out yesterday, and I can run my suspicions past him. Hopefully, Nicco and Stefano will have Dante in their custody by the end of today, and we will get some fucking answers. I tossed and turned all night long, trying to piece the puzzle together. It's like the answer is right in front of me, and I can't get out of my own way to see it. It's frustrating.

After I shower and change, I head down to the kitchen, and I find Una and Adriana having breakfast. They are laughing, and it is good to hear after last night.

"Good morning, my handsome grandson. Would you like some pancakes?"

"Yes, please." I walk over to the island and take a seat beside Adriana. "How are you feeling this morning?"

"Good. Why do you ask?"

"Because you drank almost an entire bottle of vodka by yourself last night."

"So that's how I got to bed. You found me."

Obviously, she doesn't recall our conversation.

"I did. You were out on the patio, and I noticed the light on when I came in."

"I'm sorry. I had a rough day, and I needed to blow off some steam.

Being as I have no friends, it was good ole Tito's keeping me company. Don't worry; it wasn't a full bottle."

"That's good at least. I don't think you want to be rushed to the hospital due to alcohol poisoning two weeks before your wedding. What would *Page Six* say?"

She narrows her eyes at me, and I can see that she is back to her old self again.

"Fuck you. If I want to drink an entire bottle of vodka, I will. I can handle my liquor better than you."

"That's very true. I would be on my ass right now."

"Damn straight."

Una serves up golden stacks of pancakes for us all. Grandfather joins us, and we enjoy a pleasant family breakfast. A small, motley family but still a family.

CHAPTER
Twenty-Three

Bree

"GET UP, BITCHES. IT'S WEDDING DRESS DAY!" DAWN bounces on the edge of my bed.

It's a big day. Our appointment at Catalina Omar's shop is in three hours. Afterward, we are all heading to Kleinfeld Bridal in Chelsea to pick out the bridesmaid dresses.

Later tonight, Carolyn and Susan are taking in a concert at Carnegie Hall while the three of us meet my brothers for dinner and drinks. I can't wait to see them.

We all get up and dressed and head to breakfast at The Palm Court. We are buzzing with excitement as we sip our mimosas and await our food.

"What is that?" I point to the pale pink satin-covered notebook protruding from Dawn's Valentino tote.

"It's the wedding book. She made that thing when she was nine, I believe, and she has had it ever since. Always adding to it or taking away. We would see a dress in a magazine, and she would cut it out and glue it in there. She would grab paint swatches from the hardware store and beads and sequins from the craft aisle at the supermarket, and they'd all end up in the book. She even has menus in there from past events we attended. My girl has been dreaming about this day for as long as I can remember," Dawn's mom explains with tears in her eyes.

"Wow, that's pretty cool. Can I see it?"

I reach over for the book, and Dawn grabs her fork and holds it aloft.

"Don't make me stab you, woman," she dares.

I pull the offending hand back and look at her with mock hurt.

"No one touches the book but me. It's a rule. I can show you the contents of the book, but you don't put your filthy paws on it," she informs me of the rules.

Kelsey leans in and whispers loudly, "We called it. Total bridezilla."

"Hey, watch it. I prefer Overtly Dangerous Bride. You may refer to me as ODB henceforth."

"Oh boy, she is going to be a lot of fun the next ten months," I declare to the table at large.

Everyone laughs, but we all know it's true.

We arrive at the shop right on time, and Catalina's assistant, the fabulous Rodger, leads us into a large, chic industrial space with big, soft gray sofas. A small, raised platform is directly in front of the seating, and floor-to-ceiling three-way mirrors wrap the stage. Rodger brings out a chilled bottle of Dom Pérignon and offers us each a crystal flute.

"Please, get comfortable. Catalina will join you in a few moments, and she will read your collective energy before beginning."

He flits off down a hallway, and Kelsey turns to me.

"Did he say she was going to read our energy?"

"I believe he did."

"I thought she was a designer, not a tarot card reader?"

"Actually, I can do both quite well."

We all turn to see a woman who appears to be in her late fifties, floating into the room with her colorful, billowing robes drifting behind her. She is adorned with crystals at her neck, wrists, and ankles. Her feet are bare. She has a silk headband tied at her temple that holds her long silver dreadlocks from her face. Her hands have the most beautiful henna tattoos I have ever seen. We all look around at each other, confused. This exotic creature before us is not the polished businesswoman or stylish fashionista we were expecting.

"Hello, Mrs. Omar. I cannot tell you how thrilled I am to meet you. I am so honored that you took time out of your schedule for me. I am a huge fan of your work. Your designs are far superior to anything else out there, and I couldn't imagine wearing a gown created by anyone else but you," Dawn, who is unfazed by her appearance in the least, rambles as she extends her hand to Catalina.

She takes her hand, and rather than shaking it, she turns it over. She lightly runs her fingers over her palm and closes her eyes. We all hold our breath. Not knowing if the "energy" she is reading from us will cause her to ask us all to leave. We wait in complete silence.

After a moment, she opens her eyes and smiles at Dawn. "Yes, your gown is within me. I feel it in my soul. Let's begin. Shall we?"

Catalina spends the first thirty minutes of our appointment asking Dawn questions about her life and Daniel and their love story. Dawn speaks passionately about her fiancé, how they met, Daniel's music, the proposal that went so wrong but yet so right for her.

Catalina has a sketchpad and charcoal pencil in hand, and she furiously draws the entire time without taking her eyes from Dawn once. She keeps turning the page and starting again. The rest of us watch in rapt fascination at the genius at work. Once she has a pulse of who Dawn is as a "spiritual human" and who she and Daniel are as a "cohesive life energy," Rodger appears out of thin air with a tape measure to size her.

Next, she has Dawn try on a few sample gowns, so she can get a vision for how certain fabrics will drape on her frame. She moves around Dawn on the platform, pinning and tucking, with her ethereal robes swishing around her like she is in flight. Dawn soaks it all up. She is beaming with happiness. Her mother sobs, and the rest of us cry intermittently as we sip our bubbly and watch the process unfold.

In the end, Catalina has a remarkable sketch of a one-of-a-kind gown that so perfectly fits my quirky friend's personality that we all sit and stare at the page in awe.

Dawn brushes the page with her finger as a tear slides down her right cheek. "It's perfect. It's like you took the dress in my head, in my dreams, and you drew it to life."

Catalina wraps her in her arms. "Your aura is so open; it was as easy as breathing. I can't wait to start on this masterpiece for you, my dear."

"Thank you so much."

"You are so very welcome, child."

With that, Catalina says her good-byes, and she breezes back out of the shop.

"I love her," Dawn says as she watches her go.

A moment later, Rodger appears again and leads us out.

"All right, darling, Catalina will have a simple muslin ready in a couple of days. You just stop back by, and we will let you try it on. We will make any adjustments needed then. The final creation will take about nine months to complete, as every gown is hand-stitched and all embellishments are added by hand. You will have to fly out for three to four fittings at different times during the process."

He hands Dawn a folder with all her paperwork.

"Congratulations. You have your perfect Catalina Omar original." He claps and does a little hop.

Dawn thanks him, and we leave.

We walk out onto the street, and we are all a little speechless from the strange encounter. Then, we all burst into a delightful fit of joy.

Next, we head to Chelsea on our giddy high. The staff at Kleinfeld seems so dull in comparison, but they are incredibly polite and helpful, and both Kelsey and I pick out gorgeous dresses in an emerald shade. Dawn's additional bridesmaids will wear a lighter hue, and all their dresses will be the same style, but Dawn wanted us to stand out and to pick the style we liked and that flattered our bodies best.

I take them all to Serendipity 3 for lunch.

"I would be three hundred pounds if I lived here," Kelsey muses as we finish off our frozen hot chocolates.

"No, you wouldn't. If you lived here, you wouldn't be taking a car service everywhere. Only tourists and visitors do that. Locals walk most places, or we huff it up and down the subway steps all day. We eat and drink, and then we walk our feet and those extra calories off. It's a perfect balance."

"Maybe we should walk to dinner tonight," she says as she slides her chair away from the table and places her hands on her stomach.

"We can't do that. We are meeting my brothers at La Mela. That's a very long walk from our hotel, but we can walk around Little Italy before and after if you guys are up for it?"

"Sounds good, and remind me to skip dessert," Kelsey adds.

"Girl, please. I said Little Italy. You can't skip dessert. You have never tasted cannoli until you have tasted one of Caffé Palermo's famous cannoli."

"Oh, jeez, I am definitely going to have to up the cardio when we get home."

"Totally worth it."

CHAPTER
Twenty-four

Cross

I MEET TONY AT HIS FATHER'S HOUSE. VINCENZO NEEDS TO BE IN ON this now. We have kept him on a need-to-know basis when it comes to Gabriella, but now that it appears Matteo is involved, it's time to come clean. None of this is going to go well, so Tony called in Stavros and Lorenzo for backup.

Stav and I arrive at the same time, and he leads me into the study. Vincenzo is behind his desk with Tony standing and looking over his shoulder at some papers. Lo is making a drink at the wet bar. When we walk in, Stav stops to close the door behind us, and Vincenzo looks up.

A crease forms between his brows.

"To what do I owe the honor of having not only my three sons, but also you visit me at the same time, Christoff?"

He knows instantly that something big is amiss. I walk to the front of his desk and take a seat across from him. Stavros and Lo close in as well.

"We have a story to tell you and a confession to make."

He removes his reading glasses and leans in. "I'm listening."

"First of all, this part happened years ago, and we"—I gesture to all of his sons and myself—"handled it."

He looks us all in the eye and then slightly nods his head for me to continue.

"Do you know a man by the name of Dante Calvacanti?"

"Yes, his father is an attorney, and I and some of my associates use his services when we need delicate matters handled. He is proficient and discreet. Why? Have you boys gotten yourselves into a situation that requires such discretion?"

"No, sir," I reassure him. "But, a couple of years ago, Dante set his eyes on Gabriella."

"I am aware," he acknowledges.

"You are?"

The four of us look at each other in confusion.

"Yes. He told his father he met Gabriella and Adriana at some school event when she was in high school, and he was quite smitten. He begged his father to talk to me and ask my permission to court her. I said no, of course. He seemed like a nice boy, but he was too old for my Gabriella. He asked a few more times, and I told him he would have to wait until she was at least eighteen before I would allow it. By then, she was gone off to Europe. Why?"

"Yeah, well, it was a little more intense than that. He developed an obsession with Gabby. None of us realized how much so, but when she came home and she and Adi moved to the city, he reconnected with her, and they started dating."

"Did they now?" He focuses more intently on my story.

"Yes. For a little while. Then, one night, he took her to a party at a friend's apartment, and unbeknownst to her, he was feeding her drugged drinks."

It takes a moment for him to process the last sentence. We all wait and watch as his face turns an alarming shade of red, and his eyes fill with fury.

"He did what?" He slams his hands on the desk, and papers scatter to the floor.

"She managed to get her hands on a phone and lock herself in a bathroom. She called Nicco and couldn't get him, so she called me, and I rushed to get her. When I made it, he had gotten her out in the hallway and had her pinned to the wall. He was trying to force himself on her."

"He was trying to rape my *bambina?*" he slowly enunciates every word through his clenched jaw.

"Yes, sir."

"Why am I just hearing of this if it happened when she was in school in New York?" he roars.

"Because I got her out of there before he got too far. Then, the five of us went back the next morning, and we beat him within an inch of his life. We told him, if he ever so much as breathed the same air as her again, he would be at the bottom of the Hudson, and no one would ever find his remains."

He looks around, anger growing. "I should've been told."

Tony puts his hand on his father's shoulder. "Yes, Papa, you should have been told. I'm truly sorry that we kept it from you. You had a lot of important stuff on your plate at the time, and this was something we thought we could handle for you. Plus, Gabriella begged us not to tell you. She was ashamed, and she was afraid you would have made her move back home."

"I would have," he instantly admits.

"I wouldn't have let you," I tell him.

He cuts his eyes to me. "Ah, I see. This is when you finally got up the nerve to claim her for your own."

"It is."

"Why are you telling me all of this now, Christoff?"

"We thought we'd taken care of Dante. It took him a very long time to recover. His parents sent him to a rehabilitation center Upstate, and that was the last we heard on him. Then, a few weeks ago, he turned up in California."

I look up at him and meet his eyes. He gets exactly what I am saying.

"He is still obsessed with my baby girl?"

"He is. Nicco is there. I sent Gino and his team to protect her and to aid Nicco."

"I sent Stefano and a few of our men as well to help track him down and to protect Gabriella and her friends," Tony adds.

He silently sits there, measuring his breaths as he listens to us.

"She has had a few close calls with him, and that's one of the reasons she is in New York now. We wanted her away for a few days to give Nicco and the men time to search for Dante without having to keep up with Gabby and her friends. Yesterday, they finally found where he has been staying, but he wasn't there. What they did find was evidence that someone within my organization is bankrolling him," I fill him in.

"Your organization? How can that be?"

"That's what I intend to find out. Do you know anything about my father's man Matteo di Rossi?"

"Not much. He is from an old Sicilian family that used to have a small influence here in the States, but it dwindled when his grandfather was indicted on racketeering charges decades ago. He was later brought up for the murder of a federal prosecutor, and he turned rat on his colleagues to avoid the death penalty. His son, Matteo's father, tried to hold on to the family control, but he was weak. He lost all the territory within ten months. The other families divided it. That's when your grandfather took him under his wing, and he started working for the Scutaris. I guess Matteo was about twelve or thirteen then."

"My father loves him."

"He grew up with Marcello. They were like brothers."

"He was with Papa and Emilio the night of the shooting. He had just excused himself to take a call when the bullets started flying. It was a lucky coincidence that he wasn't there."

"It would seem so," he agrees.

"Then, just this past week, Tony and I have had two shipments for the Irish weapons hijacked, and only four men know the schedule for those shipments."

"I see, and the someone within your organization that is sending Dante money is …"

"Di Rossi."

He stands from his desk and makes his way over to the bar. He pours himself a scotch, drinks it down, and then pours another. Then, he starts pacing.

"I'll deal with you all about keeping these things from me at a later time. For now, we find this boy. We find him now. Before he gets any more desperate. It's in my experience that desperate men make very dangerous adversaries. They have nothing to lose, and that is a powerful thing. Once we have him away from Gabriella, you can find out if he and di Rossi had anything to do with the hit on Marcello. In the meantime, do you have eyes on Matteo?"

"I do, and he has been fed a phony schedule for O'Neill's next shipment. We have a dummy truck going out tonight that will be expecting him."

"Good. It won't be him. He is not that foolish. It will be hired men. Perhaps you can persuade one of them to talk. It's doubtful they will know where Calvacanti is, but they might be able to confirm all your other suspicions."

Tony's phone starts to vibrate, and he looks down at it.

"It's Gabriella; we are supposed to meet her and her friends in Little Italy for dinner tonight. Should I cancel?"

"No, you boys go have dinner with your sister and her friends. I don't want her to be alarmed any more than she already is. I will talk to Nicco and Stefano, and I will contact some of my personal California resources to help get this matter taken care of swiftly."

"Thank you, Vincenzo, and I am sorry to be bringing all of this to your doorstep."

He cuts his eyes to me. "You should have brought it to me sooner."

"I know, sir. I am sorry, very sorry."

I get to my feet and walk over with my hand extended. He waves it off and clasps my shoulder.

"Christoff, we are allies, and I will always have your back, son. We will get to the bottom of all this before your wedding. I promise."

CHAPTER

Twenty-five

Bree

AFTER LUNCH, I TAKE THE GIRLS TO SEE THE 9/11 MEMORIAL AND Battery Park. We decided to admire Lady Liberty from afar and skip the ferry ride over, so we would have time to do a little shopping in SoHo before we head back to rest our poor feet until it's time to shower and dress for dinner. That's the thing about New York; no matter how much time you have, it's never enough time to do and see all the things, which means we all have to come back again.

I text Tony on our way back to the hotel to confirm our reservation time. We have three hours, so we decide to take a quick nap before we get ready for the evening. Of course, that's a bad idea. We oversleep and have to quickly throw ourselves together and then make a mad dash for the restaurant.

La Mela Ristorante is on Mulberry Street in the heart of Little Italy, and it is my favorite Italian restaurant in the city. It has been open for over twenty-five years and serves the most amazing food, second only to my nonna's cooking. The walls are papered with photographs of their customers through the years, including the likes of Frank Sinatra and Bill Murray from back in his *Saturday Night Live* days. It just feels like the best of old New York. I love it.

When we arrive, the hostess is expecting us, and she leads us to a table in the back where my three big brothers are already seated with a bottle of red wine breathing. When they spot us coming in, they all stand. I run into Tony's arms. It has been so long since I have laid eyes on the three of them, and I am overwhelmed with emotion.

"Hey, *cara.* Let me look at you." He holds me out at arm's length and looks me up and down. "*Bellissima.*" Then, he kisses the top of my head and pulls me to his side.

"Hey, what about us?" Lo gives me his sad eyes.

I disengage from Tony's hold and make my way to him and then Stavros for equally tight squeezes.

"So, who do we have here?" Stav asks over the top of my head.

I turn to see my two best friends with very stunned looks on their faces.

"These are my roommates, Dawn and Kelsey. They don't usually drool like that." I grin up at him.

Then, I turn back to my two dumbstruck friends.

Dawn blinks at me and then looks up at Tony. "Seriously, what is in the water up here? I thought Nicco was an anomaly."

Tony raises an eyebrow at her. "Ah, you must be the one Nicco is dating?" he incorrectly surmises.

She shakes herself out of her daze. "Um, no. I am the one Daniel is marrying. Kels over there is the lucky duck who gets to ride your brother every night."

"Dawn!" Kelsey and I yell her name in unison.

"What? It's the truth." She shrugs.

All the color drains from Kelsey's face, and I just shake my head.

Dawn eyes my brothers up and down.

"So, where is all your gear?" she asks Lo.

"Gear?" He looks to me. "What gear?"

"You know, the fedoras and Tommy guns, stuff like that."

When the words leave Dawn's mouth, all three of my brothers burst out in roaring laughter. Every eye in the restaurant turns our way.

"This isn't the 1940s, sweetheart; we don't wear pinstripe suits with fedoras and suspenders and shoot up joints anymore. Our family is civilized," Lorenzo informs her.

Her face falls. "Bummer, that would have been cool as shit."

Amused, the boys give us each a hug before we sit down for dinner. They ask about California, and I tell them all about my new home, school, my friends, and jobs. I leave out the details about Jake and skip everything that has to do with Dante. I figure Nicco has filled them in on both those fronts, and tonight is supposed to be fun. No need to get them all riled up.

"You and my brother, huh?"

Lo puts his arm on the back of Kelsey's chair, and she blushes under his intensity.

"Yeah, I mean, it's nothing serious. At least, I don't think it is. Honestly, I am not sure what we are," she admits.

"They are having fun and screwing like rabbits. That's what they are," Dawn interjects.

"Are you trying to embarrass me?" Kelsey grits out.

"Embarrass you? Girl, if I were you, I would be shouting that shit to the rafters. *I am fucking Nicco Mastreoni, so back off, bitches!*" Dawn welds her fork in the air like a sword.

Stavros snorts water out of his nose. "I like you. Cousin Daniel is a lucky man. I have a feeling his life will never be dull." Stav smirks.

"Nope. Not a chance," Dawn declares as she pops ravioli into her mouth. She closes her eyes and moans in delight.

All three of them stare at her.

"What? This is almost as good as an orgasm," she broadcasts loudly. "Almost."

Stav turns to me. "It's uncanny. It's like she's the blonde version of Adriana."

My smile instantly drops.

Lo punches him in the shoulder, and Stav winces as his mistake dawns on him.

"Fuck, I am sorry, Gabby. I didn't mean to bring her up," he says. His apology is dripping with remorse.

"It's okay."

"No, I am an ass. You can punch me if you want to. Free shot. Just not in the nose. I am too pretty, and I can't have you breaking this nose and breaking the hearts of every girl in Manhattan. Here, how about the ribs? I can take a broken rib." He stands and pulls his shirt up to give me access.

"I'm not hitting you. And pull your shirt down. I know you are just looking for a reason to show off your abs."

He sits down. "Gabriella, I don't need a reason to show off my abs. Just a request."

He winks at Kelsey, and she blushes again. The poor girl is going to have high blood pressure by the time we leave.

"I can't get used to everyone calling you by your real name. I'm going to give it a shot though. Do you prefer Gabriella or Gabby?" Dawn wrinkles her nose.

"That's okay; I told you that I don't expect you guys to call me anything but Brie." I playfully nudge her.

After dinner, we order coffee, and just as the affogato hits the table, my phone starts to ring. I dig in my purse to find it and cut it off when I notice it is Melanie's number. It's pretty late in California, and I can't imagine why she is calling.

I excuse myself from the table and walk out the front door onto the sidewalk.

"Hello? Melanie?"

"Brie, he's gone." Her frantic words come blaring over the line.

"What? Who's gone?"

"We were out for the evening, and Rick's mom was staying here. She put him down. A few hours later, she was awakened by a noise coming over the monitor, so she got up to check on him, and by the time she made it to his room, he was gone. Just vanished."

She is babbling rapidly, and I am trying to follow her ramblings.

"Wait, what? Do you mean, the baby?"

No, no, no. Not Cassian.

"Yes. He's gone. What do I do? Tell me what to do?" she asks, her voice laced with panic.

Oh God. My worst fears come raining down on me. *This can't be happening.*

"Are you sure?" I manage to squeak out.

"Yes, Rick found where they came in through the window in the laundry room and disabled the alarm. The cameras never caught the face. It's like they knew where the cameras were located."

I know. I know exactly who has him.

"Do I call the police?" she asks.

"Oh my God," is all I can manage as fear grips me.

"Brie?"

"Don't call the police."

"I'm so sorry. I am so, so sorry. We should have been here ..." She is hysterical.

"You didn't do anything wrong. Just sit tight. It's going to be fine. I will get help," I try to reassure her with confidence I do not feel.

She is sobbing now.

"Melanie, I need you to stay by the phone. Okay?"

"Okay, I will ..."

I don't hear anything else she says as I disconnect and drop the phone into my bag then run back into the restaurant.

They are all sitting there, sipping their coffees and chatting away. As I approach the table, their curious eyes come to me, but as soon as Tony sees my face, he is on his feet.

"What's wrong, *cara?*"

"I need you to take me to Cross."

He looks confused as he asks, "Right now?"

"Yes, right now. Please, Tony. I need to get to Cross."

He can see the panic in me, and he stops the waitress and tells her to let Mario know he will be back to settle our bill. Then, he rushes all of us out the door. A blacked-out SUV pulls up to get us a few seconds later, and we all pile in and head to New Rochelle.

Time for me to pay the piper.

CHAPTER
Twenty-Six

Cross

"I'M GOING TO ASK YOU ONE MORE TIME. WHY IS MATTEO hitting our own trucks?"

The man tied to the chair before me is bleeding from a gash on his head. He and his sidekicks, who are standing to the right with their hands cuffed to a metal support beam above them, attacked the dummy shipment a little over an hour ago. Our men were ready. Vincenzo was right. Matteo was not with them, but these three are about to talk.

"I ain't no rat," the man spits out right before the butt of my gun smacks into his jaw. The sound of cracking bone ricochets around the room as two of his teeth hit the cement floor.

"Do you have a family? Do they expect you home for dinner tonight?"

He stares into my eyes. Hate fills his.

"Go to hell." He spits blood at my feet.

I nod to one of my men, and he takes a metal baseball bat and brings it down hard on the guy's kneecap. We hear a loud snap, and the man wails before he passes out cold. Great, he will be useless for a while. I look over at the other two and see the terror on the youngest one's face.

"Him." I point to him. "He is next. Bring him to me."

He looks to his friend, who remains silent, a look of relief on his face.

"Lou? Lou?" he cries.

"Lou can't help you now," I calmly tell him.

They bring him to the chair beside our passed-out guest and securely tie him.

"What is your name?" I ask.

"J-J-Joey ..." he stutters.

"Well, Joey, it's nice to meet you. I am Christoff Scutari. Do you know who I am?"

"Yes ... yes, sir."

"I have a few questions. You see, the weapons you have been stealing are mine. I don't like being stolen from."

I twirl the gun around my trigger finger. He follows it with his eyes.

"I didn't know they were your guns. They told us they were shipments for the military," he starts to sing like a canary.

"Joey." A warning comes from his friend, who gets a pipe to the ribs for speaking.

Joey cuts his eyes back to me.

"Good. That's good that you didn't know. Now, I am not angry with you, Joey. I am angry with the person who hired you. So, if you answer my questions, I will let you go. Do you understand?"

He nods.

"I'm a man of my word, Joey."

"O-o-okay."

"Who hired you?"

"His name is Matt. He said that he was starting his own organization and that he needed soldiers. These guns we were stealing from the government were gonna make us enough money to get started. He said, if we pulled these heists off, we would be set. We would be his right-hand men and that we were gonna make a lot of money together."

"Is that all? I'm not sure that's enough information for my guys to work with. They might not want to set you free with so little to go on."

He looks around at my men, who have surrounded him. Each one with a weapon of torture in hand.

"I overheard him talking to Harv here." He gestures to the guy passed out beside him.

"They didn't know I was listening. I had gone out for a smoke, and they walked outside. I hid 'cause I was supposed to be loading the truck, and I didn't want to get into any trouble."

"I can understand that. What did you hear while you were hiding?" I coax him to continue.

"That Matt guy, he said he was gonna take over as boss, but he wasn't gonna get his hands dirty this time. He said that O'Neill was going to get impatient, and when he did, he would do the dirty work for him."

"Fuck. You idiot!" his cohort chained to the post howls.

"What? He is going to kill us!" Joey yells back at his friend.

"You think we aren't dead the second we walk out of this warehouse?"

Joey cuts his eyes to me. Fear. He pisses himself as he begs me to help them, "Please, Mr. Scutari, please don't kill us. We didn't mean no harm to you."

"Tell you what, Joey. I am going to set you free. And, if I were you, I would run. I would run far, and I would run fast. I am going to give you a twenty-four-hour head start before I send your friends here back to Matteo."

He looks over at his friend. Sadness washes over him. Then, he straightens his spine and speaks, "Thank you. Thank you, sir."

I look at my men.

"Release him. The other two go back to di Rossi in body bags tomorrow. Once he receives the message, I want you to bring him to me."

"Yes, boss."

I head home and shower and change. On the way, I place a call to Vincenzo, telling him what I found out. Matteo is making a play for me. He knew, if I kept being late with my shipments, that the Irish would get angry, and he was hoping that they would either hit and weaken me or take me out completely. Now, I have no doubt that he was the one who betrayed my father and had my brother killed.

I am about to leave to pay a visit to Marcello and explain what I found out when I receive a strange text message from Tony. Something is wrong, and he is en route to my house with Gabby and her friends. They should be arriving at any minute. I find Una in the kitchen, and I send her to warn Adriana. She stands on shaky legs and heads out to find my fiancée.

A few moments later, I see their car pulling into the drive on the monitor in my office, and I go out to meet them. Tony gets out first, followed by Stavros and Lo, all wearing looks of concern on their faces. Then, Gabriella's friends are out, and finally, Gabby bolts from the car door and up the steps. Everyone follows her in.

She turns on her heel and looks at the group. "I need to speak to Cross alone, please."

Tony steps forward. "I'm coming with you," he insists.

"No. I need to talk to him by myself first."

"Sis, whatever the fuck is going on, you are scaring me. I'm not going to stay here. Where you go, I go."

By the tone of his voice, it is apparent that he means business.

"Fine. I don't have time to argue with your stubborn ass." She gives in and turns and takes off in the direction of the living room. She starts looking around for a place to go just as Adriana comes barreling into the room with Una on her heels.

"What's going on?" Adriana asks the room at large.

Gabby just darts off in the other direction.

I gently clasp her wrist and move her toward my office. "This way."

As we move, I hear Lorenzo tell everyone that we just need a minute and that everyone should wait in there.

Once Gabby, Tony, and I are in my office, I shut and lock the door and turn toward her.

She is obviously distraught. Her breathing is erratic and panicked, and she is pacing as tears stream down her face. I look to Tony in question, and he shrugs. He's as confused as I am.

"Calm down, baby. Tell me what's wrong." I slowly walk toward her.

"He has him. He has him." She is talking to herself and not to me.

"I am not following you, *Tesoro*. Who has who?"

"Dante. He has Cassian."

I look over to see if Tony is able to make any sense of what she is saying. He just shakes his head.

"Who is Cassian?" I ask him.

"I think that is the name of the child she takes care of."

"Gabby, baby, why do you think Dante has this kid?"

"Melanie called me and said he is missing. Someone broke into their home and took him from his crib while he was sleeping. It has to be Dante. It has to be. He saw us. He saw us at the market that day. He had to have."

I walk to her and stop her pacing. She is hysterical, and I try to calm her with my touch.

"I'm sorry their baby is missing, but it's highly unlikely it's Dante. Nicco and Gino have a lock on him. They know where he has been staying, and they are waiting for him. They might already have him."

"They don't," she insists.

"Why would he take a baby?"

She looks over her shoulder at Tony, and then she looks back up at me. "To get to me."

"*Tesoro*, that would be messy and stupid on his part. Besides, if he planned to take anyone from your life, he would have done so months ago."

"No, he just saw us last week."

"Calm down. Nicco said you quit that job. Think for a minute. Why would he take the baby of the people you used to work for?"

She stops pacing and squares her shoulders. Then, she takes a deep breath. "Because I don't work for them. They work for me."

"They work for you?" I ask, confused.

Nothing she is saying is adding up.

"Please don't hate me," she says as she finally looks me in the eyes.

"You aren't making any sense, Gabby."

She glances nervously at Tony once more, and then she meets my eyes again.

"Cassian is my son."

CHAPTER
Twenty-Seven

Bre

AS SOON AS THE WORDS LEAVE MY LIPS, I COLLAPSE. THE WEIGHT of the secret falling from my shoulders and crashing around us. Cross reaches for me as I lose my footing and brings me to the edge of the desk. He is searching my face as he tries to make sense of it.

"Your son?"

I can't meet his eyes as I make my confession, "Yes, my son. Cassian is my son."

"I'm sorry, baby, but I'm going to need more of an explanation than that."

I swallow the fear, and I confess everything, "I gave birth to him fourteen months ago in a clinic in Switzerland. I had planned to give him up for adoption. To let him go and walk away. I tried. I really did, but I couldn't do it. I was selfish. I couldn't let them take him."

He starts backing up from me. His eyes are wild as he starts doing the math in his head and putting the scattered pieces of the puzzle in place.

"Fourteen months ago?"

"Yes."

"Your European backpacking trip. You went to Switzerland? To have a baby?"

"Yes."

He looks down at my stomach.

"You were pregnant," he whispers.

"Yes."

"How far along?"

"I was three months along when I found out. I had been sick for weeks. The doctor Papa had come out to the house thought it was the flu, remember? It never occurred to her to ask if I could be pregnant. It never occurred to me. I was so distracted by everything going on around us. It was the day after you found me at the hotel in the city. The day after you told me we were done. I was so sick that morning. I thought it was just my emotions, but I couldn't keep the Tamiflu she prescribed down or even water. I was so weak. Nonna made me call to tell them, and the nurse said she would send something else out, and before she did, she asked if I could be pregnant. I told her there was no way and then hung up on her. I did the math in my head, and I realized that it was more than possible. I was late, and I had just been too upset to realize it. I had a home pregnancy test stashed in my closet because Adi had had a scare, and we'd bought several, so I took it, and it was positive. Actually, I took three, and they were all positive."

I stand on shaky legs, and I walk toward him.

"Please, Cross. You can hate me. You can have me punished. I don't care what happens to me, but please, please find him. Don't let him hurt the baby," I plead.

I don't care what becomes of me. My only concern is for Cassian.

I look over to Tony, who already has his phone out, typing.

"How could you keep this from me?"

He is looking at me like I am a monster. Maybe I am.

"I had to. I had to protect him."

"Fine fucking job you did of that," he roars.

I put my head into my hands and weep because he is right. Fine fucking job I did.

"Stop crying. You did this," he accuses.

"I tried. I tried to tell you!"

"When?"

"Before I left. I called you, and I begged you to call me back. I begged you to choose us."

"Did you think to say that you were pregnant with my child, Gabby? Because I listened to that damn message over and over and over again, and never once did you mention it."

"Of course I didn't. I didn't know if my room was bugged. I didn't know if my phone or your phone were bugged. I was sick and I was scared and you were gone. Your father and brother had just been gunned down, and according to you and Papa, no one wanted me in your life, so what would they have done if they knew I was carrying your child? What would they have done to me? To the baby? Can you answer that?"

"I would have found a way to—"

"A way to what? Get rid of it like you got rid of me?"

His head snaps up at my accusation.

"You threw me away like I didn't matter. You let them throw me away. How could I trust you?"

"How could you not?"

"Because"—I place my hand on my stomach and look down—"I finally loved something more than I loved myself. More than I loved you. I had to protect him. I tried to tell you, and you would not see me, so I ran, and I hid him."

I look up, and his eyes are focused on my hand. Pain clear on his face as tears fall. He swipes at his cheek and looks back up at me.

"Why do you think Dante has him?"

"Because he wants me. Because he wants to hurt you. Because he is demented," I scream. I throw my hands up in frustration.

How the hell am I supposed to guess what is going on in Dante's head?

"Me? How would he even know he was mine—or yours for that matter? Just because he saw you with some woman and her child at a public place. Why would he make that leap?"

I reach down into the front of my shirt and pull the delicate chain to reveal his mother's locket. I open it and walk over to him. I raise it so that he can see the tiny picture tucked inside. It's of Cassian's beautiful face grinning up at the camera, his green eyes glowing with delight and his dimple in full view. He is gorgeous—the spitting image of his father.

Cross takes the charm in his hand and brings it up to his face, pulling me in close as he stares into the eyes of his son for the first time. His eyes. There is no denying, if anyone who knows Cross were to see me with Cassian in my arms, they would know instantly.

He closes the charm in his fist and squeezes his eyes tightly shut. Regret. Deep regret hits me as I watch the grief crash over him.

"I'm so sorry, Cross."

I reach up and wrap my arms around his neck. I bring my face to his as we both stand there, lost in the torment.

"I'm so sorry," I repeat against his skin.

He reaches up and takes my arms from around him, and he slightly pushes me back. There is no life in his eyes, just betrayal.

He looks over to Tony. "Get Nicco on the phone."

Tony raises his phone and waves it in our direction. "I already have him on the line."

Cross reaches his hand out for the phone. Tony releases it and comes and wraps me in his arms. I bury my face in his chest and cling to him.

"Shh, sis, everything is going to be okay. We will find him. I promise you."

I believe him. I pray that, when they do, it's not too late.

CHAPTER
Twenty-Eight

Cross

NICCO, GINO, AND STEFANO ARE CLOSING IN ON DANTE. THEY think they have him cornered in an abandoned dock house in La Mirada, not far from the apartment building where he is staying. They know he is going to make a run for the place because all his money and identification is stashed there. No way he is leaving California without it unless he finds a way to contact Matteo and get help. Which they would no doubt intercept. I told them to go in slow and easy because Dante has a child, and we need that child unharmed.

Tony took Gabriella out to calm her down. I can't even look at her right now. I take a seat at my desk, and just as I am about to pick the phone back up to call or text Nicco and see if they are in yet, a faint knock comes at the door. It opens, and Una is standing there.

"It's not a good time, Una."

"I am sorry, Christoff, but I must speak with you, and it can't wait."

I set the phone down and gesture for her to come in.

She walks in, and Grandfather follows behind her. She looks nervous.

"Now is really not the best time, Una. I have urgent business to attend to."

"Now is the time."

I look up just as she takes a seat on the opposite side of the desk. She slides a photograph in front of me. It's a photo of Gabriella. Her hands are holding the sides of her swollen belly, and she is smiling up at the camera. I don't look at Una as I examine the photograph.

"You knew."

There is no bite in my accusation, only grief. She knew this entire time. The one person I trusted most in this world. *How could she keep this from me?*

"I knew," she confirms. Her voice cracks as she continues, "She needed help. She came to me, and I helped her."

I take my eyes from Gabby's stomach and lift them to my grandmother. The woman who raised me.

"How could you? I trusted you."

"Christoff—"

"No, I don't want to hear any more lies. Get out."

"No more lies. I am going to tell you everything," she starts.

I cut her off, "Why should I believe anything you say?"

I have never once in my life raised my voice to her, but now, I can barely contain my fury as I stand.

"Sit down, Christoff."

It's a command. I am not used to my grandfather using such an authoritative tone. It catches me off guard. In fact, he rarely speaks at all, so when he does, I pay attention.

"You're not a boy anymore. You are a man. A man who has had a lot of responsibly thrust upon him, yes, but you will listen to your grandmother. You will show her respect, and you will not interrupt her until she is finished."

I begrudgingly take a seat. I raise my eyes and meet Una's, and I nod for her to go on as Grandfather brings her a glass of water and stands behind her. A united front. They always have been.

"Gabriella called me and told me she was pregnant. She was terrified, but she was determined. She said that she had to run to protect her baby, and she needed my help. She hoped that I would understand because I had lost my daughter and two of my grandsons."

She lifts a shaky hand to her throat and takes a sip of water.

"She knew her father wouldn't just let her go, so she devised the ruse all on her own. She was going to leave in the middle of the night, and she was going to go somewhere overseas. She had a little bit of cash but nothing else. All she asked was that I help her get to the airport. She didn't want to take her car, and she didn't want to call a taxi because she knew Vincenzo would be able to find out where it had taken her. I couldn't send her off without any assistance and without her knowing where to go. So, I made some calls, and I arranged for her to go to the clinic in Switzerland.

"The plan was for her to stay through the duration of the pregnancy, and then, once she gave birth, the baby would be placed with a family for adoption. She was so brave. She snuck out of her house with only a small bag of belongings. She was very sick, and she flew all alone to Zürich. I gave her a throwaway phone, so she could call me if she met any trouble along the way, but she made it safely. She was in a small room there with one other girl. She did well at the clinic, making the best of it. They spoke very highly of her. I was proud. She made friends, and after the morning sickness subsided, she was healthy and cheerful. The nuns adored her."

That's my Gabby. Everyone loves her.

"Do you remember when I flew to London with my friend to do the cruise?"

I nod in response.

"Yes, well, I actually took the train from London to Zürich, so I could be with her when she gave birth. I didn't want her to be frightened and to go through it alone. The baby came a little earlier than expected. His delivery was complicated. She was in labor for a long time. They thought, at one point, they were going to have to do an emergency C-section. She was in a lot of pain, and she refused any drugs."

She looks up at me, her chin trembling.

"She cried out for you the entire time."

At that, I lose my shit. Right there in front of my grandparents. I am angry. Angry for Gabby. Angry for me and that moment I missed.

"When he finally made it into the world, he wasn't breathing. Gabriella was hysterical. The nurses immediately started to work on him, and I tried to keep Gabby calm. It was chaos in the room. Finally, we heard his faint little cry and then a stronger one. Gabby begged to hold him. She wasn't supposed to hold him. He was supposed to be taken away at once to make it easier, but she was in such distress, and so was the baby. I just nodded for the nurse to bring him over. As soon as she laid him against his mamma's skin, he started to calm, and she started to calm. She looked down at him and said, 'Hello. There's that face Mamma has been waiting to see.' Then, she looked up at me and said, 'He looks just like his papa.' That's when I knew. She would never be able to let him go completely. I couldn't do it to either one of them. My great-grandson. So handsome."

She brings her hands to the sides of her face, lost in the memories, and it's as if I can see it all through her eyes.

"All of a sudden, the monitors started blaring, and alarms started going off. Gabriella's body began to shake uncontrollably, and I reached and took the baby from her arms. The doctors and nurses swarmed her. She had gone into shock. They said she was bleeding internally, and they rushed the babe and me from the room. I sat there, holding him close and praying that his mamma would be okay. I made a promise to God that, if he would just spare her life, I would find a way for them to be together. It was terrifying."

She is wringing her hands, and I move to sit beside her. She lays her head on my shoulder, and I wrap my arm around her. I take a good look at her. She has always been a force. Strong. Beautiful. Sophisticated. I see now how the past few years have taken a toll on her. The lines around her eyes are a little more pronounced.

"I should've been there. I could have lost her, lost both of them. They were my responsibility. You shouldn't have had to bear this alone."

I squeeze her frail frame, and she pats my cheek like she did when I was a little boy.

Then, she continues with her story, "She was in the hospital for several days, but she recovered, and she got stronger. While she was there, we found Rick and Melanie. They were foster parents in California, who came very highly recommended. Gabriella's story was explained to them in great detail. Melanie agreed to fly to Zürich to meet both of them, and she fell under their spell instantly. She spent a week there. By the time she flew home, she and Gabby had bonded, and they had worked out all the details. Melanie would take the baby home with her. Gabby would return home from her backpacking trip, and she would tell her family she was moving to California to finish school. She would move close to Rick and Melanie. She would attend school and find work and pretend to be their nanny, so she could see the baby as much as possible. No one would be the wiser until she was on her feet and felt it was safe enough to take him back. If ever."

"You just happened to find a couple who was okay with all of that?"

"Well, Lilliana might have had something to do with it."

"Lilliana knows?"

"Yes. I had to tell her. I needed her help once Gabriella had a change of heart about the adoption. I had to get her home at once because Vincenzo's patience had run out, and he was going to go searching for her. We had to figure out how to hide the baby from him. Bringing him back to New York would be taking too big a chance of discovery. Lilliana was the one who suggested she go to California be-cause she had a cousin out there, and she wouldn't be all alone. She did some digging and found that Rick and Melanie had fostered many chil-dren until they could be reunited with their birth parents. They lived in Santa Monica. She did the background checks and everything. Then, she flew out there to meet with them before arranging for Melanie to come to Zürich. We—Lilliana and me—have been paying them privately for the baby's care so that no agency or government service would be involved."

"Does Gabby know her mother is involved?"

"No. Lilliana doesn't want her to know. She had to be angry with all of them in order to leave and not look back, to get a clean start. You can never tell Gabriella or Vincenzo that Lilliana knew about the baby."

It's a lot of information for me to absorb. I sit here in silence as my grandfather walks behind me and places his big hand on my shoulder.

"I know you are angry, son. I know you feel betrayed, but that girl in there did the best she could on her own. You forced her hand. You all did, and she more than likely saved your son's life. Ripping her own heart to shreds in the process. That's what mothers and grandmothers do. They sacrifice. You think it's hard for you to find out you had a son you didn't know about? Imagine being a mother and knowing and not being able to keep him? Living with that. She is out there, waiting, filled with guilt and fear, and she needs you to be the strong one now. She did what she had to do to give you time to come into your own. It's time for you to get over your pride and anger, son, and go take your family back."

CHAPTER
Twenty-Nine

Brie

AFTER TAKING A MOMENT TO COMPOSE MYSELF, I WALK INTO THE living room with Tony at my back and face my friends. Dawn and Kelsey are seated by the fireplace, and Lorenzo and Stavros are standing by the French doors. Adriana is sitting in a corner, glaring at their backs.

When Dawn spots us, she sits up at attention. "What is going on? You're freaking us out! Are you okay?"

Worried. She sounds very worried. I hate that I dragged them into this mess with me. This part of my life was never meant to touch them.

"Not really," I say as I move further into the room and sit in front of them.

"What's happened? Is it that scary guy?" Kelsey looks at me with fear in her eyes.

"Scary guy? What scary guy?" Adriana asks from her perch.

I look over her way. I can't exactly ask her to leave. This is her house after all, not mine.

I look back at my concerned friends. "Yes, but before I get into that, I have one more secret to confess."

They look at each other, and then Dawn turns back to me.

"Okay. We are listening."

I nervously look over at Adi. Maybe I shouldn't tell them in front of her. She is marrying Cross. It's probably something he doesn't want her to know, or he'd rather tell her himself.

"Oh, for fuck's sake, Gabby. Whatever it is, just spit it out," Adi belts out in exasperation.

"Don't rush her!" Dawn snaps.

Adi rolls her eyes. "You can't handle her with kid gloves. She responds better to goading. Raise her hackles, and she'll spout the truth out. You let her sit and hem and haw, and we'll be here all night."

"Don't act like you know me anymore," I spit at her through gritted teeth.

"Whatever. Just trying to help." She sits back in a huff.

"Not helping," I snap at her.

"Okay, jeez, just say it already," she insists.

I look back at Dawn. She is glaring at Adi.

"Back off, backstabber," Dawn hurls in her direction.

Adi sits back up at attention and opens her mouth to spill her retort. "Stop!" I yell.

All eyes turn to me. Dawn's are filled with apology.

Kelsey takes my hand in hers. "It's okay, Brie. Whatever it is, we have your back. Just tell us."

"I ... I ... I have a son," I whisper in her direction as I scan the faces of everyone in the room.

All their eyes are trained on me. Including my brothers.

"What?" Dawn squeaks.

I take a deep breath, and then I spill it all, "When I said I left New York and toured Europe for a year before moving to California, I actually went to Europe to have my baby."

I hear a gasp and look over to see Adi with her hand covering her mouth. Lo and Stav look confused, but she knows instantly.

"You have a baby? A son. Where is he?" Kelsey asks me.

"He's in California."

"Where have you been hiding him all this time? I know you haven't had a baby in your closet or anything. I might be flighty, but I am not that flighty."

I see the wheels turning as Dawn struggles to make sense of my story.

"You guys have met him," I admit.

"Cassian," Kelsey guesses. "It's Cassian, isn't it?"

Dawn looks to me for the answer. Shock is dripping from her expression.

I nod. "Yes, Cassian is my son," I confirm.

"Who the hell are Rick and Melanie then?"

"They are his guardians. My friends."

I shake my head at my muddled, half-assed explanation. It is difficult to describe the nature of my relationship with Rick and Mel.

"Whoa." Dawn sits back, absorbing the information.

"Why are you telling us this now? Has something happened to them or the baby?" Kelsey asks.

A sob escapes me, and she gets up and puts her arm around me.

"Melanie was the one who called while we were at dinner. Rick's mom was keeping the baby tonight while they were out. Someone broke in while she was sleeping and took him."

"Oh my God. Do you think it's Dante?"

"Dante?" Adriana stands. "Gabby? Is she talking about Dante Calvacanti?"

"Yes," I say calmly as I turn my eyes to Adi.

She knows exactly how terrifying this is for me.

"He has been following me again," I answer her.

"What? He can't be that fucking crazy," she bellows angrily. Then, she focuses her attention on Lorenzo. "Why the hell didn't you guys take care of him years ago?" she demands from him.

"Adi, please," I plead.

None of this is my brothers' fault, and the last thing I want is for any of them to feel responsible for Dante's actions.

"No. These assholes should have put a bullet in him two years ago," she accuses as she points a furious finger into Lo's chest.

"They are not to blame, Adi."

"I agree with the disloyal bitch," Dawn throws in.

165

"Who are you calling a bitch?"

"That would be you. Bitch."

"Guys!" I scream. "Can we not right now? My son is missing. A lunatic has him. He is probably scared and wondering where I am. I don't know if Dante will hurt him. I don't know what kind of mental state he is in. I don't know what he is feeding him. If he is feeding him."

I give in to the hysteria and start spouting off all the worst-case scenarios in my head.

"Oh, honey." Dawn embraces me and tries to offer comfort. "He's going to be okay. Nicco will find him. He will."

Adriana has a pained expression as she watches us. When Dawn lets me go, I walk to Adi.

"I'm sorry we came barreling into your home like this. I didn't know where else to go when I got the call."

"Of course you would come here. Cross will find your son. His son. He won't stop until he finds him, and he will make Dante pay."

We stand there, looking at each other. There is so much to say, but neither of us knows how to start. I hear a phone ringing, and Tony calls out to me.

"Gabby, I think that is your phone."

He is holding up my bag. I run over and grab the phone just before it goes to voice mail. Hoping it is Nicco with good news.

"Hello?"

"Gabriella."

I look over at Tony. "Dante."

Tony heads to Cross's office, and I try to keep my composure and keep him on the line.

"Hey, baby. I have a surprise for you."

"A surprise? What kind of surprise?" I try to keep my voice steady and give nothing away. I don't want him to know that Nicco and the boys are on to him.

"I have your little boy."

"So, that's where he is. Whew. His mother called me. We have been worried." I force relief into my response.

"You don't have to keep up the charade now, baby. I know he is yours, and I know that you are hiding him from Scutari, but you don't have to do that anymore. I am going to take you home. Both of you. You don't have to fear him any longer. Christoff is about to fall, and he won't be able to hurt you anymore. I promise."

Tony, Cross, and his grandparents come rushing into the room. I put my hand up to stop them. I want to keep him talking until I know the baby is okay.

"What do you mean, he is about to fall?"

"I mean, he is about to meet the same fate as his brother. There is about to be a changing of the guard in the Scutari family, and he will no longer be a problem for you. I will take you guys home, and we can finally be a family."

"I see. Where is the baby now?"

"He is right here. Sleeping. He's fine; don't worry."

"Has he eaten? He needs formula and baby food."

"We will get that. Where are you? We will come to get you."

"I'm home."

"You haven't been to your apartment in days, Gabby. I have been watching for you."

"No, home, as in New York. I came for a visit."

"Gabriella, don't lie to me. I'm not in the mood. I am tired, and I am ready to go home. Call your brother and his goons off of me, and get your ass to your apartment, so I can come get you."

"I'm not lying to you. I swear. I am in New York. I have been out to dinner at La Mela with Tony and Lorenzo. We were just heading out for drinks and cannoli."

"Damn it, Gabby. Stay there. I will get us on a plane and come to you," he huffs his demand, and I hear Cassian rouse with a startled cry.

"No, Dante. Take the baby back to his home. I bet Melanie is a worried mess. She has his clothes and diapers and food. Give him back to her, and I will wait for you here. You can come get me in New York. Then, you and I will go back together and get the baby when we are more prepared."

"No, he comes with me."

"Please, Dante," I plead with him as the tears start to slide down my face. "Please, take him home. I promise I'll be here, waiting for you."

"We'll see you soon, Gabriella."

The line goes dead.

I lift my eyes to Cross. "He hung up. He has him. He has the baby. He says he is going to get them on a flight and come get me."

CHAPTER
Thirty

Cross

I START WALKING SLOWLY TOWARD HER. SHE LOOKS LIKE SHE MIGHT pass out or bolt. She is staring at the phone in her hand as I approach. I reach out and gently take it from her, and I wind my arm around her waist just as her knees give way. I take her weight as I hand the phone off to Tony.

"Call Gino. Let them know that he is about to be on the move, and it's confirmed that he has the baby with him. They are not to engage him in any high-speed chase or gunfight unless they have a clear shot. He will be heading for an airport."

Gabby's body jerks, and she twists to look up at me. "He doesn't have a car seat. He doesn't have a car seat for Cassian. He has him in a car without protection."

"Shh, it's okay, *Tesoro*. They are going to follow him and make sure they get where they are going safely."

"You don't know that. What if they are in an accident?"

"They won't be in an accident, baby."

"You can't control that."

I pull her in closer.

"Cross," she whimpers, "he's so little. He needs his car seat. He is probably hungry. He needs me. He needs me, and I am three thousand miles away." She is becoming hysterical again.

I try my best to reassure her, "We'll get him back to you. I will get him back to you. I promise, baby."

She is clinging to me now. I have never seen her this scared before. I can't stand it. As angry as I was with her earlier, now, I just want to take her fear and make it better. I gently run my hands up and down her back to soothe her.

When she finally stops trembling, I look up, and every eye in the room is on us.

"Brie?" Dawn cautiously approaches.

She dries her eyes and turns to answer her friend, "Yes?"

"Your, um ... his"—she gestures toward me—"she"—she then points to Adriana—"has offered to let us stay here tonight. I'm going to call Mom and tell her that we drove out to see your parents after dinner and have decided to stay over because it's late. Is that okay? Are you okay, staying here?"

Gabby swipes at her nose and looks between Adriana and me. "I don't know. I ..."

Adriana steps up beside Kelsey. "Stay, Gabby. You're all welcome here, and you want to be close if we get any word from Nicco or the other guys. Besides, you look exhausted. I can have Marie get the guest wing rooms readied for you all."

Dawn speaks up, "You don't have to stay here if you don't want to. I'll get us a room at the closest hotel, and Tony can keep us informed," she offers the alternative.

"I would prefer you guys stay." I draw Gabby's attention back to me. "If he calls you again, I want to be there."

I can see the indecision written all over her. It's clear she doesn't want to be in my and Adriana's home.

"But, if you want to go, it's okay. Just please take Lo or Stav with you."

"Cross ..." Adi begins.

"It's her decision, Adriana," I say with a little extra emphasis. I won't force her to do anything she doesn't want to do. Not ever again.

"We'll stay. I don't want to divide your focus. Any of you." She looks around at her brothers. "Kels, call Aunt Susan, and, Adi, please have the rooms set up."

Dawn and Kelsey walk off in the direction of the kitchen.

Once they are out of earshot, Gabby shares, "Dante said that you were about to fall. That you were going to meet the same fate as your brother. What does he mean?"

I look over her head at Tony. "Did he say anything else?"

"Something about a changing of the guard in the Scutari family."

She shakes her head like it doesn't make any sense. But it makes perfect sense to me.

"Nothing for you to worry about."

I look over my shoulder to Lorenzo and Stavros. "I need you two to track down Matteo di Rossi. Take all the men you need. Just bring him to me."

Stav grins wide.

"We're going to have to tell Papa what's going on," he states what I already know is true.

I promised Vincenzo that I wouldn't keep him in the dark anymore, concerning Gabby. I am a man of my word.

"No," Gabby says more to herself than to us.

"Not yet. Let's give Gabby some time," I tell him in answer.

The girls come walking back in, and Lorenzo looks at Dawn.

"Looks like you are going to get your wish after all, sweetheart."

"What wish?" she asks.

"We're about to have a little fun, Tommy guns blazing."

She just turns and looks at Gabby with her eyes wide as saucers. "What did we miss?"

"Nothing," we all reply in unison.

Una clears her throat. "I'll go find some pajamas that you girls can wear and gather some extra towels."

"Thank you. Do you need any help?" Kelsey offers.

"Yes, dear, that would be lovely."

She walks off with Dawn and Kelsey in tow.

Adriana approaches us, and she looks from Gabby to me.

"I'm going to go have coffee started. It looks like it's going to be a long night." She pauses and then looks Gabby in the eye. "It's going to be okay, Gabs."

Gabby watches her leave. I can feel the hurt vibrating off of her as her eyes follow Adriana out of the room.

"Can you stand?"

She starts at my question. "Yes, I'm sorry." She rights herself and steps out of my hold. "I am sorry, Cross. For everything."

"I know. Me, too."

She looks down at my hand. The hand that is still holding the photograph of her. She walks over and takes it from me.

"Una gave it to me," I offer in explanation.

She steps over to the fireplace and takes a seat in front of it, still looking at the photo.

I sit next to her, and she starts to speak softly, "You know they wouldn't let me hear his heartbeat—before he was born, I mean. When they examined me, they would check for it. I wanted to listen, but they wouldn't let me. I didn't get to see the ultrasound photos either. They said it would be easier to let the baby go if I didn't hear or see him or her." She laughs bitterly. "But I didn't have to hear him or see him to get attached. I could feel him. I could feel him growing inside of me. First, it was just a flutter, like butterfly wings. Then, it was more persistent, like a little hummingbird. He moved a lot at night. He liked to keep his mamma up into the wee hours. When he was a little bigger, I would sing to him, and he would start bouncing around like he was dancing, and if I laughed, he would kick up a storm. He knew me. He knew my voice. And I knew him."

I wrap my arm around her shoulders and pull her into me. As painful as it is, I need to hear her story. "Tell me."

"I was supposed to have a scheduled C-section. They were going to put me to sleep, and by the time I woke up, the baby would have been delivered and gone, placed with his new family. Una came to be there, so she could help me after the surgery. Take me to a hotel to recover and fly me home. I wasn't supposed to be conscious for any of it, but my water broke that morning. I thought I had peed the bed while I was asleep, but I hadn't. I went into labor early."

She gets a faraway look as she tells her story, "The baby was under duress, so they rushed me in, and everything happened so fast. He got stuck. His shoulders got stuck, and they couldn't get him turned and get him out. I pushed, and I pushed. I tried so hard, and he just wasn't coming. I was exhausted and so scared. I thought he was going to die.

"When the doctor finally got him turned and he came out, he wasn't crying; he was silent. I could see the panic on all of their faces, and I just started praying, praying that God would take me and not him. Una held my hand and prayed with me. Then, after a few minutes, we finally heard his cry, and it was the most wonderful sound I had ever heard in my entire life. I wanted to see him. I was in so much pain, but he was upset. He started screaming, and I knew he needed me. I begged them. I begged Una. I just wanted to hold him one time. To calm him down. I knew he was upset because he was searching for me. One time. That was all I asked for. The nurse brought him and laid him on my chest. I sang to him, and he calmed down. He snuggled up under my chin, and he just looked up at me. He was perfect."

She looks up at me, tears in her eyes, but her mind is in a different place. She raises her hand and brushes it against my cheek. "It was you. Like a piece of you, a piece of our love broke off and grew inside of me. He looked just like his papa. I loved him so much. It was like he healed that shattered part of me with one little look.

"After that, it gets fuzzy. I don't remember much. I was just drifting off, looking at his face. I guess I coded. Something about hemorrhaging and internal bleeding. When I woke back up a few hours later, I was in an actual hospital emergency room, and Una was there. I panicked and ripped the IV out. Una was trying to calm me down, but I thought he was gone. I thought the baby was gone, and I was never going to see him again. It was the most terrified I had ever been in my life. Until now."

I hold her as she trembles, reliving her nightmare.

"They didn't though. Una wouldn't let them take him. I think she had to pay the clinic a lot of money to get out of the agreement. I owe her so much. She stayed with me while I recovered, and she helped me take care of Cassian. That's his name, by the way—Cassian Antonio Mastreoni."

"After my grandfather and your brother."

"Yes, Una told me your grandfather's full name is Agostino Pieri Cassian Silvestri. I knew I was going to have to hide him, and I knew that I wasn't going to be able to be his mother, but I wanted him to carry a name that linked him to us. To have that connection."

She sighs as she looks at the photograph once more.

"I didn't get to enjoy being pregnant. I didn't get to have a big baby shower to celebrate expecting him with friends and family. I didn't get to set up his nursery. I only got to nurse him for a couple of days before we had to leave, and he had to go home with Melanie. I didn't even get to buy him his first outfit to come home in. Una did that while I was in the hospital."

Her body shakes as she tries to hold it together.

"It's not fair to him. There was no joy, no celebrating his entry into the world."

She brings the photo to her chest and holds it to her heart.

"I was selfish by keeping him close. Now, he is with a madman. All because of me, because I was too weak to just follow the plan. To let him go. This is all my fault, Cross. Our baby is in danger because of me."

That's when she falls apart. I hold her body close to me as she shatters, and I whisper soothingly into her hair and try to bring her back from that dark place. She is not to blame for this. I am. I failed them. I failed her. All because I wasn't strong enough to fight for her.

CHAPTER
Thirty-One

Brie

I AM STARTLED BACK FROM MY MEMORIES WHEN CROSS'S PHONE STARTS to ring. He releases me and reaches in his pocket to retrieve it.

"It's Lo," he tells me.

I move over, so he can stand.

"I'll be right back."

He walks into his office, and I stand and warm myself in front of the fire.

Dawn calls down the stairs, "Brie, we have pajamas for you if you want to change."

I follow her voice. It's been a long time since I have been in this house. I finally take a moment to look around me. To look at the house Cross and his brothers grew up in. I barely recognize it. The decor is so different. It is every bit Adriana, top to bottom. From the glittering chandeliers to the marble staircase. The crystal palace she always dreamed of. There is no trace of Cross here. Not the Cross I knew and loved anyway. I wonder if he is happy in this grandeur.

We had a plan. A plan to build our own dream house in the woods. A large A-frame with floor-to-ceiling windows, dark wood floors, a large stone fireplace, and a farmhouse kitchen with a massive deck off the back that overlooked the garden that I would plant and tend to myself. We wanted to be able to begin our days on that deck with coffee and fresh air and end our nights curled up in blankets, watching the sun set over our land. It is a far cry from this magnificent home.

I climb the stairs and find Dawn in one of the bedrooms at the top of the landing.

"Hi. How are you holding up?"

"I'm okay," I lie.

I am far from okay at the moment.

"Liar." She calls me on it. "They'll find him. I still can't believe Cassian is your baby. Although, thinking back, I should have seen it. You were always more involved than your average nanny. I just thought you really, really liked your job, and I mean, who wouldn't be head over heels for that adorable little chubster?"

"I'm sorry I kept it from you guys. I was protecting him. At least, I thought I was."

"It's okay. I get it."

"Thank you."

I don't deserve them.

"You don't have any other bombs to drop on us, do you? I mean, do we need to brace for anything else? I'm totally cool if you do, but you are kind of upstaging my bridal weekend, you know. I'm going to have to do something seriously twisted to take the attention back at this point, and you know I have no limits. I'll probably have to start a bitch-slap fight with your man's fiancée or something."

She looks at me with complete sincerity, and I start laughing in spite of myself.

"What? I am serious."

I know she is just trying to take my mind off of things, and I love her for it.

"Make sure you pull her hair. It's her Achilles heel. Oh, and she favors her left side."

"Got it! Thanks for the tips." She gives me a high five, and then she hands me the pajamas Una provided. "I'm going to jump into the shower if you are okay?"

"I'm good. I am just going to change and maybe go grab a cup of coffee."

I get dressed in the PJs and head back downstairs. Adi is standing in the formal living room, staring at the ceiling.

I walk up to her and look up to the ceiling to see what she is looking at.

"What are you doing?" I ask because I don't see anything.

"Do you hear that?" She tilts her head to the side and concentrates.

"Hear what?"

I strain to listen for what she is hearing, and I get nothing.

"The echo. Every time someone speaks, it echoes. It drives me insane."

I look around the vast space. It's an old manor, and the acoustics are like that of a stone cavern. The sound bounces around with nothing to absorb it.

"Maybe you should have some drapes made for the back wall," I suggest.

She glances over to the large floor-to-ceiling windows that cover the back wall and look out onto the veranda. "You think? I like the light that comes in during the afternoon. It brightens this old, stuffy place up. It's my favorite thing about this room."

"Yes, but you could have sheer silk drapes made, just something to absorb some of the sounds. It could help."

She ponders that for a minute. "I think you might be right. I have a lady who is making blush window treatments for my bedroom. I bet she could do sheer drapes for this room."

"Blush window treatments." I snort. "Cross is going to kill you. He likes his bedroom dark and cold."

She coughs. "Ha. I know. He's like a vampire with that shit. He can have pitch-black drapes made for all I care or have the windows cemented shut and live like a bear in a cave."

That confuses me.

She looks at me with a wide smile, but then she frowns as she takes in my expression. Sadness washes over me because we can't be this version of ourselves anymore.

I turn to walk to the kitchen.

"Gabs, wait."

I pivot back toward her. "For what, Adi? There is nothing for us to say to each other."

"I'm sorry," she blurts out.

"For which part?"

She hesitates, so I keep going, "Sorry for telling everyone I wasn't capable of being in a relationship with Cross if he took over for his papa? For helping them run me off? For sliding into my place once I was out of the picture? For accepting his ring and moving into his house? For planning your wedding? Which part are you sorry for exactly?" I bite out.

"All of it," she murmurs. "I know I have done some pretty fucked-up stuff, but I love you, Gabby. My biggest regret is not talking you into staying in Paris. You could have gone to university there, opened up a little bistro or something. Married Antoine and had a perfect life. Instead, I did everything I could to try and entice you to come home. I even constantly brought up Cross to try and lure you back because I missed you so damn much. You could have gotten over him and been happy, but I was selfish. You were the only person who could put up with my shit and the only person I could tolerate most of the time. I needed you."

It sounds nice, and maybe it would have saved me a lot of heartache, but it wasn't my destiny.

"I wouldn't do a thing differently. Not one single thing. Because, if I did, I wouldn't have Cassian, and he is worth every single ounce of pain. Being his mamma is the best thing that has ever happened to me. It is a love like I have never known. I would literally walk through hellfire for him."

She inclines her head. "I wish I could meet him, that I could be the fabulous auntie I was always meant to be."

"You and Cross will have your own children one day."

"I don't think so; I'm not sure motherhood is my thing. Can you imagine?"

"Sure you will. He wants a house full, and you guys definitely have a lot of house to fill." I gesture around the room.

She follows my hand and then looks back at me in horror. "Yeah, I am not having ten babies."

"Maybe not ten, but you have to give him at least one. He needs to be a father."

She cocks an eyebrow at me and points out, "He is a father."

Damn it. She's right. I haven't considered the repercussions of him knowing about Cassian. *What will he do? Will he try to take him from me?*

"Don't look so scared, Gabs. Cross won't do anything to hurt you."

"All Cross does is hurt me."

She purses her lips into a tight, sad smile. "It's not intentional. Believe me, I know. I don't hurt you intentionally either. I know you don't believe that, but it doesn't mean it's not true."

"You want to know the worst part? You knew. You of all people knew how I felt about him. How deep my love for him ran. How could you do that to me?"

"I just wanted you to be happy, Gabs."

"Happy?" I ask disbelievingly.

"Yes, you have no idea how much."

"What does that even mean? You thought I would be happy, being exiled from my family? Living without Cross? You weren't thinking of me. You were thinking of yourself."

She looks up at me and bites her lip. It's her tell. She wants to tell me something, but she is holding back.

"It's fine. You can hate me. I don't even blame you, but I did what I did, so you could have a good life in California. I don't regret that."

"More riddles. Everyone talks to me in fucking riddles. What does that mean?"

She doesn't give me anything else.

I turn on my heels and escape into the kitchen in search of coffee.

CHAPTER
Thirty-Two

Cross

"WE HAVE HIM. WE TRACKED HIM DOWN AT CLUB Macanudo." Lorenzo fills me in that they were able to apprehend Matteo at his favorite cigar lounge in Manhattan.

It doesn't surprise me.

"Did he give you much resistance?" I ask.

"Oddly enough, no."

That doesn't surprise me either. Matteo doesn't like to cause a scene. I'm sure he definitely did not want to cause a scene in front of his close acquaintances at his club.

"Where do you want us to take him? Your house?"

"No. All of the women are here. I don't want to freak them out any more than they already are," I answer.

"Hmm, we can take him to Papa's. We have a soundproof basement with an exterior entrance."

"That sounds like a good plan."

"Okay, I'll call Papa and tell him we are on our way and have him disarm the alarm. He's going to want an explanation though."

"We'll tell him everything. Hopefully, we can calm him down before he sees Gabby."

"All right. I'll make the call. You coming now?"

"No. I have a meeting with Diego Aguilar first. I will come right after."

"Aguilar?"

I hear the alarm in his voice.

"Yes. Vincenzo arranged a meeting with him tonight at an out-of-the-way location. It was set before you all showed up. I can't cancel it. It might be my only chance with him."

"Why are you meeting with that guy?"

"I think he might know something about what happened to Papa and Emilio."

He blows out a long, weighted breath. "He's dangerous. You need some backup?"

"Thanks, Lo, but I want to walk in there alone. Nonthreatening. I just want to talk, and I think he will be more open to a conversation if it's just me."

"Okay, man. Be careful, and we will see you once you are done."

He disconnects, and I sit back on my seat. I hate to leave Gabby right now. What if Dante makes contact with her again, and I am not here? I know Tony will take care of her, of all of them, while I am gone, but I want to be the one comforting her. I should be the one. However, I can't miss this meeting with Aguilar, and then I have to deal with Matteo.

I hang up and look at my watch. It's just after midnight. I close my eyes and rub my temple. It's been the longest day of my life, and it's far from over.

I walk out of my office in search of Gabby and Tony. I have to be at the bar for my meeting with Diego shortly.

I find Adriana standing in the living room, gazing blankly toward the hallway.

"Have you seen Tony or Gabby?" I ask as I approach.

She startles slightly. "Gabby is in the kitchen. I am not sure where

Tony is," she answers me in a dead tone and doesn't take her eyes from the direction of the kitchen.

"Are you okay?" There is clear concern in my question.

She finally turns her sad eyes to me. "It's hard, having her here and seeing how much she hates me. I knew she did, but having her look at me like I am some kind of evil stranger is awful."

I know this is difficult for her. I pull her into my arms and whisper into her ear, "Just remember that she doesn't know everything. You are not a horrible person, Adriana."

She presses deep into my hold, seeking comfort, and I give it to her.

Then, I hear footsteps come in behind me, and I loosen my hold and turn.

Gabby is coming down the hall, carrying a mug of coffee. She stops short when she sees us. Hurt washes over her before she can hide it. She pulls her mask back into place as she misreads our embrace.

Her hair is piled in a messy knot on top of her head. Unruly wisps of hair have escaped the knot, dancing around her face. She is wearing a pair of Una's ill-fitted pajamas, and her feet are bare. Even with her puffy eyes and the dark circles, she takes my breath away.

"I'm sorry. I didn't mean to interrupt," she says as she tries quickly to skirt around us.

I step in front of her to halt her escape. She looks up at me. Her hurt changes to annoyance.

"Excuse me," she demands.

"I was just coming to look for you."

She looks from me to Adi and back. "Yes, I can see that."

I smile in spite of myself at her jealousy. "I have to go into town for a little while. I want you to let Tony know right away if you get any more calls from Dante before I return."

That causes her to deflate a little.

"You haven't heard anything from Nicco, have you?" she concludes.

"No, nothing yet."

I see the panic beginning to rise in her again, and I step closer. She doesn't move away, so I place my hands on her shoulders and command her to look at me.

She does as I asked.

"It's only been a few hours. You have to give them time. I am going to town to handle something. It's critical, or I wouldn't go. I will be back as soon as I can. I promise."

"Okay." Her voice is small.

There is no fight in her. Which I hate.

"You should try to get a little sleep if you can," I suggest.

She looks as if she can barely stand upright at this point.

She shakes her head and scurries around me. Then, she sits on the sofa in front of the fire and brings her legs up under her. She mindlessly blows over her mug and brings it to her lips as she stares blankly into the flames.

I look at Adriana, and she is watching her, too. Concern clear on her face.

"Stay with her, Adriana. Even if she doesn't want you here, she needs you."

"I'm not going anywhere. I'll sit here in silence with her if I have to." She looks up at me. "I don't know what kind of trouble you are getting into, but it must be pretty urgent if you are leaving this house right now."

"It is."

"Go. Be careful and hurry back to us."

I nod, take one last glance at Gabriella, and go off in search of Tony.

I walk into the bar thirty minutes later. Aguilar is seated at a private table in the back corner, out of the view and earshot of the other patrons.

He is an older gentleman with golden leathery skin, black hair, and a thick mustache peppered with black and gray. He is dressed casually in a navy sports coat and slacks, but his demeanor is anything but. I can tell he is a man who is always alert and aware of his surroundings. I spot several suspicious men around the room, and I assume he has himself covered quite well.

I approach the table, and he stands when he sees me. He extends his right hand, and I take it in a firm handshake.

"Christoff Scutari, I presume." It's a statement, not a question. He has done his homework and knows my face.

"Yes. Thank you for meeting with me, Mr. Aguilar," I return his greeting as I take my seat across from him.

"Please, no need for such formality. Call me Diego. Now, tell me, how can I help you?"

He is cutting through the pleasantries and getting straight to business. His keen eyes focus on me as he waits for me to fill him in on why I wanted this meeting. I can see that he might have years on me, but he is still an intimidating figure.

"I want to know how you knew my brother Emilio."

He sits back and folds his hands in front of him.

"What makes you think I knew your brother?"

I lean in. "Let's not play games or talk in circles. You are a busy man, and I have very important matters to tend to at the moment. I know that you know why I asked you here. Can we please speak openly?"

He watches me for a few beats, and then he signals for the waitress to come over. He orders three shots of tequila, and I order a brandy. When the drinks arrive, he tells the waitress not to disturb us until he signals for the check. She doesn't argue and scurries away.

He takes and downs the first shot. Then, he starts talking, "I was contacted by an associate of your father. He wanted to propose a business partnership between myself and your family's organization to move my product and some of my girls through your casinos in New Jersey. His proposal was appealing. I already had distributors in place in Atlantic City, but he presented a mutually beneficial proposition."

"One of my father's associates, but not my father or Emilio?"

"Correct. I was surprised. I had approached your father with a similar proposal before, and he was adamant that he was not interested in my line of business. So, I told this associate that I would consider an agreement between us, but I needed to meet with Marcello personally."

"Did you?"

"No. Not long after that is when I heard about your father's and brother's unfortunate accident. This man reached out to me again and said that, once things calmed down, he would be in touch."

"This man, his name is Matteo di Rossi, correct?"

"It is."

I swallow a drink from my glass as rage rumbles through me.

His assessing eyes never leave mine.

"Did you have anything to do with the hit on my family?" I ask him the question point-blank. No use in tiptoeing around it. He knows it is why I am here.

"No, Christoff, I did not. An execution in broad daylight in a family-friendly restaurant is not my style. When necessary, I prefer my dirty work to be handled in the dark."

"You didn't hire it out?"

He takes the second shot of tequila and slides the other one to me. I take it and set the empty glass upside down beside his.

"No. I got a call from your brother a few days before he was gunned down. He had found out about my conversations with di Rossi. He was very unhappy. He informed me that the man had no authority to make deals on behalf of your family and that he had contacted me behind Marcello's back. He was going to take the info to your father, but he wanted to speak to me and have proof that moves were being made without their knowledge before he did."

I let the information rattle around in my mind as the picture starts to become more evident.

"Matteo wanted Emilio out of the picture."

He sits back, and his sharp eyes say it all.

"I would surmise that he wanted both of them out of the way," he agrees.

There is no doubt in my mind who is responsible now.

"Thank you for speaking with me, Diego. I'm sorry you were pulled into the middle of this."

He shrugs. "If there is one thing I hate, it's disloyalty. I have had to deal with it within my own organization lately. There is no honor among thieves anymore. It sickens me."

I stand. "I need to get back home."

"Of course. And, Christoff? If you ever want to explore a partnership, do call me."

He needs not to hold his breath on that one, but I do not voice that. I just agree and head out.

CHAPTER
Thirty-Three

Bree

I FEEL HIM SIT DOWN ON THE SOFA BESIDE ME. I KNOW IT'S HIM BEFORE I even open an eye. I must have drifted off to sleep. I lift my head and look in his direction. Something is wrong, and I feel the tension radiating off of him. I rub the sleep from my eyes and sit up.

"What's wrong?" I ask, and his eyes slide to me.

"What's right?" he answers.

His voice is tight, and he is clenching and unclenching his fists, which he does when he is agitated or upset. Alarm bells start going off in my head.

"No, Cross. What happened while you were gone? Did you hear from Nicco? Did Dante get away?"

"I haven't heard from Nicco."

"Then, what is it?"

He lays his head back against the sofa and closes his eyes.

Despair ripples through me.

"You're not going to tell me. I don't know why I bothered to ask."

I start to curl back into myself when he begins to speak, "Is it so bad that I want to protect you from the ugly parts of this life, *Tesoro*?"

"Hiding things from me. Keeping secrets and deciding what you think I can and cannot handle, taking choices away from me—none of that is protecting me, Cross. It doesn't save me from one ounce of pain. Don't you see that?"

"I don't want any of this to touch you. I've never wanted any of this to touch you," he whispers his confession more to himself than to me.

"I'm not made of glass. I can handle so much more than you give me credit for. Cross, I am not sixteen years old anymore. The reason we are here now, with our son missing, is because of us keeping secrets from each other."

He opens his eyes and looks at me. Really looks at me. His gaze is weary. He lets out a heavy sigh, and he starts to share, "I know who killed Emilio and tried to kill Atelo and Papa. I had my suspicions, and they were confirmed tonight."

That is not what I anticipated him confessing.

"You know who pulled the trigger?"

"No, he didn't do it. Not by his own hand, but with hired hit men, like the coward he is." He pauses for just a moment, like he is searching for the right words, and then continues, "It was someone Papa trusted. Someone we all trusted."

Every word of his revelation is dripping with pain.

"A rat among our own family, someone my father considers a friend, and I didn't see it. It's taken me two years to see what was right in front of me."

I move in closer to him. I shouldn't, but I know that he needs comfort right now. So, I burrow into his side and lay my head on his chest. His hand finds my throat, and he starts rubbing his thumb over my pulse beneath my ear. It's what he does to calm me; now, it seems he is doing it to calm himself.

"What are you going to do now?" I softly ask him.

"I don't know. I have him secured, and I need to go deal with him, but I don't want to leave you."

I look up at him, and his face is right there, just a breath away. Pain and indecision are written all over him.

"I will be okay, Cross."

He reaches over and tucks a stray strand of hair behind my ear. "There's more."

"More?"

"I think he sent Dante after you." He furrows his brow and slightly shakes his head.

"He did?" I ask in confusion.

He nods. "I don't know why, but Nicco found evidence that he was sending Dante money."

He's right; it doesn't make sense. Why would the person who had Cross's brother killed bother with me now? Especially after all this time. I was gone. Cross had moved on. What could he benefit by sending Dante after me? It seems like unnecessary aggravation and use of resources. It would have made more sense if he had threatened Adi.

"The only way you are going to get any answers is to go to the source, and he might know where Dante is. You should go. I can hold myself together. Besides, my girls are sleeping upstairs if I need them."

He gently runs his knuckles down my cheek. "It might take a while."

"That's okay. Do what you have to do."

He looks at me like he is seeing me for the very first time. "What do you think I should do?"

I think hard for a moment. Surprised that he is asking my opinion. Yet I honestly don't know what he should do.

"Maybe you should ask your papa. After all, he is the one who was left crippled, and Emilio was his son. If his friend betrayed him, he deserves the chance to confront him and find out why. After he gets his answers, let him decide the man's fate."

He sucks his bottom lip between his teeth as he ponders my suggestion. "I think you're right. I was going to try to protect Papa from all of this as well, but that's not fair. I shouldn't treat him like a child. He has every right to confront him."

He kisses the top of my head. His mouth lingering at my temple. "Thank you, *Tesoro.*"

I wrap my arm around his middle and squeeze him tight. "You're welcome. Thank you for confiding in me."

He kisses me one more time, and then he stands. "I'm going to go brief Tony, and then I am going to head to Papa's. If anything happens and you need me, have Tony call me immediately, and I will be here as fast as I can."

I look up at him. The look of defeat is gone and replaced with a look of determination.

I smile. "Okay, I will."

He takes a blanket from a basket beside the hearth and covers me. Then, he walks out of the room.

I sit there in silence, watching the orange flames dance in the fireplace for several minutes, when a voice carries from across the room.

"He listened to you. He never listens to me."

An ache balls up and settles in my chest. I forgot Adi was sleeping on the chaise across the dark room.

She continues, "They were wrong about you, you know. I was wrong about you."

"Wrong how?"

"They thought you were weak. Too weak to handle this life. That you wouldn't be woman enough to stand beside him while he rebuilt his family. They were mistaken. You have never been weak, Gabby. A weak woman wouldn't have taken off to have her baby alone. A weak woman wouldn't have moved across the country by herself and started her life over to protect that baby. Only to watch him grow up without her. That takes strength. More strength than I possess. You are stronger than any other woman I know."

Her words pour over me like a soothing balm.

"Yeah, well, I didn't do such a great job at protecting him, did I?"

"That's not your fault. You are not responsible. The person who hurt Cross's family and sent Dante looking for you is the one responsible, and he is no doubt about to get what he deserves."

We sit there in the darkness, quiet for a long time. Then, I prepare myself to ask the question I need to know.

"Adi?"

"Yes?"

"Did you plot with them to get rid of me because you wanted Cross for yourself?"

"Of course not. I never wanted Cross back then. You have loved him since you were four. You were my best friend. All I ever wanted was for you to finally get the guy and live happily ever after."

"Then, why?"

She walks over and joins me. She lies on the couch opposite me and pulls half the blanket I am clenching over her.

"Because things are different now. At first, it was because we were both so miserable without you, and he was never going to fall in love with anyone else. My father wanted us to marry, and he kept pressing for it. Your father thought it was a good idea as well. I never thought you would come back here. I know that doesn't sound good, but it's the truth." She shrugs. "So, we figured, why not? Misery loves company, right?"

I let the information sink in, trying to decipher how I feel about it.

It doesn't lessen the feeling of betrayal.

A few minutes later, we hear footsteps coming down the stairs. Dawn emerges with Kelsey on her heels. They look from me to Adi.

"Everything all right down here?" Dawn asks.

"Yes, everything is fine," I tell her.

I'm too spent to fight anymore.

She walks all the way in. "Well, Kels and I couldn't sleep, and we decided to come down and raid her"—she gestures toward Adi, refusing to say her name—"kitchen. Care to join us?"

I look at the grandfather clock in the corner of the room. It's now almost two a.m.

"Sure, I can make eggs or something," I offer. I look over at Adi. "If that's okay? Do you have eggs?"

She snorts at me. "How the hell would I know if we have eggs? I only open that refrigerator to grab bottled water or wine."

I giggle. Yes, I giggle at her.

"Right."

"You guys are more than welcome to anything in this house. Go for it." She motions toward the kitchen.

Dawn and Kelsey head down the hall, and I get up to follow.

I stop, turn around, and look back at Adi. "You hungry?"

She looks up with hope in her eyes. "I could eat."

I tamp down some of my bitterness and beckon with my head for her to follow us.

CHAPTER
Thirty-four

Cross

I WAIT FOR THE ELEVATOR TO OPEN TO MY FATHER'S CONDO. I CALLED and woke him as I left the manor. His night nurse was conveniently close by, and he said she would help him get ready and he would be up and waiting for my arrival.

I didn't tell him much, just that I had a situation and that it was urgent and that he and I were going to have to take a drive to deal with it.

He seemed pleased that I was coming to him, even at this ungodly hour.

The doors open to his foyer, and when I walk in, he is up and dressed and waiting for me in his wheelchair.

"Son," he greets me.

He is completely alert and looks every bit the formidable man he used to be.

"Hello, Papa."

He eyes me intently. "Shall we go, or do you want to fill me in first?"

"I think I should prepare you before we go."

He nods and turns to wheel himself into the living space.

"I dismissed the nurse so that we could have some privacy," he informs me as I follow him.

"How is Candy?" I ask with a hint of humor in my voice.

He glances at me over his shoulder with a devilish smirk on his face. "Oh, she is exceptional."

"I bet she is."

Once we make it to the room, he stops and turns. "Will I need a drink to hear this news?"

Instead of answering, I walk to the wet bar on the far wall and begin to pour him a drink. He watches me with assessing eyes. I hand him his glass, and I take a seat in the wing chair opposite him.

"Go ahead, son. Whatever it is, just spit it out."

I do as he said, and I don't beat around the bush.

"I know who ordered the hits on you, Emilio, and Atelo. And I think I know why."

He sets the glass down on the table to his right and focuses on me. "All right. Tell me," he bites out.

He has been waiting for this moment as anxiously as I have for the last two years.

"It was Matteo."

I see the flinch and then confusion pass over his face, followed by acceptance and betrayal.

"You are sure of this?" he asks the question, but he knows that there is no way I would make this accusation, unfounded.

"I wouldn't have come to you if I wasn't."

He sits back, and I can see him trying to figure out the whys in his mind.

I continue, "Apparently, he had been trying to make a backdoor deal with Diego Aguilar to run drugs and prostitutes through our New Jersey casinos and hotels. Emilio got wind of it and put the brakes on it. He was planning to bring the proof to you right before the hit. The hit that conveniently happened after Matteo stepped away from you that night."

His face is starting to turn red as he relives the night. "And you know this how?"

"Gio remembered Emilio mentioning a meeting with Aguilar. So,

I asked Vincenzo to reach out and see if Aguilar would be open to a sit-down with me. I met him earlier tonight. He told me about Matteo coming to him with the proposition and his conversation with Emilio when he found out. Emilio immediately shot the deal down. I think he planned to tell you all about it that night. Then, I asked Aguilar point-blank if he had anything to do with the hit."

His eyes shoot to mine. "That was a very dangerous thing to do, son."

"I had to know. I had to know if he and Matteo were in cahoots to take you all out."

"And?"

"He denied any involvement, and I believed him. It was all Matteo. Trying to cover his ass and, at the same time, get control of the family."

He nods stoically.

"He meant for that bullet to kill you, and he meant for Atelo to go down, too. Evidently, he didn't think I was worth wasting the money for a fourth hit. No doubt he never thought I would rise to the occasion."

"A grave mistake on his part, underestimating you, my son." He finishes his scotch and waits.

"He has been the one behind the hits on our arms shipments as well. He is the only one besides Tony and me who knows the details of those shipments. He tried to make it look like it was Pauly who was leaking the schedule, but it wasn't. He was hoping that the Irish would get angry enough to take care of me for him before I figured it out."

I pause, letting him absorb each bit of information before moving to the next.

"What else? I can see there is more."

He is tired of waiting.

"He sent someone to California after Gabriella."

I furrow my brow because that one still makes no sense to me.

"A distraction."

I look up at my father and question, "What?"

"A distraction. He wanted your focus elsewhere. He knows how you feel about Gabriella. He and I have had a long discussion about the matter over cards. I can see now that my old friend was playing me for information to use against you."

The bastard. I can't wait to get my hands on him and make him pay for all the suffering he has caused those I love.

"I'm sorry, son. I did not see the dishonor in him."

I can't let him take that burden on himself.

"No, Papa, you have nothing to be sorry for. He betrayed you. He betrayed us all. None of us saw through him."

"Emilio did."

Yes, Emilio did, and it cost him his life. And Matteo will pay with his.

We pull around to the back entrance of Vincenzo's home, and Stavros comes out to help me get Papa from the car.

Once he is settled, we wheel him into the side entrance that leads to the basement where Lorenzo and Vincenzo sit, smoking cigars.

Matteo sits in a chair in the center of the room. He looks casual and calm, as if he were just there for a friendly visit.

He turns his head toward the door as I enter and acknowledges me with a blank expression, but a slight flicker of remorse hits his eyes when Papa is wheeled in behind me.

They stare at one another for a long moment before Vincenzo gets to his feet and comes to stand beside my father, placing his hand on his shoulder in a sign of solidarity and friendship. Matteo's eyes follow the gesture, and then he looks up to us standing before him and smirks.

"Marcello, how nice it is to see you out of that prison cell your son banished you to."

Papa doesn't react; he just sits there, watching his old friend.

"Cross," he greets me.

Papa clears his throat, and then he begins to speak, "What I want to know is, why? Did I not treat you well? You had money and authority. You wanted for nothing."

Matteo feigns puzzlement, and Papa raises his hand to stop his denial.

"I know you did it, Matt. There is no point in denying it, but I think I deserve to hear from your own mouth what you hoped to gain by killing my sons and me. You owe me that much, old friend."

Matteo's eyes grow hard, and he bites out, "You caused this yourself. Listening to those boys whispering in your ear, trying to get you to turn from lucrative deals, deals that would have made us all very rich and powerful. Worrying you with a conscience. We are not men of conscience. That is for the weak. We are men who do what we must to remain on top. If we do not, then someone will come along to take it from us."

"And you decided that person would be you?"

"That person had to be me. You were letting them run all over you. There was going to be nothing left if I didn't take it from you."

Rage hits me like a lightning bolt, and I lunge for him. My fist lands, and I hear his teeth crash together as I open my knuckles against his jaw. He lists to the right, momentarily stunned, before righting himself and wiping the blood from his mouth.

"Go ahead; kill me." He grins like he has a secret.

"He isn't going to kill you." Papa pulls our attention back to him. "I will get that pleasure."

Just then, my phone starts to ring in my pocket. The tone is Nicco's, and I have to take it.

"Papa, I have to take this call. Don't do anything until I return."

I look over to Vincenzo, and he looks confused that I would take a call now. I walk to the other side of the room and answer.

"Nicco."

"Hey, man. I have good news and bad news."

"Go ahead," I urge.

"We found Dante."

I let out a relieved breath at the news. "What's the bad news?"

"Someone got to him first."

"What do you mean, someone got to him first?"

"We found him in his apartment. With his brains blown all over the back of the sofa. The place has been ransacked, and bags of smack are beside him. Staged to look like a drug deal gone wrong."

What the fuck?

"The baby?"

"Gone. Like he was never here. So is everything else that had to do with Gabby or you or di Rossi. All the photos he had of Gabby. The paperwork. Wire transfers. His phone. All gone."

Shit, Gabriella is going to lose it. How am I going to tell her the baby is gone?

"Look, we are leaving him here for whoever to find. Stefano and Gino are going to do all they can on the ground here to find a trail, and I am heading to the airport. I am coming to New York. Gabby is going to need me. I should be there in six hours."

I don't argue with him. He is right; Gabby will need him.

"See you soon."

I end the call and race across the room. An indecipherable sound wrenching from my throat as I launch myself at the man behind all of this. Lorenzo calls to me and reaches for me before we both go toppling to the floor.

Lo pulls me back and holds me with his arm tightly across my chest as I scream, "Where is my son, you son of a bitch?"

He has the nerve to look perplexed. "I have no idea what you are talking about."

"Where the fuck is he, you sick bastard?"

He straightens his features and gives nothing away. "I have no idea where your son is, Christoff, and if I did, I wouldn't tell you. I am a dead man anyway."

"Son?"

The booming question comes from behind me. I turn to face Vincenzo.

"What are you talking about?"

Now, his and Papa's questioning eyes are focused on me.

"Ah, Nonno doesn't know," Matteo says with a wicked glint in his eye.

I turn back to him. "You sent him after them. How did you know?"

He grins. "I didn't. I knew about the unfortunate incident that happened to your Gabriella years ago. So, I sought out this young man to make him a proposition. He was all too eager to take me up on it. I just wanted your focus elsewhere for a while. I had no idea you would send Nicco instead. So, I cut him off and came up with plan B. That is, until he called to tell me of your clever girl's little secret."

"I will gut you."

"Uh-uh-uh … not if you want to know where they are."

I start to lunge for him again when it hits me. He thinks Dante still has the baby. He has no idea that someone took him out of play.

Shit. He was my only hope for answers.

"Someone had better start explaining now!" Vincenzo booms from behind us.

We hear the clicking of heels across the concrete floor, and our attention is drawn to the door.

Lilliana enters. "I will explain to them. Go to her. She needs you now."

"You will explain?" Vincenzo questions his wife.

"Yes, I will. Everything." She turns back to me. "Go, Christoff. I will handle things here. We will dispose of"—she gestures toward Matteo—"and Marcello can stay the night here. I will fill in the blanks for him and my husband."

"Are you sure?"

I know Vincenzo is going to lose his mind at her confession. I don't want to leave her without backup.

"Yes, I have this. Go take care of my baby girl," she says softly as she pats my back.

I need no other prompting. I head straight for the exit.

Before I can get the door open, I hear two gunshots being fired. I turn back to see the gun being held aloft in my father's hand and two holes between Matteo's open eyes. Perfect shot.

CHAPTER
Thirty-five

Bree

WE RIFLE THROUGH ADI'S KITCHEN. LUCKILY, THE HOUSEKEEPER stocks the refrigerator and the pantry pretty well. I decide to make French toast for us.

The girls busy themselves, helping me prep. Dawn and Kelsey are carefully avoiding Adi as much as possible.

Adi gives up on trying to help with them elbowing her out of the way and sets to the task of making mimosas. Then, she sets the table off to the side of the kitchen.

Tony smells the aroma and joins us.

Once we all have our plates, we settle in uncomfortable silence and eat. I pick at my plate, not able to eat. I look around at my friends. We are all so exhausted.

I feel incredibly guilty for dragging them into my mess. Here we were, in New York, to celebrate Dawn's engagement, and my crisis overrides her excitement at having her perfect gown designed.

I truly am a wrecking ball, wreaking havoc through the lives of all the people I love.

"This is amazing, Gabs," Adi compliments as she takes a bite.

"Thanks. French toast is hard to mess up. It's just eggs and bread." I shrug.

She snickers. "Remember when I tried to make scrambled eggs for you that morning while you slept in with Antoine? I nearly burned our apartment to the ground."

"How could I forget? Everyone rushing out of the building and creepy Chad slithering down his fire escape in nothing but his socks. The entire building hated us from that moment on."

"Except for Chad."

We both start laughing at the memory.

Dawn and Kelsey watch us as they eat.

Dawn decides to leap into the conversation. "So, Tonya, um, I mean … I'm sorry, what was your name?"

"Traitor?" Adi spits at her.

Tony coughs as he chokes on his food.

"Oh, yeah, that's right."

Adi turns in her direction and smiles. "I get it. You are a better friend. Happy?"

"You're damn right, I'm the better friend."

"Stop, guys, please. Let's just eat in peace."

Dawn gives me an apologetic look. "Sorry, Brie. The food is fabulous. Maybe we should do breakfast tacos next Taco Tuesday. Oh, we could wear our pajamas with our sombreros and serve Bloody Mary margaritas!" She claps her hands and looks at Kelsey in question.

"Bellini Margaritas?"

"Definitely sounds better than Bloody Mary margaritas. Clamato juice and tequila. Ew," Kelsey answers.

"Are they high?" Adi whispers across the table to me.

"I'm not sure. I keep forgetting to ask them if they get high."

"You know, if they weren't such possessive bitches, I could totally like them."

I glance over at my roommates as they animatedly plan our next Tuesday at home. I am so lucky that I landed on their doorstep.

"Yeah, they are pretty awesome."

"I envy that. All I have ever had was one friend, and I fucked up and lost her."

I look over, and her eyes are full of unshed tears, which is unsettling. Adriana Ferraro is not a crier. She is a roll-with-the-punches-with-sarcasm-and-a-whatever-attitude kind of girl.

I want to forgive her. I wish we could go back to the way we were, but I don't think it's possible. Some things, once broken, can never be mended.

After we finish eating and as we are cleaning the table, we hear Cross arrive back home. My instinct is to run to him and find out how things went with his papa and to see if they were able to find out anything about Dante's whereabouts.

With effort, I keep my feet planted in the kitchen with my girls.

Adi eyes me from her spot at the table as I rinse plates and load them into the dishwasher.

Then, she calls out to him, "Cross, we are in the kitchen."

I give her an appreciative glance before I shut the machine and hit the on button.

A few seconds later, he waltzes in from the hallway. The sight of him still causes a thrill to sliver up my spine even though he looks beat down and as exhausted as I feel.

I tamp down my reaction and school my face. Then, I take a moment to really look at him. Alarms start going off in my head. Something is very wrong.

I ignore my resolve to stay put, and I rush to him.

"What happened?" I ask as I reach him.

His jaw is twitching, which is another one of his tells. He is either angry or worried. Neither of which is good.

He looks behind me and addresses my friends, "Ladies, I need a moment with Gabby, please."

Dawn and Kelsey give each other a concerned look and set the dishcloths they were using to clean the table and counter into the sink.

They walk toward us, and each one places a comforting hand on my shoulder as they pass.

"Don't go far. She is going to need you," he warns them as they make their exit.

Kelsey glances back at me with fear in her eyes.

I look back to him, growing more and more frantic as he waits for Adi to join us.

"Can you wake Una? I know it's early, but I need her."

She inclines her head and scurries off after the girls.

"Tony, can you call Lo and check on things at your parents' house?"

Tony looks between us, and I can see that he wants to stay put, but he nods once and disappears down the hallway.

Once we are alone, Cross takes a deep breath, and I can see him mentally calculating how to break whatever news he has to me.

"Just spit it out. Whatever it is, we will deal with it, but just say it."

I close my eyes tightly and wait for the words I know are about to come from his mouth. Something has happened to Cassian. Nothing else would be this hard for him to reveal to me.

He moves in close, and I feel his fingers thread through mine as he tilts his head down to press against my forehead. I'm too scared of what he is about to say to open my eyes.

We stand there, tension dancing between us, and I work up the nerve to pull back and look up at him. His eyes are still closed.

"Cross?" His name is a plea as I step closer into him. I think I will have to hold him together this time. I wrap my arms around his middle. "Say it."

He finally brings his eyes to mine and goes to open his mouth when a ring comes from his left pants pocket.

"Damn it," he mutters as he reaches in and pulls the phone out.

He hits Ignore and starts to place it back when another chime sounds, and he looks down at it.

Confusion crosses his face before he masks it.

Then, he looks up at me. "I need to take this."

What? Now?

I start to protest, but he places a finger to my lips and presses a button.

I thought he was going to walk into another room or out of my earshot, but he doesn't.

"Hello?" It is a question, not a greeting.

CHAPTER
Thirty-Six

Cross

"HELLO, BROTHER," HE CONFIRMS.

When I saw the text that read, *Pick up the phone, prick*, I suspected that it was him.

I cut my eyes to Gabby, who is looking at me with perplexity on her face.

"Did I catch you at a bad time?" he asks with exasperation in his voice.

"As a matter of fact, yes."

"Sorry, Christoff, but I thought you would want to know that I have your boy."

I take my eyes from Gabby and concentrate on what he is saying. "You have who?"

"Your boy. I have him. He is safe."

My eyes snap to Gabby's as my heart starts to slam wildly against my chest. She can see the change in my demeanor, and she clasps my forearm tightly.

"How?"

"I had my ears to the ground. I heard that some funds were being funneled from our accounts, and I followed the money. It led me to California. Imagine that. I have been watching your girl for a few weeks now. Got the beat on that Calvacanti character."

My mind is whirling as he recounts his story. I walk from the kitchen to the living room and take a seat. Gabby is on my heels, and she walks swiftly behind me. She sits across from me, so she can watch my face and read me.

He continues, "It hasn't been easy, skirting around Gino and Nicco. Luckily, they were so laser-focused on the girls that I was able to be smoke." He chuckles. "Of course, Mastreoni is gonna hear about it when I see him next."

I growl in the phone. I don't need his amused blow-by-blow account. I need him to get to the point.

"Anyway, I was tailing this guy to see if I could find where he was staying and why you were sending him such large sums of money. When I get into his place, I find all this crazy shit. Photograph after photograph of your Gabriella. Everything from her walking to her car to playing tennis and kissing some blond guy. There had to be hundreds of pictures scattered around the place. Now, I deduce that you are not sending this head case to keep tabs on Gabriella, so I start looking, and I find that Papa's good friend Matt is the one sending him the cash."

He has now moved on to telling me shit I already know, and I am about to let him know this when he gets to the point.

"After the girls took off, he started going nuts, man. Gabby not being where he expected her to be tripped some switch in him. When he broke into that couple's house and snatched their kid, I started to bail and take my ass on out of California and let the cops have him. That was, until I got a good look at his tiny hostage." He stops and then softly says, "Man, he looks just like you did, baby brother."

My chest tightens as I remember the tiny face smiling back at me from my mother's locket around Gabby's neck.

"It didn't take a genius to figure out what your clever little lady had done. Would have worked, too, if Matt hadn't sent that lunatic after her. So, I waited. He rode around with the kid for a few hours. Then, he made a run for his place to grab his shit and I guess head for Gabby. He had thrown Nicco off by first abandoning the car he had rented and cell he was using with some teenagers who took it on a joy-ride. While they were chasing the decoy, he hightailed it to his apartment. I followed."

With every word he divulges, the knot in my chest eases a little more.

I glance over, and Gabby still has a look of terror on her face. I need to ease her fear. I pull her attention to my face and reassuringly wink at her. The crease between her brows lets up, and her expression changes to puzzlement.

"Then, what happened?" I urge him to finish his story so that I can relay the good news to Gabby.

"I ambushed the asshole. Put a bullet in his sick head. Then, I cleaned up any crumbs that could connect him back to you or your girl, including the paper trail back to Matteo, and I grabbed my nephew and bolted."

I blow out a long, relieved breath and run my free hand through my hair.

Thank God.

"Where are you now?" I need to get my son back to his mother as soon as possible.

"On a plane, headed for you."

"ETA?"

"We've been in the air about three and a half hours, so I would say another two before we land in Queens."

"Why the hell did it take you so long to call me?"

"Sorry, baby brother. I've been a little busy trying to get us the fuck out of town without anyone asking too many questions. Luckily, Dante had some cash on hand, fake IDs for him and the kid, and a pair of plane tickets to New York. We barely made it to the airport in time. It took a while, but I was finally able to talk the lovely flight attendant into watching the baby and letting me take her phone to the toilet to make a Wi-Fi call. Poor thing could get in big trouble. I'm going to have to find a creative way to thank her."

Fuck

"I'll have a car waiting for you when you land. Is the baby okay?"

At that, a strangled gasp escapes Gabby, and her hand flies to her mouth. Tears well up in her eyes and threaten to spill down her cheeks at any moment.

"Yeah, he's been through a lot. Ripped from his bed in the middle of the night and yanked around by that psycho, but I think he is a fan of his uncle. I went to a store before we headed to the airport, and a sweet young cashier helped this poor single dad pick up all the essentials he needed. By the way, if I never change another diaper in my life, it will be too soon. Little fucker's been dropping deuces all night."

I chuckle to myself at the thought of him attempting to care for an infant.

"Thank you, brother."

"You're welcome. I'll see you soon."

I end the call and set the phone aside. The immense relief that washes over me is overwhelming. Then, I hear a murmured plea.

"Please, please, please ..." It's a prayer as she wrings her hands and waits for me to fill her in.

"It's okay, *Tesoro*." I bring my hands to either side of her face and gently caress her.

Footsteps come thundering down the staircase at that moment, and the girls burst into the room, followed closely by Una.

"Oh my God, Brie. What happened?"

Dawn and Kelsey run to her and kneel on either side of the chair she occupies.

"What did you do?" Dawn turns fiery eyes to me.

I open my mouth to answer, and Una interrupts, "Christoff, what is going on? They said you had bad news and needed me to help you break it to Gabriella."

She is standing behind the sofa with Adriana at her back. I take a moment to look around at this room full of women—all strong and fiercely protective of Gabriella and each other. I can't help but fill with pride. We think of them as the weaker sex, but in reality, they are a force, especially when they stand together. There is really no love quite like it. Men, we love our friends, our brothers, but we do not know how to emotionally support one another in this manner. We will put a bullet in your enemy, sure, but if that doesn't fix your situation, we are at a complete loss. These women are literally ready to hold her up if she can't stand up of her own accord.

"Well?" Una's patience is wearing thin.

I cut my eyes to her. "Calvacanti is dead."

A collective gasp hits the air as each one of them absorbs the news.

"And what of my great-grandson?" she asks as she clutches her robe next to her heart. Her voice cracks as she lets the reality of what it could be settle while trying to school her reaction.

Rather than answer her, I turn my attention back to Gabby as I relay, "He is fine. He is on a plane with his uncle, on his way to us."

A sob of relief releases from her throat.

She collapses on me. "Nicco has him?" she asks into my chest.

"No." I look from her to Una. "Atelo."

CHAPTER
Thirty-Seven

Brie

I DON'T HEAR MUCH OF ANYTHING AFTER HE SAYS CASSIAN IS OKAY. I leap into his arms. Every cell in my body is singing. He catches me and pulls me into his lap. I wrap my arms around him and bury my face into his throat as I empty myself of all the guilt and fear and grief that has been like a chain around my neck the past twenty-four hours.

"Who is Atelo again?" Dawn's voice cuts through my elation.

Then, the weight of what he just said hits me.

"Atelo? Wait, I thought he had taken off?" I sit up and look at him. "Did you know where he was this whole time?" I am so confused.

He takes my hands in his and focuses his attention on me. "No, I had no idea he was in California. Last we spoke, he was in Mexico, following a lead."

"You let me think he had taken off without a word, and you were in contact with him?"

He guiltily looks at me and then sighs. "The night that Papa and Emilio were shot and Atelo was targeted, he came to me. He had been hiding, and when I left the hospital, he was waiting for me in the car."

He looks up at Una, who is crying. She has been so worried about Atelo. Not knowing where he was or if she would ever see him again has been excruciating for her.

"What's this?" Cross's grandfather comes up behind Una and pulls her back into his arms.

"Grandfather," Cross acknowledges, "I was just explaining the arrangement with Atelo."

He gives his grandfather a pointed look, and I don't miss the moment of acceptance that flashes across his face.

Una doesn't miss the exchange either. She breaks from his hold and turns to face her husband. "You knew about this?"

He lovingly looks down at his wife and answers, "I knew only what I needed to. I had to help Atelo get out of the city that night. We had to make it look believable that he had taken off like a coward."

"But why?" I ask.

Cross moves in closer to me and continues, "We came up with a plan that night. I would take control of the family while Atelo ghosted. We needed everyone to believe he'd run. That would allow him to move around undetected and investigate, trying to find out who was after our family. I had to assume leadership."

I jerk my hands from his. Fury hitting me like a lightning bolt. "What? You made up the story? Bastard. You made me think you had no choice, that Atelo was gone and you had to stay. The entire thing was a lie! He could have been here, and you could have been with me. With us."

He blanches like I physically struck him. Good. I hope the truth stings.

"No, *Tesoro*. It wouldn't have made sense for me to leave. I had no reason to go to ground. It made more sense that he would take off after nearly being hit. Plus, he had connections and friends in this life that I didn't have. He could be vapor. I couldn't."

My mind is a whirl with all this new information. It was all a game. "You tore my life apart."

"I didn't mean to. I thought—Atelo and I thought that it would be over quickly. That I would stand in until he and Gino were able to take out the threat, and then I would come for you. But you took off, and we kept running into dead ends."

"So, what? You figured you would marry Adi and keep up the charade forever?"

Adriana walks over to stand beside him. "Not forever, just until it was safe," she says as she removes the diamond from her left hand and places it in his. Then, she addresses me, "It was never going to be a real marriage, Gabs. We were playing the part as plausible as possible, so no one, not even my papa, would be suspicious. There were real threats against you and against the rest of Cross's family. We all knew that the only way attention was going to be taken off of you was for Cross to move on."

"It was a ruse? The whole thing?" I look at Una, my only ally. "Did you know? This entire time, did you know?"

She comes to me and takes my face into her strong hands. "No, Gabriella, I didn't know. I'm as stunned as you. I thought Atelo was lost forever, and I thought Christoff and Adriana were getting married forever. I thought it was a loveless marriage of convenience but a real marriage all the same."

"Everyone lied to me," I whisper to her through my tears.

"The only people who knew were the two of us and your papa," Adi admits.

"Nicco?" I need to know if he was in on their scheme.

"No, not even Nicco," she confirms.

Cross cautiously approaches me. I'm so angry and relieved. The two emotions are warring within me.

"The one thing I didn't plan for, the one thing I didn't know, was that you were pregnant. I would have never—baby, never—have gone through with any of this had I known. I would have left with you. I swear. I was trying to protect you, protect Marcello and my grandparents, avenge Emilio's death, and give Atelo enough time and cover to figure out what the fuck had happened. I knew you were upset and heartbroken, but I thought you would move back to the city and go back to school with Adriana, and as soon as everything settled, I was going to beg you for forgiveness. Then, you were gone. Just gone. I had no idea where. Vincenzo had no idea. Until we got that first letter from Scotland, I was a mess, thinking someone had taken you."

"I had no choice."

"I told you to never take off without leaving me a way to find you. It was one of the last things I said to you. I needed you to trust me."

"Trust you?"

His expression fills with amused exasperation. "Yes, you keep taking off when I need you to trust me and stay put. You did that when you took off to Paris, again the night you took off and stayed in the hotel, and then ..."

"This was different."

"I know."

"You should have told me the truth. I could have handled it. I could have played along."

"Could you?"

"I deserved the chance to try."

"You're right. You did deserve that. I am so fucking sorry."

"Hey, guys, maybe we should give them a little privacy. I think they have a lot to work out. Why don't we go make a second breakfast?" Kelsey corrals the group back toward the kitchen.

Cross waits until they are down the hallway, and then he speaks, "I am so sorry, *Tesoro.*"

"You and Papa still treat me like I am a child. You should have trusted me. I would have moved back to the city."

He looks at me. "How would you have explained the baby bump?"

"That's something we could have figured out together."

He nods. "It was too risky," he says more to himself than to me. "We took a bad situation, and we beat the hell out of it and made it so much worse," he admits.

I watch him as he takes a seat and puts his head in his hands.

Instead of feeling relief at this entire saga coming to an end, he looks more burdened than ever. I stand there and try to set aside my anger and look at the situation through his eyes. He was grief-stricken, scared, and thrust into a position he wasn't ready for. Same as I was. Maybe we both did the best we could with the cards we were dealt. I have asked him to forgive me. Perhaps I need to show mercy as well.

I sit beside him.

"I don't know. You did what you'd set out to do. You protected everyone. You restored your family's reputation. You found out who'd hurt your father and killed your brother. And I did what I'd set out to do. I protected Cassian. He is on his way home to us now. Safe and sound. Your brother is coming home. I don't think we did such a bad job."

"I hurt you."

"You did."

"I don't mean to keep doing that."

"Then, don't do it again."

He reaches up, twines his hand into my hair, and pulls me to him. Then, he crashes his lips to mine. I don't stop him. I move in closer and open to him. This kiss is passionate. It's loaded with apology, relief, forgiveness, and longing.

He ends the kiss and stands. He reaches his hand out to me in invitation.

In that moment, I decide to stop running. Nicco was right all along. I can't be two people any longer. I am not Brie. I am Gabby.

I take his hand and let him help me to my feet. Then, he sweeps me up into his arms and heads for the stairs.

CHAPTER
Thirty-Eight

Cross

I CARRY HER UP TO MY ROOM. THE ROOM I RARELY SLEEP IN. THE room that used to be my father's. I want to take her out back to our loft, but I don't have the patience. She locks her mouth to mine, and I fumble with the doorknob. Once inside, I kick the door shut behind me and walk her to the lush king-size bed without disengaging.

She is frantic, and so am I. Like all the frustration and panic of the last forty-eight hours—or, hell, the last two years—are finally bubbling over and threatening to burn us. To burn the whole damn house to the ground.

I lay her down and move to sit up, and she grabs the lapel of my shirt and pulls me back down. I chuckle as she wraps her legs around my hips and holds me in place.

"Baby, I am not going anywhere. I just want to look at you," I whisper against her lips.

She doesn't let me up. She arches her back and flexes her hips to force me over. I am lying on my back, and I let her have control. She looks down at me and licks her lips.

"Maybe I want to look at you," she utters as she slides her hands down the front of my shirt and starts to slowly unbutton it.

I surrender to her. She can do whatever she likes to me for the rest of our lives.

She spreads my shirt open, and she glides her hands over my chest and down my rib cage. She stops as she gets to my lower left side.

She gasps as she gently fingers the ink that I had added when I came home from California. An anatomical heart with a cross stabbing through it, breaking it, making it bleed.

A large tattoo that matches the smaller one she has on her hip.

Her eyes come up to meet mine. "Why?" she asks softly.

"Because you needed a reminder of why you left. A tattoo of me breaking your heart. I needed one, too—a reminder, so I'd never do it again."

A tear slides down her face, and I catch it with my finger.

She moves down and brings her lips to my side, lightly peppering the ink with kisses.

I take her hair and weave it into my hand, so I can lift it and see her face. Her beautiful face. I have missed it so much.

She shifts back up and unbuttons the pajama top she is wearing, and I move my hands to help her slide it from her shoulders. I caress her neck right below her ears, and I come up to a sitting position, so I can bring my mouth to the sensitive valley where her neck meets her shoulder.

I feel her shudder atop me, and I slowly trail my mouth up the slope of her neck.

She releases a sharp intake of breath as her head falls back, giving me full access to her throat.

God, she is exquisite.

I take my time, savoring the taste of her skin. Absorbing every gasp and moan as I love her.

She arches her back and bears her chest into me, and I feel her seeking my hardness with her core as she starts to move her hips against me. My cock grows painfully hard at the contact, and I fight the urge to flip her onto her back and sink myself deep inside of her.

I want her to take what she wants at the pace she wants it.

I lean back and watch as her breath grows ragged, and her eyes roll back as she rides my hips. I grow thicker beneath her. I bring my mouth to her breast and take a taut nipple between my lips. I give it a tiny nip and gently suck it.

Her hand glides up my left bicep, and she sharply digs her fingernails in as a tremor runs the length of her body.

"Crrrosss ..." she moans my name, and it is the sweetest sound I have ever heard. I never thought I would hear it again.

It breaks the thread of restraint I am holding on to.

I clasp her by the waist and twist, her back hits the bed and her eyes fly open.

"Hips up, baby. I need to taste you."

She does as I said and lifts her hips from the bed. I slide her bottoms off. She isn't wearing any underwear, and I growl as I see how slick and ready she is for me.

I hold her hip with one hand and bring my other to her center. I slide a finger through her wetness. Her legs start to tremble with anticipation as I circle her clit with my thumb.

I remove my hand and stand. She is lying there, naked, completely open to me, and I have never seen anything so fucking beautiful in my life.

I quickly remove my slacks and return to her.

I slide my hands under her and pull her to the edge of the bed. Then, I kneel before her and bring my mouth to her core. I lick and suck and take every drop. She threads her fingers into my hair and holds me where she wants me, and I bury my tongue inside of her and let her ride it. Then, I add a finger and then another till she is full. Her hips start vibrating uncontrollably, and she starts holding her breath as her orgasm hits her.

She cries out, and I don't give a fuck if the entire house full of people hear her.

I lick every last drop from her before I crawl up her body and take her mouth in a possessive kiss.

I bring my throbbing cock to her entrance, and I thrust into her.

She is so hot and ready and perfect. I try to go slowly, but I am too far gone. I move into her over and over as she scores my back with her nails. She raises her hips to meet each thrust and to drive me deeper and deeper inside.

I pull back, trying to get control of myself because I am about to come, and I want it to last longer, but she blocks me by tightening her legs around me and quickening her movements. So, I give in, and I move harder and faster until I explode. My release rocketing down my spine. She wraps her arms around my neck and bites down hard into the flesh of my shoulder as she spasms rhythmically around me once more.

I stretch out, covering her, as my breath evens out. We are a tangle of sweaty limbs and twisted sheets.

When my heart rate finally calms back down, I look up into her beautiful brown eyes, and for the first time in years, I feel like myself. Like I am home. She is home.

I get up and run to the bathroom. I return with a warm towel to find her in a deep, peaceful sleep. She hasn't rested at all in days, and I know that her body needs it. I bring a pillow, gently lift her head, and place it under her. Then, I wrap her in the soft comforter and turn out the light.

I quietly close the door and tiptoe back down the stairs.

I am met by four very concerned women when I make it downstairs.

"Where's Brie?" Dawn demands.

"She is sleeping."

She folds her arms over her chest and gives me the stare-down.

"Okay, Romeo, wipe the sex smirk off of your face. What exactly are your intentions with her? I mean, you just shook the tramp off. Don't think you can just snap your handsome fingers, and our girl is going to forgive everything and come running back to you. Not. Gonna. Happen."

Adriana rolls her eyes and elbows past Dawn to address me, "She is not wrong, Cross. It is not going to be that easy, you know. You had better not be strong-arming her, or I will—"

"Stop!" I cut her off. "Ladies, I appreciate how much you all love Gabriella. But we are done making choices for her. All of us. No more thinking we know what's best for her without ever asking her."

All their eyes are trained on me, including Una's.

"I want my family. But it is her decision. I don't expect it to be easy, and I will accept whatever she decides."

Their gazes soften, and it is Kelsey who speaks up, "It might not be you. She might want to go back to California"—pain slices through me at the thought—"with Cassian."

My son. The son I haven't even met yet.

"Then, I will let them go," I say as I look them all in the eye. "It will kill me, but I will let them both go."

Smiles—big, relieved smiles—wash over them.

"Oh, don't look so fucking sad there, handsome. Our girl is not going anywhere. We just had to make sure you wouldn't stop her if she did want to leave." Dawn pats my chest. "Damn. Now, those are some rock-solid pecs." She sighs.

"Stop feeling him up, Dawn," Kelsey chides as she shoos her toward the stairs.

"Come on; it's still early. Let's get a couple of hours of sleep before the baby gets here. We are going to have to face our mothers soon, and we have to figure out what in the hell we are going to tell them." She stops at me. "You're stealing my roommate." She pouts.

"He does that," Adriana shouts after her as she drags Dawn up the steps.

I watch them disappear at the top and then turn back to Adriana and Una.

"Well, it sure has been an eventful night," Adi muses. "Think I'll go grab a few winks myself. Rest up before I get the pleasure of breaking the news to Papa that his little arranged marriage isn't going to happen."

"Adi, wait." I stop her as she heads toward her room.

"Yeah?"

"Are you okay? I mean, about the wedding?"

"Are you shitting me? No offense, but thank God I don't have to marry you. Especially with those haughty bitches as my bridesmaids. I can't wait to tell Papa to take his dream of our happy marriage and shove it up his ass. Let him cut me off. I don't care."

I walk to her and wrap her in my arms. "I won't let him cut you off. Even if he tries, I won't let you go without anything."

"I know," she murmurs against my chest. Then, she gives me one quick squeeze and heads to bed.

"Well"—I face Una—"what now?"

She comes over and takes my hand into her tiny one. She smiles up at me with tears of joy in her eyes. "Now, my Christoff, we settle in and wait for your brother and your baby boy to finally come home, where they belong."

Una's head pops up from Grandfather's shoulder when we hear the gate bell chime. I walk over to the monitor and see the black SUV pulling up. I am nervous as we all hurry to the door to greet them.

I open the front doors just as Atelo emerges from the back seat with a wailing baby clinging to him. I would be amused at the look of distress on my brother's face if I wasn't laser-focused on the upset infant.

I rush down the stoop and reach for him, and Atelo gladly releases him to my open arms.

He continues to scream as I cradle his wiggling body to me. I take a moment to look at my son. His face is red and soaked with tears. He has a tuft of dark hair and large green eyes that are wide and bloodshot. Two tiny teeth are cutting through his bottom gum, and he is mumbling incoherent sobs as he gasps for air.

He is perfect.

No sooner do I have him through the entryway than I hear a fast-paced gallop coming down the stairs. Gabriella rushes at us full speed.

As soon as the little man catches sight of her, his chubby arms reach out, and he starts crying, "BB," over and over.

CHAPTER
Thirty-Nine

Brie

I SLAM TO A HALT AGAINST CROSS. I'M SO RELIEVED TO HEAR Cassian's distressed cries that I don't even panic at the sight of his father holding him for the first time.

Cassian reaches for me, and Cross instantly relinquishes him.

I hold him close and start murmuring reassurances to him, "It's okay. Shh. BB's here. I've got you, baby."

I bounce him until I have mollified him into a quiet, hiccupping calm. I pace back and forth, softly rocking him, and he clings to me.

The relief I feel is great.

I say a silent prayer of thanks, and then I turn to Atelo. "Thank you. Thank you so much for finding him."

He nods to me and then points to the bag at his feet. "There is formula, diapers, wipes, and baby food in there," he informs me. "A lady at the store helped me. I am not sure if any of it is the right stuff or not. He didn't seem to care for the milk, but he finally drank some of it."

"I'm sure it's all great," I assure him. "Thank you for taking care of him."

I repeatedly kiss the top of Cassian's head.

"Yeah, well, he is my only nephew. And I have a lot of Mastreoni competition for Best Uncle, so I get to claim this victory forever."

I laugh. "That's true. You get to be the hero."

"Hey now, what's that?" Tony comes around the corner.

"Sorry, but he did bring him home," I declare as he walks over to shake Atelo's hand.

Then, he comes to us, so he can get a better look at the baby.

He places his big hand on his head, and Cassian looks up at him with wide eyes. Then, he grins, and the dimple in his left cheek pops out.

"Ah, but he likes me already," Tony gloats.

"Pssst, that's only because he is in his mamma's arms," Atelo retaliates.

"Move, move, move." Una shoos Tony away as she comes up beside us. "There is my precious great-grandson," she declares. "My, have we been worried about you. Look at how big you are. And handsome," she speaks softly to Cassian and then looks up at me. "I called Marianna. She is on her way with more baby supplies. Clothes, diapers, blankets, food, and formula. She is going to check him over to make sure everything is okay, and he is all good."

"Thank you, Una."

She smiles up at me.

"I mean, for everything."

She cups my cheek with her hand. "Oh, Gabriella, thank you for bringing this beautiful creature into our lives."

I turn to tell Cross that I am going to go upstairs to call Rick and Melanie and let them know Cassian is safe and then wait for Marianna. I catch the unguarded way he is watching us. Love in his eyes for us. Both of us.

Pride and pain are written all over him. I start toward him, and he opens his arms for us to walk right into. He pulls us both in close. Cassian grunts, and Cross pulls back and looks down at him.

"Hey, little one, you are gonna have to get used to sharing your mamma."

Cassian looks up at me and coos. Then, he nuzzles into my chest and reaches up to Cross's chin and rubs the stubble with his hand.

Cross nips at his fingers, and Cassian starts to snicker. Then, he leans in and lets Cross pluck him from my arms as he reaches for his face once more. Cross starts gobbling his hand again, and Cassian erupts in a fit of giggles.

I stand back and watch my two boys play, and my heart starts to beat wildly in my chest. I never thought I would see this day.

Marianna finishes checking Cassian over, and then she packs her bag. "He is absolutely fine. Maybe a little dehydrated, and he might sleep a long while once he does wind down, but don't be alarmed; it's just jet lag. Give him the Pedialyte I 8brought in his bottle and let him sleep it off."

She heads to the door just as Dawn and Kelsey come bounding in the room.

"Yay, he's here. Gimme. Auntie Kelsey needs some baby snuggles." Kelsey reaches for Cassian.

"Everything okay?" Dawn looks to Marianna.

"Yes, he is perfect," she answers.

"Well, thank goodness," Dawn says as she tickles his belly while Kelsey peppers his face with kisses.

Cassian loves the attention.

While they are mooning over the baby, Marianna looks at me and asks quietly, "How is Nicco?"

From the corner of my eye, I see Kelsey's posture stiffen slightly. She definitely caught the question.

"He's good. Great actually. He moved to California and got an apartment on the beach with our cousin. He is working for one of Papa's marketing companies."

She nods and looks away for a moment. "That's good. I bet he loves living on the water. He's always been a fan of the ocean," she muses.

"He does," I agree.

She sighs. "Will you tell him hello for me when you see him?"

"Of course."

"Thanks, Gabby."

"Thank you for coming out here after working a double. I know you have to be exhausted."

She does look completely worn out. "No problem. I would do anything for you; you know that. I'm so happy to meet the little fellow. He is beautiful, Gabby. The perfect mix of you and Cross. I always knew you two would make the most adorable babies." She gives me a huge, genuine smile.

"I'll walk you out," I offer, and Dawn and Kelsey follow with the baby.

When we round the hall to the living room, I catch sight of my parents and grandparents as they enter. They are followed in by Lorenzo, Stavros, and ... *Nicco?*

I freeze. I haven't seen or spoken to my parents in over a year, and now, here I am, with a baby in tow.

When Papa's eyes land on me, they immediately fill with tears. It catches me off guard. I have never seen my papa cry before. Ever.

He walks rapidly toward me as he lets them spill.

"*La mia bellissima bambina,*" he speaks.

I run into his arms, and he stands there, tightly holding me as we both sob quietly.

"*Il mio cuore,*" he whispers into my hair.

I have missed him so much. All of them. I look over his shoulder and see Mamma trembling. I release Papa and head to her.

"Hi, Mamma."

"Hi, baby."

She opens her arms, and I hug her. All the anger and hostility I have been holding on to the last couple of years just melting away.

"There is someone I would like for you guys to meet," I say as I step back toward Kelsey and reach for Cassian.

He leaps into my arms, and I carefully walk him back toward them.

"This is your grandson, Cassian."

Cassian clings to me as he curiously eyes the new strangers.

Mamma instantly erupts in a flood of tears, and Papa pulls her into his side then he places a proud hand atop the baby's head.

Cassian just looks up as his larger-than-life grandfather in wonder as Papa booms, "What a fine boy he is. You did good, my Gabriella."

Cassian grins up at him, and I can see my papa's heart grow four sizes before my eyes.

Mamma looks at me in question as she steps forward, and I nod as she reaches her arms out in invitation to Cassian, who timidly looks at her and then to me. I tell him it's okay, that his nonna wants to meet him.

Mamma lets out a little gurgle when she hears herself being called Nonna, and Cassian finally decides to accept her bidding and dives for her outstretched arms. She catches him and swings him up onto her hip.

I look from them to the rest of my family, and I spot Nicco looking very uncomfortable as Marianna approaches him.

She whispers something to him under her breath, and he nods and follows her outside. Before he disappears, he glances back at Kelsey, who is trying hard to look impassive but has turned pale. Dawn gives me a concerned glance, and I slightly shake my head to let her know that there is nothing to be concerned about. At least, I don't think so. That is yet another mess to be sorted out.

I just hope that Kelsey doesn't get her heart broken.

Nicco returns a few minutes later, and he comes straight for me.

"Hey, sis." He squeezes me.

"When did you get to New York?" I ask.

"A couple of hours ago. I took the next flight out after I talked to Cross. I expected to land and find you a mess because I had failed to get him back for you. I had no idea about Atelo until Lo picked me up at the airport. I swear, that was the longest six hours of my life."

I can still feel the tension rolling off him in waves.

"Hey." I grab his face with both hands and make him look me in the eyes. "It's okay; we are all okay."

He breathes out a sigh of relief.

I feel a tap on my shoulder.

"Brie, um … I mean, Gabby …" Dawn interrupts. "Kelsey and I are going to head back into the city to meet Mom and Susan. We have a little bit of explaining to do, and my muslin should be ready."

"Oh my God, of course. I forgot. That's the whole reason we are here," I exclaim.

Then, I look around at my family and deflate.

"It's okay. You saw the sketch, and we are just approving and getting a few more measurements. You aren't going to miss much, and you need to be here. You have a lot of catching up to do and some decisions to make."

Kelsey steps up behind her. "Yeah, we will pack your things at the hotel and come back here before we head to the airport. I'm sure our moms are going to want to meet your family and see Cassian once we fill them in." Her eyes fall on Nicco.

He looks nervous.

"Let me take you guys to the city," he offers.

Kelsey starts to protest, but Dawn answers before she can, "Sure thing, handsome. Get your ass in gear. My dream gown is waiting."

He smirks at her. "Yes, ma'am. Let's go."

I hug them both one more time, and the three of them disappear.

Cross comes to my back as I stare after them. "Don't worry, *Tesoro*; everything will work out as it should," he assures me.

"I just don't want her to get hurt."

"I know, but it's a risk you take when you put your heart out there."

I know that all too well. It was my biggest concern when they first started this dance. I knew Marianna still had a piece of Nicco's heart even if he denied it.

I turn to face him. "Why does it have to be so complicated?"

He smiles down on me. "Because, if love were easy, no one would ever appreciate it and respect it as they should," he answers.

Maybe he is right. Maybe the fact that you have to fight so hard for it is what makes it worth everything.

I walk off toward my mamma and Nonna, who have Cassian playing on a blanket on the floor. I don't know where I stand with any of them, and it's an uneasy feeling.

Cross summons Papa and Tony to his office as I sit on the floor beside my son. My decisions aren't just mine anymore. Now, I have to base everything on what's best for both of us.

CHAPTER

forty

Cross

VINCENZO TAKES THE SEAT ACROSS FROM ME AS TONY STANDS AT his back. His stern gaze is concentrated on me as I lean back in my chair.

"Thank you for handling the cleanup with Matteo," I start.

"It was my pleasure," he earnestly answers.

"How was Papa?"

He shrugs. "He was upset to know his oldest friend had betrayed him. He feels guilty that he didn't see it and that it cost Emilio his life."

"It wasn't his fault."

"I told him this."

"I don't want him carrying that."

"This cannot be helped. He is your father, and as you will soon learn, as a father, you take the responsibility of protecting your family very seriously. Failure is hard to swallow. He will get there. He just needs time."

I lift my chin in agreement.

"What else is on your mind, Christoff?" he asks.

I blow out a breath and proceed. No use in tiptoeing around the subject.

"I'm sorry, Vincenzo, but I have to renege on our agreement."

He raises an eyebrow at my declaration, and I continue, "The wedding is off. Adriana returned the ring last night, and she is telling Salvatore this afternoon."

He takes in the information without giving anything away. "I see."

It is the only response he shares, so I go on, "Atelo is back and ready to take on responsibilities, and rather than go through an upheaval as before, he and I will handle business together. A team. I am going to offer the house to him as long as he agrees Una and Grandfather can stay on in their wing."

I pause to look around the office.

"It's never really felt like home anyway. I still have the piece of land I purchased for Gabriella, and I will stay in the loft until I build on it."

He inclines his head to let me know that he is still listening.

"Atelo is at our father's condo now, explaining everything to him— where he has been and why we deceived him."

At that, his jaw tightens, and I know I have hit a nerve.

"I am sorry that I didn't tell you about Atelo. You have been my biggest ally, and you deserve an explanation. We needed everyone to think he had taken off. Not because we didn't trust you, but because, honestly, we didn't trust Salvatore. He and you are so close. We were afraid, if he were a part of this, he would be able to use your friendship to avoid detection."

He does not look convinced.

"Salvatore is very ambitious, and he can be extremely rigid, but he had nothing to do with what happened to your father and brother. Of that I am certain," he says pointedly.

"I know that now, but I was suspicious of everyone then," I admit.

"You could have confided this to me, and I could have helped you," he says through gritted teeth.

"I'm sorry. I was out of my element, and I made some poor choices. I see now that I could have and should have told you."

Facing him now, I truly am sorry that Atelo and I excluded him in our plan.

He nods his head in acceptance of my apology.

"I'm just glad that it all worked out satisfactory," he admits.

"Me, too."

"Now, out with the rest," he pushes.

I take a deep breath. "I want my family." I look him in the eye. "If she will have me. I want Gabriella and my son. I missed a year. An entire year of his life was stolen from me. She had to endure the pregnancy and birth alone." I hear my own voice crack.

"I can't promise there will never be danger, but sending her away didn't keep danger at bay. What I can promise is that Atelo and I will run our business with integrity and as close to the fence as possible. We will be mindful of making enemies. Whatever comes our way, I will love them and protect them with my life."

I can't get a read on him. I look to Tony for help, and he just shrugs.

"I want your blessing, Vincenzo, but I will be honest. With or without it, I will beg her to come home to me."

With that, he smiles a wide, pleased smile. "Well, it is about time, son."

I'm confused at his words. "About time?"

"Yes, I have been waiting for you to tell us all to go to hell and go get her for over a year now."

"Wait, what? I thought you wanted me to marry Adriana."

"No, Cross. It was what was for the best, what made sense, but it was never what I wanted for you, son. Do you not think I saw the misery on your face every time I saw you? Do you not think I wished for things to be different for my Gabriella? Keeping you apart … this never pleased me."

"Then, I have your blessing to ask Gabby to marry me?"

He laughs. "You have my blessing, but I am not the one you have to convince."

I sink in my chair. "Lilliana. She has always hated me."

He roars with laughter. "No, my boy, Lilliana will be your biggest fan if you move her baby girl and grandson home. I am talking about Gabriella. She is headstrong and determined, even more so than she was when she left. I don't see this going easy for you."

"She still loves me." Of that I am certain.

"Yes, she does, but now, she has more than her own feelings to consider. What will matter most to her is whether or not she feels safe, bringing that baby boy home."

"I'll convince her."

He stands. "I have no doubt."

Nonna and Una prepare lunch, and after we have all eaten, everyone says their good-byes with plans to return for dinner at eight p.m., which is when Dawn and Kelsey are returning with their mothers.

Gabriella puts Cassian down for a nap and returns to the kitchen to help clean up.

I ask Una if she can give us a minute, and she pats my back in silent support and takes her leave.

Gabby is putting away leftovers. I come up behind her, take the container from her hand, and set it aside. Then, I pick her up at the waist and set her on the counter in front of me. I step in between her legs, and she allows me into her space. I plant my hands on either side of her and lean in. She rests her forehead to mine, and we stand like that for a few moments.

"What happens now?" she asks in a small voice.

"What do you want to happen now, *Tesoro?*"

"I honestly don't know," she admits. A tremor in her voice. "I love California. I love living with Dawn and Kelsey. I love having Daniel and his dad there. Plus, Rick and Melanie ... and I have school."

My heart rate spikes with each word from her mouth. She wants to go back.

"But," she continues, "Dawn's getting married. Now, I have the baby, and I don't think it's fair to saddle Kelsey with an infant roommate. And I want Cassian to have his family, his grandparents, and his uncles.

They've missed so much time with him. You have missed so much time with him. It's not fair to take him away again. Plus, there's you and me."

She is crying now, and I realize, no matter what she chooses, her heart will break. I can't save her from that.

"Can I tell you want I want?" I ask her.

She nods her head against mine.

"I want you and my son. I want us to be a family. I want to build our house and fill it with more babies." She sniffles as I continue, "But what I want most of all is for you to do what you want. No more forcing you to do what I want."

She bears back and looks at me, and I see the pain written all over her. So, I decide to make it easy for her.

"Tell you what. You go back."

Her body jerks slightly at my statement.

"Listen to me. I don't want you to go, but you want to be there while Dawn plans the wedding. You want to finish school there, and it will be good for Cassian to have Melanie nearby while he gets used to the change."

She bites her bottom lip and nods in agreement.

"I'll come out a couple of times a month. Now that Atelo is home, I will be able to get away more. You can come home with the baby whenever classes are on break and all holidays. It's for a year. Not even a full year. We got this. After the two years we were apart when you were in Paris and the last two years, I know we can survive."

She laughs through her tears.

"But no Antoines and no Jakes," I sternly bite out.

"Same goes for you," she says as she fidgets with the collar of my shirt.

"There will be no one else, *Tesoro*. There has never really been anyone but you. I need you to understand that I won't abandon my father and Atelo. I will continue to run this family with him. I have moved as much as I can to our legitimate businesses, but my hands are dirty. I have done things I'm not proud of. I might have to get them in the dirt again from time to time, but I will try to keep that as minimal as possible, and I will never let it touch you or Cassian."

While that confession sinks in, I pull the box from my pocket. When she sees it, she gasps.

"You still have it?"

I look down in confusion at the royal-blue velvet.

"I found it once, in your drawer, before everything went sideways."

Fuck me. She knew I had a ring for her. I am the biggest asshole on the planet.

She doesn't look up at me as she fingers the box in my hand.

I open it, and the engagement ring that I picked out all that time ago because I saw it and knew it had been made for her twinkles up at us.

"When you are ready, I want you to be my wife, Gabriella Mastreoni. Whenever that is. If you can't say yes now, then I will be patient and ask you every single time I see you until you are."

"I love you, but I want to finish school, and I want to open my own restaurant," she starts.

"Okay."

"I want it to be mine. No laundering. No backroom deals. No family business. I want a place that is mine, to be proud of, a safe place where families can come to eat good food and drink and celebrate big moments and enjoy each other."

"Anything you want," I agree.

"I'll stand beside you and support you, but I want you always to be honest with me and include me in all parts of your life. Even the things you think I won't like."

"No more secrets. I promise."

She takes her eyes from the ring and brings them to me. Then, she gives me the greatest gift I have ever been given.

"Okay."

"Is that a yes, *Tesoro?*"

She nods her head. "It has always been you."

CHAPTER
Forty-One

Bree

"WELL, HE IS JUST ABOUT THE CUTEST THING I HAVE EVER seen." Aunt Susan is bouncing Cassian on her knee as he cackles with glee.

Dawn and Kelsey spent the afternoon explaining my very twisted tale to their moms after Dawn's muslin fitting.

Needless to say, they were speechless when they first arrived.

Being Daniel's stepmom, Susan knew part of my story and she had seen Cassian in passing before but never really gave him much thought. He was just the baby I watched.

The whole organized crime family, fake identity, and secret baby news was, however, a lot for Dawn's mom to absorb at once. At least, Dawn and Kelsey had been fed it all in small doses, which had made it easier to digest. Honestly, it probably sounded like the plot for one of Aunt Susan's evening soap operas.

After meeting Cross and Cassian, they melted pretty quickly though, which was a relief. I was afraid Carolyn was going to force Dawn to omit me from the wedding and toss me out of the apartment.

Before the rest of my family arrives, I sit the girls down and tell them my plans.

They are so relieved. Kelsey confesses they thought I wouldn't return to California, and they cried all the way back into the city.

"We love having you as a roommate. And our last months together before Dawn and Daniel's wedding would have sucked without you," Kelsey says as she throws her arms around me.

"Don't celebrate just yet. I come with a tiny human now. He will put a cramp in our style. No more hungover Wednesdays or late nights out. Not for me anyway."

"Oh, pshaw." That's from Aunt Susan. "You have a couple of built-in babysitters right here." She points between herself and Carolyn.

"I'm sure we can cover a couple of Tuesday nights and the occasional night you girls need to study or to go out and blow off steam."

"Yes, and I am sure Rick and Melanie are still going to need their Cassian time," Dawn agrees.

"He is not through teething yet, and you guys remember how fun that was, right?" I ask.

"Are you trying to talk us out of letting you come home or what?" Kelsey asks with her hands on her hips.

"No, I just want you to know what you are agreeing to."

"We know what we are agreeing to. You are our family, and now, so is Cassian," Dawn states matter-of-factly.

That ends the debate, and I look up to see Cross watching us. He is leaning in the doorway. His feet are bare. He has on a pair of faded jeans that hug his hips. His henley is stretched across his chest, accenting his broad shoulders and thick arms. The sleeves are pushed up to his elbows, and his arms are crossed. His dark hair is messy, and his green eyes are dancing. He looks completely relaxed and happy. He looks like my Cross.

"I'm going to stay here through the rest of this summer though," I tell them. "I think Cross needs time with Cassian."

"Uh-huh," Dawn teases. "That's why."

"It is."

"Sure it is."

My family arrives, and we all have dinner in the large dining room. Cross had one of the local restaurants cater in, so no one had to cook. It's an impressive buffet.

Marcello, Atelo, and Adriana join us. I forgot in all the commotion of the past day that she does still live here.

Her father didn't take the news of the broken engagement very well, which doesn't surprise anyone. Cross tells her she is welcome to stay as long as she wants. I start to protest, and he tells me that he is moving back into the loft this weekend. Atelo is moving into the master here. I see Adriana's eyebrow rise at that as she watches Atelo across the table. He winks at her, and she scowls at him. This arrangement should be interesting.

"You need to forgive her, too," Cross whispers into my ear.

"I don't know if I can," I admit.

"She deserves forgiveness, even more than I do, *Tesoro*."

She glances over at us, and she smiles a small, sad smile.

"I'll try," I concede.

"Thank you." He kisses the side of my head.

Mamma didn't take the news too well that Cassian and I would be returning to California after the summer. She hoped we were home to stay. Merging my two worlds isn't going to be easy, but my family has expanded this past year, and I have to make enough room in my and Cassian's life to accommodate them all.

I'm a far cry from that scared, lonely girl who arrived at LAX. A lot can happen in a year.

After dessert and coffee, everyone starts dispersing. I follow Dawn and Kelsey and their moms to the door. I tightly squeeze them both.

"Don't start." I point to Dawn, whose eyes have filled with tears. "I will see you guys in six weeks," I remind her.

"I know; I know," she says as she shakes off the emotion. Then, she turns her focus on my brother. "What about you, stud? You coming back to California, or is Daniel putting a Roommate Wanted ad in the paper?"

Nicco glances at Kelsey, who has stealthily avoided him all evening. "I might stay here another week or so, visit with family, but I will be home after that."

Kelsey doesn't react or say anything, but I notice the look of relief that passes over her when he refers to California as home.

Dawn doesn't miss it either. "Good. I will let Daniel know, and we will see you in a couple of weeks." She turns back to me. "We have to go. The plane is waiting for us. You have a great summer, and don't do anything I wouldn't do." She waggles her eyebrows at me. Then, she heads to the car.

Kelsey takes another glance around and gives me one more hug. She quickly looks up at Nicco and then back to me as she says goodbye and follows Dawn. Aunt Susan and Carolyn slide in next, and they pull off.

I hate to see them go, but they can't stay all summer.

Nicco comes up behind me and tugs my hair. "It'll be okay, sis. The summer is going to fly by, and then you will be sad, saying goodbye to everyone here to head back to them."

I know he is right. No matter where I am headed, I will be leaving a piece of my heart where I am.

I sigh.

"I wish I could have everyone in one place."

He chuckles. "You should have thought about that before you made a whole new family on the opposite side of the country."

I know that is true, but I wouldn't change a thing. If I hadn't left, I wouldn't have them.

"So," I carefully begin my interrogation, "what exactly is going on with you and Kelsey?"

He blows out a long breath. "I don't know. I guess finding

everything out about our family was a lot for her to process, and running into Marianna was a little startling for her." He runs his fingers through his hair in frustration.

I know that they both kept trying to say their relationship was casual, but they obviously caught deeper feelings for one another.

A little startling for him, too, I bet.

"How did you guys leave things?"

"Pretty much how you saw it. She hasn't really spoken to me since I arrived. Just avoided me at every turn, and I gave her space. Honestly, seeing Marianna after all this time was a little jolting for me, too."

"Are you going to pursue that while you are here?" I try to ask the question as delicately as I can, but this is precisely the predicament I was afraid of when he and Kelsey started this relationship.

He gives me a pained look, and some of the edge leaves me. I know my brother. I know his heart. He has loved Marianna for most of his adult life, and the last thing he wants to do is hurt either one of them.

I walk over and wrap my arms around him. "I guess we both ended up in messy situations, huh?"

He props his chin on the top of my head. "Yep, but I think that you have finally found your way back to where you belong. I am so happy for you, Gabby."

"Thank you for coming to California to look after me, Nicco. I love you."

"I love you, too, *cara*."

Nicco heads home with our parents.

After saying my good-byes to them all, I come into the living room to find Cross lying on the couch with a sleeping baby sprawled across him.

My heart skips a beat at the sight.

My boys.

Oh, how I love them.

I'm not sure what the future has in store for us. All I know is that I will love them with all I have. It's a vow I make to them.

Cross my heart.

Epilogue

Gabby

I STAND HERE AND LET MAMMA FUSS WITH MY DRESS. IT'S AN OFF-THE-shoulder, flowing white chiffon gown. I bought it off the rack. I walked into a boutique in Malibu last fall, and it just called to me. Simple, elegant, and perfect for a beach wedding. Dawn calls it my hippie gown. I think it's the most beautiful thing I have ever seen. I love the way it floats around me like a gossamer-winged butterfly when the wind catches it.

Mamma stands behind me and runs her fingers through my long hair. I left it down in a cascade of curls, only braiding the crown at the top. She takes the headband of wildflowers and places it on my head. It's a threaded branch of eucalyptus and baby's breath with white daisies and tiny cornflower-blue roses and pink-bells. The sweet aroma envelops us.

She helps me attach the locket around my neck, and then she stands back with tears in her eyes as we both look at the final product in the mirror.

"I hope he likes it," I whisper.

"Oh, Gabriella, he is going to love it. You are the most stunning bride I have ever seen."

"I think you might be a tad biased."

"Doesn't make it any less true."

We hear a commotion outside, and then the door swings open. In burst Dawn and Adi with Kelsey on their heels.

"I'm the maid of honor, and the maid of honor walks down the aisle last and stands beside the bride. Tell her, Gabby," Adi demands.

"Well, I am the matron of honor, and matron trumps maid," Dawn huffs.

"Maybe in age," Adi retorts.

I just watch them spar in their gorgeous glass-blue dresses, pointing their ivory bouquets at each other. Instead of getting frustrated, I count myself lucky that they love me enough to argue over who gets to stand beside me today.

"Oh, for fuck's sake. I'm going to walk down the aisle last, and I am going to stand beside her. You two are ridiculous. It's her day, and she loves you both." Kelsey fakes exasperation as she turns to me. "How does that sound, Gab—oh my goodness, you look exquisite!"

They all finally look up to see me, and moisture fills all their eyes.

"Don't cry, or you will make me cry and mess up my makeup," I command as I hold back my tears.

"Wow, you were right about that dress, Gabs. You look like an angel." Adi sighs.

"He's going to get an instant boner."

"Dawn!" Kelsey chastises, but we all erupt into a fit of giggles, and the threat of tears immediately dissipates.

This is why I love them so.

"It doesn't matter who walks down the aisle when, guys. You can even rotate during the ceremony if you want to. I don't care. I love each of you equally."

They seem to ponder that for a moment.

"Oh, fine, you can stand beside her. As long as we rotate in the photographs," Dawn relents.

Adi triumphantly grins at me as we hear a knock.

"Are you ladies decent?" Papa's voice booms from behind the door.

"Yes," we sing in unison.

He opens the door and walks in, carrying Cassian in his arms. When he spots me, a look of unmistakable pride overcomes him.

"La mia bellissima figlia."

They make their way to me. Papa is dressed in a white linen dress shirt and sand-colored linen pants, and so is my little man. Cassian is playing with the white rose boutonniere on Papa's shirt pocket until he spots me.

"Mamma!" he exclaims as he tries to leap from Papa's arms and into mine.

Papa tightens his hold. "Whoa, my boy."

He turns to Papa. "Whoa, Nonno," he mimics as he pats Papa's cheek.

"It's time to go. We have to walk your mamma down the aisle."

Cassian turns his curious face to me and points. "Mamma, pretty."

Papa's eyes get misty as he agrees, "The prettiest."

Mamma turns to my friends. "Okay, girls, it's showtime."

She kisses me on the cheek, and she and the girls rush out to take their places.

"Are you ready, baby?"

"I have never been more ready for anything, Papa," I admit.

He gives me his arm, and he, Cassian, and I walk out of the room and toward the back of the beach house.

It's turned out to be a gorgeous day. There was a threat of rain earlier that had Mamma in a tizzy.

"What if it's pouring at sunset?" she asked me, panicked.

"Then, we will get wet." That was my response because nothing, not even a monsoon, was going to ruin this day.

A day I have been dreaming about since I was four years old.

When we hear the beginning notes strumming from Daniel's guitar, we start toward the ocean as the music hums above the crash of the waves. The guests stand from their seats as we make our way down the makeshift aisle, which is sprinkled with white rose petals.

Everyone I love is here. I smile at each face as I pass. Rick passes Melanie a handkerchief, and she dabs at her eyes. Uncle Matt grins wide at me as Aunt Susan claps. Una has her hand over her heart, and

Nonno and Nonna stand proudly beside Mamma. Marcello glides out and stops us to kiss my hand as we go by.

When my eyes find Cross, standing with the pastor at the front of the small crowd with Atelo and my brothers at his side, all I want to do is run to him. He is wearing the same long-sleeved white shirt and linen pants as Papa and Cassian. His hair is mussed, like he has been impatiently running his fingers through it. He has been waiting for this day, and it's been a long year.

Tears are spilling down his cheeks as he silently mouths, *Beautiful, Tesoro.*

When we reach them, the pastor asks, "Who gives this woman to be wed?"

Papa proudly declares, "Her mother, Cassian, and I do."

Then, he leans in to kiss my cheek, and Cassian copies him before Papa gives my hand to Cross, and they join Mamma.

"I now pronounce you husband and wife. You may kiss your bride."

Cross places his hands on my cheeks and brings me to him for a tender kiss.

Then, we hear our son's voice, "Yay. Me kiss Papa."

Cassian escapes Mamma's lap and toddles in the sand toward us. Cross scoops him up into his arms and kisses him, and then my two boys walk me up the aisle.

Bliss.

My perfect ending.

It might have taken us a while to get here, but the important thing is, we've finally made it. After all, every good fairy tale starts out messy.

The End

Acknowledgments

Where to start? There are so many people who had a hand in this book. The conclusion of Cross and Gabby's saga was truly a labor of love.

First, I want to thank every single reader, blogger, and fellow author who took a chance on Both of Me. Each message, text, email, share, giveaway, and review meant the world to me. To my friends and family who not only encouraged me to chase my dream but supported me every step of the way, I love you all with my whole heart.

Autumn Gantz, once again, where would I be without you? Most days I don't know up from down and without you keeping me straight I could never pull this publishing thing off.

Jovana Shirley, I promise that I will improve. I have to, right? There is nowhere to go from here but up. Thank you for taking my manuscript and cleaning it up so beautifully. You are an angel and commas are still the devil.

Mackenzie Trotter, thank you for your artwork beautiful girl. You are so talented. Keep up the good work and follow your dreams. KK loves you.

Judy Zweifel, Stacey Blake, James Pulido, Taylor Rhodenbaugh, and Scott Hoover, thank you for your contribution to the Cross My Heart Duet. You are each the best at what you do and I am so blessed to have had you all be a part of this journey with me.

Thank you to my early readers that took a choppy, discombobulated first draft and helped shape it into a cohesive story. Autumn and Gloria, your input is invaluable. I love you and I trust you.

I would thank David, but nobody knows who the hell he is anyway.

About the Author

Amber Kelly is a romance author that calls North Carolina home. She has been a avid reader from a young age and you could always find her with her nose in a book completely enthralled in an adventure. With the support of her husband and family, in 2018, she decided to finally give a voice to the stories in her head and her debut novel, Both of Me was born. You can connect with Amber on Facebook at facebook.com/AuthorAmberKelly, on IG @authoramberkelly, on twitter @AuthorAmberKel1 or via her website www.authoramberkelly.com.

Made in the USA
Middletown, DE
01 October 2023

39893403R00139